A COVID ODYSSEY VARIANT RESET

A fictional COVID-19 pandemic story

Graham Elder

Herb,
Thanks for all the years of virtual mentorship ← oops, plane hiccup!
& Thanks for reading!
Mark

G.M. Elder Publishing
www.twodocswriting.com

Printed in Canada
Cover design by Rebecacovers
ISBN: 978-0-9958907-9-4 (ebook)
ISBN: 978-0-9958907-8-7 (pbk)

To my children, Emily and Charles.
A father's love knows no bounds.

In memory of Maija Nenonen, who shined brighter than a million suns and was taken from us at the blossoming age of 21 as I was penning the last words of this novel. The reality of our world struck hard. No matter the desperate want, there are some life events that even a father or a mother's love can't circumvent.

To all the burned-out healthcare workers around the globe who continue to hope for light at the end of the tunnel

CONTENTS

FOREWORD

The information in this novel reflects the scientific thinking and general status of the world leading up to the end of November 2021. Vaccines and boosters were all the rage. A plethora of treatment options ranging from brand new (Paxlovid) to old and repurposed (fluvoxamine, an antidepressant) flooded the markets. Yet, still, the virus evolved from one variant to the next, becoming less deadly but more contagious, and the world evolved with it ...

PRESENT DAY

December 8th, 2021

Invisible rain clouds çaressed my face and tickled my ears as a rush of warm air lifted us to dizzying heights a mile or more into the sky. We hovered in darkness for several more heartbeats, and then a loud, "Whoosh," like a dragon releasing its fire breath, propelled us even higher until we broke through the cloud coverage and emerged into a blazing moonlit night.

"Quite something, isn't it, my friend?" Rufus said, standing next to me. He placed an arm over my shoulders.

"I've never seen anything like it," I replied, letting go of the railing and putting my arm over his shoulders. My stomach was decidedly unhappy with this sudden, unexpected gain in altitude, and it reminded me of that one particular amusement park ride that you went on once, and then never again. The splendor of the view and the camaraderie seemed to settle my intestinal turmoil.

"The Caribbean Ocean as far as the eye can

see," he said.

"Um, all I see are the backsides of the clouds."

"Look more closely." Rufus disengaged from me, grabbed the railing with one hand, leaned forward, and pointed with his other. "There are holes in the clouds. Places where they thin out, and you can see right through."

I leaned over the edge and followed the direction of Rufus' index finger straight down. "I see the breaks in the clouds, and beyond that I see only darkness."

"I'm telling you, every now and then the moon pokes through, and you can see the water. I can even see moonlight dancing on the crests of waves."

I strained my eyes but saw nothing. "Rufus, I think you have an extraordinary imagination."

He released a deep belly laugh. "Yes, mon. This is very true. But I tell you –"

A heavy wind suddenly picked up from the east and pushed us hard. I grabbed for the railing but was knocked off kilter by Rufus' heavy frame impacting my shoulder. We both fell to the floor in a tangle, much to the amusement of the other two passengers.

"What part of 'keep both your hands on the railing at all times' didn't you two understand," a gruff female voice yelled.

"It is to be expected of my comrades,

Yara," the fourth passenger said. "They have an uncanny knack for falling, crashing, sinking, and things of that nature."

"Bah," Rufus said, "did we really have to bring him along?"

"Since he's the only one of us who knows exactly what we're looking for," I grumbled, "I guess so."

When both Rufus and I had finally disentangled ourselves and were standing upright, I asked, "Are we still on course, Yara?"

She glanced at her instruments and nodded her head. "Dead on track and straight on until sunrise. The winds could not be better."

"We will be there *before* sunrise, won't we? The stealth nature of our plan depends on it."

"I'm sure Yara was just playing with words, Hitchhiker," Rufus said. "Peter Pan's directions to Netherland?"

In the glow of the moonlight, I could see Yara smiling at Rufus, who had a goofy grin that I recognized from our medical school bar crawling evenings in Montreal.

They did seem a good match.

"Haven't you read Peter Pan, Hitchhiker?" Rufus asked. "Or seen one of the movies?

"Harumph," Hitchhiker responded dryly. He was sitting on the floor with his back against the wall. He lifted his head and looked first at me and then at Yara. "How much longer until we arrive?"

"Hot air ballooning is not an exact science," Yara said. "We will get there when we get there. Hopefully, for all our sakes, while it's still dark."

***

"We're not going to make it," Rufus declared, staring off into the horizon.

The first hint of dawn glowed far in the distance, throwing enough light to outline a land mass.

"Is that our destination?"

Yara checked her GPS and said, "I believe so."

"Will we be seen?" Hitchhiker asked, still sitting on the floor, cupping his face with his hands.

"Hopefully not," she replied.

"How bad do you think it is there?" I put the question out to everyone.

As was typically the case with questions requiring detailed information for an answer, Hitchhiker responded first.

"The Delta Variant has all but destroyed their healthcare system. There has been a recent dramatic spike in cases, and the numbers are the highest the country has ever seen."

"Not surprising, given that only eight percent of the population is fully vaccinated."

Hitchhiker looked up at me and said,

"Eight and a half percent, actually."

I smiled, "I think you're feeling better."

He shrugged, "A little. In any case, all the borders are closed, and we can expect military everywhere. If we are observed landing, our mission will be over."

"Yara will get us there unseen," Rufus said confidently. He was looking over her shoulder at her GPS and other instrumentation, fascinated by any vessel pushed by the winds. He had been crowding her space more and more during the latter part of this trip, and she didn't seem at all annoyed by it. I was happy for my old friend.

"I hope you're right," she said. "Otherwise, those of us without proper papers are going to be spending time in prison. And the military aren't known for their hospitality."

She adjusted the burner, turning it down a little, and I could feel a slow drop in altitude.

"Are we beginning our descent?" I asked. "It seems early."

Yara's silhouette motioned an arm to the east, from where we had come. "There's something creeping up on us."

"Something?" Rufus said.

"She's obviously referring to a storm with high winds." Hitchhiker sighed, hugging himself tighter, tucking his forehead deep into the crook of one elbow.

"How can you tell?" I asked Yara.

"Pressure is dropping fast, and we are

accelerating," she said. Even in the pre-dawn darkness, I could see she was fidgety, slowly turning around in circles, staring for long moments off into the distance, into black nothingness, repeatedly checking her instrumentation.

"Isn't that a good thing?" I asked. "Won't that get us there faster and under cover of darkness?"

"My friend," Rufus said. "Do you remember our transatlantic crossing? There is such a thing as too much wind."

I remembered our trip all too well, and every blood vessel in my body turned to ice.

***

The smattering of pre-dawn light that we had enjoyed for a few moments disappeared in the blink of an eye as dark and heavy clouds overtook us. Yara's efforts to lose altitude and pass beneath the storm were only marginally successful. Her last check of the speedometer marked the wind speed at over seventy knots, and the screeching blow laid into our balloon, dragging our basket almost into a horizontal position and us to the floor in the process. It was like the G forces felt on takeoff in a jet airplane, except that the pressure wasn't into my back but through my arse. I was reminded of the bucking bronco ride Rufus and I endured at the bow of the *Rumrunner* before she sank the previous year, right before Rufus died ... for a while. A shiver ran through me.

Initially, there was random yelling and general pandemonium in the basket. And then the howl of the wind silenced all conversation as crew members curled up into their respective corners, clutching tightly to whatever parts of the basket could be clutched to. Yara's idea was to keep the weight distributed evenly to balance out the basket. It seemed logical, except that in the darkness, at more than an arm's reach from my friends, this chaotic world became a very lonely and terrifying place.

In the beginning, as the wind speed accelerated, we were simply dragged straight as an arrow behind the balloon making incredible time towards the coast, but then we were caught in some kind of circular downdraft, and the basket spun out of control, pushing us deeply into the wicker and metal struts that reinforced the contour of the basket. I imagined my body being sucked between the struts and through the wicker, falling helplessly into emptiness. I reflexively tightened the straps to the small survival backpack that I had been wearing since boarding the balloon, wishing it was a parachute.

It seemed to go on interminably, and it was hard to imagine a worse scenario. Four bodies tossed around like jelly beans in a clothes dryer, some unknown distance above the Caribbean Sea with a dozen ways to die: impact with the water; immediate drowning while unconscious or drowning later from fatigue, eaten by sharks; or perhaps making it as far as the mainland in the balloon and belly flopping a landing. Suddenly, I felt beyond horrible for my friends. They were here for me and my quest. They had nothing to gain but my gratitude, and what was that worth? Certainly not their lives.

I wondered if my friends were still there. In their respective corners. I couldn't see or hear them. I might be the only person still on this wild ride.

A red glow suddenly emanated from the other side of the basket, and I realized someone – Yara? – had cracked a glow stick and thrown it to the floor. She must have been wondering the same thing. Now I could see my friends: Hitchhiker curled into a ball with his head buried, his worst air-terror nightmares coming true; Yara, our pilot, digging through her backpack looking for God knows what that could improve the situation; Rufus, my oldest and dearest friend, his face stricken by a horror that mirrored my own. How could we not die? And with it all of Sarah's hopes.

Yara was yelling something now, but it was impossible to make out. She closed her eyes and tucked her knees to her chest. That wasn't reassuring.

The impact was staccato-like at first, as if the rectangular basket was skimming off waves.

I could feel the drag for a few seconds and would catch a spray of salt water in my eyes and hair. Then it would stop, and I could feel the lift with the wind blowing me dry. Then it would start again until finally the lower edge of the basket dug in deep and caught like an anchor, propelling me through the air and over the heads of Yara and Hitchhiker, out of the basket. I grabbed frantically for anything, and my left wrist coiled around a thick rope, the dropline used to hold the hot air balloon to the ground upon landing.

Of course, my leaving the basket was the best thing that could happen for my friends. The instant loss of weight allowed the balloon to rise, pulling the basket out of the water. At this point, I was already taking a wavy saltwater bath and was doing everything I could to gasp for air. Then I felt the pull on the dropline and was lifted sky bound from the water. Lightning bolts of pain arced down my left arm and into my shoulder. My one arm wasn't designed to carry my full body weight, and I felt like I was being drawn and quartered.

And then I was no longer rising. There was now just enough dawn light radiating through the clouds to offer a visual of my predicament. The balloon had found some kind of stasis going neither up nor down, and I was dangling maybe thirty feet off the water, and an equal distance from the basket. I was twisting around in circles on the rope as the natural tension of the tether unwound itself, giving me a dizzying 360-degree view. That's when I noticed the coastline coming at us like a freight train. I looked down and realized we were still moving ridiculously fast, as if you were to open a car door at a 100 km/hr to watch the pavement zip by. We were minutes from shore, followed by a wall of towering palm trees.

I felt a jerk on the rope and looked up. Rufus and Hitchhiker were both trying to pull me back up into the basket, but I realized it wouldn't be fast enough, and it wouldn't solve the problem. With my weight, the balloon would not be able to rise high enough and quickly enough to avoid the trees. At this speed we would certainly crash and ....

I didn't see any alternative. If I detached myself, at least we would all stand a chance. A thirty-foot fall into the ocean was survivable. I took a deep breath, closed my eyes, and let go.

Nothing happened.

I looked up and realized that I wasn't just holding the rope, the rope was holding me, coiled around my wrist.

The end of our journey was fast approaching, and all I could think of was my baby daughter.

ACT I

The First Circle of Hell

12 Days Earlier

November 26th, 2021

"**He was riding a dirt bike** on a singletrack mountain biking trail?"

"That's what his dad says. Apparently, he does it all the time," I answered.

"And he's only ten?" Rick, the orthopaedic surgeon, asked.

"Actually," I was looking at the patient's EMR chart, "it's his birthday today. Just turned ten. He was with a half dozen other dirt bikers. Must have been a birthday party rally of some sort."

"And he went off a jump?"

"Overshot the berm off a booter and went down the other side."

"What? Berm off a booter?"

"It's what the dad said. It apparently means he landed wrong off a very large jump."

"Right. I tell you, everyday there's a new and interesting way to hurt yourself."

"You got that right."

"I looked at his x-rays," Rick added. "Anything else besides the broken tibia?"

"He's got a bad headache, probably a concussion, so he's off getting a CT head. Back in a few minutes."

"Okay. I've got a break between cases. I'll be right down, slap a cast on him and save the day. Can you knock him out while I do it?"

"Sure thing. See you shortly."

I tapped out on my cell, checked the weight of the ten-year-old, and then closed the EMR chart. I was staring off into space calculating the various dosages of medications I would need to sedate a ten-year-old, when a hand appeared in front of my face shield.

"Earth to Mark, anyone home? Over?"

I turned and was surprised to see the masked and shielded face of my wife, Sarah. She was also wearing a hair bonnet, so only her beautiful green eyes were visible. There was a small wrinkle between them as she asked, "You look deep in thought. What's up?"

I smiled. "Just running some calculations for a conscious sedation procedure. A ten-year-old with a broken tibia, and it's his birthday today. Hell of a birthday present. Rick's coming down to, and I quote, 'slap a cast on him and save the day.'"

Sarah laughed, "That man is ten percent doctor and ninety percent ego."

"Ten percent *surgeon*," I corrected, grinning at her. "Don't ever call him *just* a doctor, he's a *surgeon*. Remember?" I had both hands in the air making little quotation fingers.

"Right. I forgot," Sarah said. "I still don't understand what my sister sees in that neanderthal."

"Oh. I do," I whispered, "and it apparently has nothing to do with what's between his ears." I winked at her.

"You two been spending some time in the shower together?" Sarah asked, the adorable wrinkle between her eyes apparent again.

"Just rumors, my dear, just rumors."

"Yeah. Probably started by Rick. He reminds me of The Todd from the Scrubs TV show."

"Biceps and all," I added.

"So," I asked, glancing at the trauma bay to see if my ten-year-old had returned from CT yet, "what is the head pharmacist, love of my life and mother of my four-month-old daughter, doing here at the hospital, today? What kind of mat leave is this anyway?"

"It was a totally spontaneous thing. Jenna needed a break, and I was going crazy at home. She called me this morning after you left for work, and we pulled a switcheroo. She's watching June, and I'm doing Med reconciliation here in the ER. It feels great to get out of the house, but I'd forgotten how screwed up people's medication lists are. A lot of patients literally have no idea what they're taking. You know – she lowered her voice and made it scratchy – 'I mostly take red ones and blue ones.'"

"Mmm," I said, "like they're in a Matrix movie, or something."

"Yeah. Exactly. Without the cool, Bullet Time, special effects."

I grabbed her around the waist and leaned my forehead into hers, our shields touching, eye to eye, and gave her a sultry smirk. "Well … it's a pleasure to have you here, Mrs. Spencer. How are *you* today?"

She grimaced, pushed me back a little and whispered, "My breasts are freaking killing me. I don't think I pumped enough this morning."

"Mmm. Not sure I have anything in my armamentarium that can help. Hot packs?"

A passing nurse commented slyly, "Hey, this is a PG ER department here, kids. Can we move this lovey-dovey moment into a closet, or something?"

I rolled my eyes and yelled, "There are some perks to being chief of the department again, Shelley."

"Hah! Long live the Chief!" She retorted.

I looked back at Sarah. "Yeah, the hot packs are a good idea. I can put up with it until I get –"

The overhead erupted, "Code blue, CT scanner. Code blue, CT scanner."

"Shit. That must be my ten-year-old."

Sarah quickly stepped aside and said, "Go do what you do, Dr. Spencer. I'll see you at dinner. Remember, we're ordering in tonight."

Sarah's last comment barely registered as I ran in the direction of diagnostic imaging only to be met by a nurse and a CT tech rushing a gurney into the ER towards the trauma bay. They had an oxygen mask on the child's face hooked up to a portable tank at the foot of the bed. A man in plainclothes with a terrified look on his face was trailing behind: the boy's father.

The nurse yelled, "He crashed while he was being scanned. He's not breathing, but he's got a pulse."

As they whizzed by and into the room, I caught a brief look at the boy. He was small for his age with a big head of disheveled black hair. The splint on his right leg was half off, no doubt because of his rapid exit from the scanner, leaving his tibia flapping in the wind. His eyes were closed, and his head was turned to the side with his jaw hanging slackly, his mouth wide-open. There was a swelling just visible at his hairline on the left of his forehead that wasn't so obvious earlier, before he went to CT.

Fuck, it's gotta be the head injury.

"Call the RT and prep for an intubation," I yelled. Bodies everywhere flew into action. All eyes were on the child.

I stepped forward to examine him more closely, and a hand clasped my right shoulder, pulling me back abruptly. I turned to look into wide, angry eyes.

"What's happening to my son? What's going on? Did the scanner do this to him?"

The scanner? Where do people come up with this stuff?

"I suspect it's from the head injury," I replied, trying to maintain a calm voice. "It must have been more severe than we thought."

"Well. Don't just stand there. Do something about it," he commanded forcefully.

Yeah, well, I would already be doing something about it, if you hadn't stopped me.

For all their love and best intentions, parents were mostly in the way in the ER, blockades to progress and the wellbeing of those they cherished most in life.

"Mr. Glassford," I said evenly, "please go outside to the waiting room. We'll come and get you when we have news."

The look on his masked face registered as anything but compliant with this plan. However, a nurse's gentle prodding at his elbow and some comforting words in his ear seem to finally persuade him. Before he left, though, he darted in quickly to kiss his son on the forehead and, in that moment, the world for me became nothing but this ten-year-old kid named Aidan.

I approached the child, quickly looked under his eyelids, and my worst fears were realized: He had a blown pupil. The pupil of his left eye was fixed and dilated on the same side as the swelling and hematoma that was now visible over his temple. I took a deep breath and said, "He's got a subdural."

The respiratory technician and a nurse both said, "Ready."

I positioned myself at the head of the bed and grabbed a laryngoscope off the mayo stand. I tilted the child's head back and opened his mouth, negotiating the blade around the tongue, and then pulled up and away to visualize the vocal cords. Normally, a patient would require IV medications to sedate and paralyse before intubating, but Aidan was effectively already comatose. A nurse passed me a smaller sized pediatric endotracheal tube, and I inserted it, passing it through the vocal cords and into his trachea – his breathing tube. The RT attached an Ambu bag to the tube and began squeezing. Aidan's chest began to rise and fall rhythmically with each compression of the bag, and I released my own held breath.

Okay, first problem solved.

"What's his GCS?" A nurse asked. The GCS, or Glasgow Coma Scale, was one of the indicators used to assess the severity of a patient's coma. It was based on verbal, eye, and motor response to external stimuli and the lower the score, the worse the coma and prognosis.

I shouted, "Aidan, move your left hand."

I repeated this several times, but he made

no attempt to move.

I then pinched his left hand, and he withdrew it. That was good and gave him a score of 4 out of 6 for withdrawing from a painful stimulus. He was not verbalizing anything before I intubated him. That was bad and gave him a score of 1 out of 5.

"Aidan, open your eyes." Again, I repeated this several times, but to no avail. I pinched the skin on his chest, and there was no response, which gave him a score of 1 out of 4, for a total of 6 out of 15. Grand conclusion: Aidan had a severe traumatic brain injury and a high likelihood of death unless we did something to help him.

"His GCS is only 6," I whispered heavily. A blanket of murmurs and gasps enveloped Aidan as everyone digested what that meant. "We have to do something," a younger nurse mumbled.

No shit Sherlock. We have to do something. But what? I doubt he'll make it to a trauma center with neurosurgery available.

I ran to a computer terminal and flashed my ID badge over it to open the PACS system that would allow me to look at imaging. Maybe, just maybe, they were able to get enough of the CT scan done to localize the bleed. I pulled up his head CT and scanned the images settling on one in particular.

"I can see it! He's got a left temporal subdural hematoma, and it's a big one. Shelley, get neurosurgery on the line through CritiCall."

Shelley picked up a landline and looked over a series of telephone numbers on a sheet taped to the wall above the phone. She punched in the numbers. Other than the hiss of oxygen flowing and the Ambu bag compressing and expanding, the room was deathly silent. I looked at a monitor displaying Aidan's vital signs, and everything seemed stable. He was holding his own. For now. But I knew it wouldn't last. As the hematoma expanded against the bony hardness of his skull, his soft brain tissue would be compressed and would have nowhere to go but out through the hole at the base of the skull where the spinal cord entered. The parts of the brain that would be pushed through and compressed first controlled all his vital signs: the breathing, the blood pressure, the pulse. It was called "coning," and it was a terminal event.

"I've got neurosurg in Sudbury." Shelley passed the phone, and I explained the situation. There was a pause as the neurosurgeon accessed the same imaging through PACS. When he came back on, I listened intently, and then shouted, "NO! WAY! There's no way we can decompress him here. You want me to drill a hole in his skull?"

As if to emphasize the neurosurgeon's point, an alarm erupted from the monitor: Aidan's blood pressure was slowly rising, as was his pulse. He was deteriorating. There was clearly no time to transfer him to another center.

"Tell me what to do," I sighed into the receiver. She explained in detail the steps involved. This was nothing I'd ever done before. In fact, I'd never even seen it done. The principle was simple, though: make a hole in the skull to allow the blood to evacuate and relieve the pressure on the brain. The faster this happened, the greater his chance of recovery. I hung up the phone and called the operating room.

"I need a burr hole set, stat."

I was given the nurse in charge of the OR, and we spoke.

"What do you mean, 'we don't have a burr hole set?'"

She answered, "We've never had a need before."

"Well," I stammered, "can you throw something together? A drill and some retractors. This kid's going to die if we don't do something stat." I was losing my cool. This was way outside of my comfort zone and training. Everyone in residency talked about doing heroic emergency burr holes to save a life, but no one ever did it. In the bigger institutions, the patient would be rushed to the OR and neurosurgery would take care of it. In smaller hospitals, like ours, the patient would be stabilized and airlifted out. Right now, there was no time. If we didn't drain the blood clot, Aidan was as good as dead.

The charge nurse promised she would rush the necessary equipment down as fast as possible. And she wasn't lying. The OR moved with superhuman speed when they had to. No sooner had I checked Aidan's vitals again, readjusted his leg splint (intubated patients in comas can still feel pain), and given him some IV sedation, that I heard a cocky voice bellow, "Special delivery for Dr. Spencer."

My eyes flicked to the entrance of the trauma bay and found Rick standing with a tray of instruments, holding it like a pizza in one hand, his bulging bicep quivering ever so slightly.

"Rick, I need your help. We have to drill a burr hole. I talked to neurosurgery in Sudbury, and they think that, given the size of the hematoma, he'll never make it to their center."

"I heard. That's crazy. I did a six-month rotation of neurosurgery at a level 4 trauma centre and never saw it done once."

"Well," I said, "now's your opportunity. You're the surgeon. Do you want the honour?"

Rick placed the tray on a mayo stand that had been cleared by a nurse and then took a long step back. He put both his hands up and said, "Way out of my malpractice insurance wheelhouse, man."

I shook my head in disgust. "You're thinking about malpractice insurance while this ten-year-old kid is dying? What happened to saving the day? This is your chance."

Rick shrugged his shoulders. "Hey, it's the

sad reality of this litigious world we live in. This kid's got a terrible prognosis, even if the procedure's successful, and someone's going to pay."

My eyes were drilling *burr holes* into Rick's head, and he saw it.

He stepped towards the bed and lifted Aidan's eyelids, noting the blown pupil. He sighed and locked eyes with me. "Okay. I'll assist you any way I can, but you've got the lead on this."

"Fair enough," I said.

A nurse passed me a razor, and I shaved a swath of long black matted curls from the left side of his head. The hair clumped to the floor as I donned sterile gloves and opened the tray. The CT image of Aidan's head was on the screen. I drew some local anesthetic with epinephrine and hovered the tip of the needle over his temple, not quite sure where to freeze.

Rick was also studying the head CT and said, "Yeah, you got it right there. Freeze that whole area."

I gulped and jabbed the tip of the needle into the skin that was just behind the bruised area on the side of his forehead. I wheeled an area a few centimeters in diameter with local anesthetic. Rick donned sterile gloves as well and passed me the scalpel.

"You sure you don't want to do this?" I asked, "You *are* the surgeon here."

"You're gonna do fine. Best if I sit back and take in the overall picture. Like you're my resident."

"I'm sure as hell not your resident, my friend."

"Right. Now cut."

I drew the scalpel across the area from front to back, reassured that Rick was nodding his head, confirming what I was doing. I came down through skin and there was some bleeding.

"Watch that bigger vessel. There." Rick pointed with a hemostat.

"Okay."

Rick passed me the hemostat and said, "Use this to bluntly dissect down to bone."

I slowly spread the tips of the hemostat, working my way through fat until I reached something hard, his skull. "Alright. Now what?"

I was trying to remember everything the neurosurgeon had explained over the phone but, under the stress of the moment, the info had all blended into a quagmire of word spaghetti.

"Now," Rick said, "You drill."

An alarm went off on the monitor again; his blood pressure was diving. "I think he's coning," someone said.

"Shit," I yelled, "pass the drill."

Rick gave me a small power drill with a large drill bit on the end about the size of my index finger.

"Power?" I asked. "I thought this was

supposed to be done with a hand drill?"

"They couldn't find one. It's ancient technology now."

"And this drill doesn't seem to have any kind of stopper to prevent me from drilling right into his brain."

"Yeah. You're talking about a drill bit that's specialized for burr holes. We don't have that. Just don't plunge."

"Don't fucking plunge? That's your advice?" I shrieked.

Rick tilted his head to the side, as if to say, "Sorry, best the OR could do on short notice."

"Anyway, the hematoma will have pushed the brain away from the inner table of the skull. So ... lots of room for error."

"Yeah, as long as I'm exactly in the right spot where the hematoma is. It's not like I can tell."

Rick glanced at the CT again. "You should be right over top."

Should, is the key word in that sentence.

As I placed the tip of the drill bit through the incision and on the bone, I made a mental note to order a full and proper burr hole set for the emergency dept. A small demonstration of my recently reacquired chiefly powers.

"Don't worry, Mark. The power gives you better control. Less jerky than a hand drill."

"Jerky," I muttered, "You're the jerky, here. You should be doing this. Not me."

Rick acted like he hadn't heard me and said, "Okay, squeeze the trigger and push."

I did as he recommended, a low-pitched whirring sound emanating from the drill, but wasn't sure how hard to push. As if reading my thoughts, he said, "Push and ease off in a rhythmical way. That way if you plunge, it won't be too bad. And hold the drill with your other hand also, with your elbow on the kid's shoulder, for better support."

I did all these things and began to drill into the skull, the pitch of the whirring sound increasing as I squeezed the trigger more boldly, advancing ever so slowly, a millimeter at a time. My entire being was focused on the tip of the drill bit. Flakes of bone began to emerge from the hole, much like drilling into a piece of pine in a workshop.

"Hurry it up, boys. He's really not doing well," a new voice said at the head of the bed.

Rick glanced quickly before returning his attention to the incision area. "Good to have anesthesia here, Phil."

"Thought you could use a hand." Phil was doing his part to keep Aidan alive, administering the necessary medications. He had taken over the Ambu bag as well. "But you have to speed it up. He's only got a few minutes."

Great. No pressure.

"Alright, everyone, be quiet," Rick said loudly. "Mark, you have to listen for a change in sound as the tip of the drill bit reaches the inner table."

"What kind of freaking change in sound?"

"You'll know it when you hear it."

And I did. The sound of the whirling drill bit became higher pitched, and I eased off and could feel the tip penetrate through the inner table. I pulled the drill bit back and a gush of dark blood oozed out."

"Jackpot!" Rick said.

We both looked up to Phil, who was checking the monitor.

"Nicely done boys. Vitals are already improving."

I stood and sucked in a heavy, deep breath – I hadn't taken one since I began drilling – and then released it slowly, as if I was meditating. This, of course, caused my visor to completely fog up. Rivulets of salty sweat then dripped from my forehead into my eyes, irritating the hell out of them. I tried to wipe them off, but my shield got in the way, so I pulled off my face shield, and my N-95 mask came with it, leaving my face bear and unprotected, radiating a ridiculously large smile.

Rick slapped me on the back, Todd style, and said, "Great job. Just put a heavy bandage on the wound to let it drain. Then he can go to the ICU. I'm gonna take care of that tibia and then run back to the OR."

As if the child was just another hiccup in

his day, Rick began manipulating Aidan's tibia and reapplying the splint. All the while arguing with Phil, the anesthesiologist, who felt it was a little early to be stimulating the poor kid after what he'd just been through.

I placed a heavy dressing on the wound and backed away, forgetting about my face shield and mask, naked to the world. Someone had to deliver the good news to Aidan's father.

As I was heading to the waiting room, a tune popped unbiddenly into my head. All the sounds of the ER – the alarms, the beeps, the wailing, the cursing – faded away to be replaced, at first, by a beat – Da-Da-Dump-Dump-Dump – and then the bravado of Freddie Mercury's soaring vocals singing, *We Are The Champions*. I shuffled a little here and a little there to the rhythm in my head and was completely encapsulated in my own little victorious world where good triumphs over evil and little kids didn't die. Life simply could not feel any better than this.

11 DAYS EARLIER

November 27th, 2021

I stepped out of my post-work "sterilization" shower and toweled off. This was a habit that had waned somewhat over the late summer into early fall as the number of daily Covid cases plummeted, and we enjoyed a return to some degree of normalcy. The truth is, though, we all knew it wouldn't last. We knew nothing would ever be normal again.

As a result, pandemic habits that we had developed to keep ourselves – and everyone around us – safe had dropped off. Six feet of social distancing and wide-arc detours around people in hallways and on sidewalks had gradually diminished to five feet ... and then four feet or less. We were all still acutely aware that someone else was nearby, we just didn't go to as much effort to make space since the threat seemed so much less. More than eighty percent of the population in our province was vaccinated at this point, and a rising number had also received a booster. Things, however, were changing rapidly again as the fourth wave struck, and old pandemic habits were being reignited; the good times were over. When I crossed the threshold of our front door after my day shift, Sarah was quick to remind me to sanitize my hands and jump into the shower.

It was nearing dinnertime, and I donned my favorite sweatpants and a comfortable long sleeve shirt, my go to stay-at-home pandemic clothes. I could hear rustling sounds followed by slobbery blurping noises coming from June's crib. I peered in and was rewarded with a smile and some gaga sounds. I picked her up and was further rewarded with the stench of a smelly diaper.

"You're as stinky as you are cute, my little angel," I cooed to her.

Breathing through my mouth, I brought her into the laundry room and placed her on the changing table. I stood back, handed her a rattler, and then hit the timer start button on my phone. It had become a little game to see how quickly I could swap out a dirty diaper.

Faster than you can say, "That's really gross," I had the old diaper off, her bum washed, and a new diaper in place. After launching the balled up, dirty diaper through the hinged lid of the dedicated trash can, I stopped the timer.

"Oh, yeah, June! A new record." She giggled and waved her arms in the air, whereupon I high fived each tiny hand using only two fingers. I was determined that one of her earliest developed motor skills would be the "high-fiver."

I lodged the new, cleaner, and less smelly version of June into the crook of my elbow and ran downstairs.

"Ooh," I yelled out, "dinner smells delicious, Sarah. What's on the –"

Simultaneously, the doorbell chimed, and Archie galloped to the door snarling and barking. We had a visitor.

"I'll get it," I screamed over the noise.

I opened the inner door to the vestibule, stepped around a variety of footwear, glanced fleetingly at the gallon-size container of hand sanitizer that was still half full, sitting on a table in the corner, and then peered through the large window of the outside door. Someone wearing a green Packer's baseball cap was placing a small rectangular box on the doormat. As he stood up, I unlocked and opened the door with one hand, my other still holding June. I stepped out on to the front porch, closing the inner door with Archie whining on the other side.

"Hi, Mark," a vaguely familiar man's voice said. "Just delivering a package."

"Darrell?" I asked.

"It is."

I almost didn't recognize him. He had grown a large Ron Swanson walrus mustache since I'd last seen him, in addition to a few new Covid pounds.

"What's with the facial hair?"

"It's my Mo-vember stash. Haven't got around to shaving it off. The wife kinda likes it."

He bent down, picked the package off the deck, and handed it to me. I placed it hesitantly under my armpit, a sudden flashback to a year earlier when we would leave all packages and mail in the front vestibule for 72 hours before opening them, worried that fomites on the package might transmit the new deadly SARS CoV-2 disease to us. Most of this had been disproven with further studies, although transmission of Covid-19 via fomites was still possible, it was much less likely than initially thought.

Darrell looked at June, smiled and commented, "So this is the new addition to the Spencer family?"

"It certainly is. This is our little June."

Darrell waved his hand, "It's a pleasure to meet you, June."

She giggled in return.

He pointed at the package I was now holding. "I'm guessing this might be a gift for someone's first Christmas?"

I put my index to my lips and made a, "Shhh," sound as I eyed June.

Darrell was a retired dentist, well known in the community, and lived a few houses down the road. I looked over his shoulder at the shiny red Tesla parked in the driveway, next to my beat-up old Highlander.

Maybe I should have been a dentist.

"What's with delivering packages?" I asked.

"Well, with the Christmas rush upon us, a friend asked me to help out with his new private delivery business. Giving Fedex and Purolator a little more competition."

I nudged my elbow towards the Tesla. "Nice ride."

A huge grin formed under his mustache and his face took on a childish look. "A little retirement present to myself." He winked at me. "It's actually the real reason I'm doing these deliveries. I just love driving it around and, with the pandemic still going on, there's really no where I want to go."

I laughed and June, trying to imitate me, let out a ferocious burp.

"I think it might be dinnertime for your young lady. Good seeing you, Mark, and best of the holidays." He turned and scooted down the stairs, sliding happily into his Tesla.

"My regards to the family, Darrell," I yelled after him.

I negotiated my way back into the house, tip toeing around the footwear, the package under one arm, June on my other. I pushed the inner door open with my knee, and Archie began jumping excitedly all over me as I worked my way to the kitchen,

"That took you a while. Who was at the

door?" Sarah asked, after I placed the package on the counter and dropped June into her car seat. I strapped her in and handed her a teething ring to play with.

"That was Darrell, the dentist from down the street, in his new Tesla. He's doing some delivery work to keep busy. You should see his new stash. Reminds me, we need to finish *Parks and Recreation*."

Sarah was mixing ingredients into a large sizzling frying pan on the stove. "Sure. Parks and Rec tonight it is. Wait, don't you have a phone call, or something."

I glanced at the clock above the door. "Almost forgot. Short business call with Rufus at 6 PM," which was in a couple of minutes.

"Are you okay to watch June while you cook?"

Sarah looked at me and raised an eyebrow pointedly. "Pretty sure I can handle it. You must wonder how we poor girls survive here at the homestead when you're off saving lives."

I turned the palms of both raised hands towards her and grimaced. "Sorry. You know I didn't mean it that way. I'll try and keep it short."

"Humph," was all Sarah replied.

I pulled my phone out and FaceTimed Rufus as I rushed downstairs to my basement office – my lair, my mancave. I settled into my office chair just as his great bearded face filled the screen. The beard and mustache were a relatively new addition and, along with his flaming red Rastafarian dreadlocks and diamond studded right ear, made him look more like Jack Sparrow than Gordon Gekko.

"Hello, my friend," he said. "What new adventures are filling your life?"

"Ha! You're funny, Rufus. I'm a father now. It's nothing but work, eat, sleep, and change diapers. The closest to adventure I get is the latest Netflix show I fall asleep in front of."

"Don't worry, mon, it doesn't last forever."

"Yes, I know. And, to be honest, I'm loving every minute of it."

"Excellent. Listen, I have some important news."

"Good or bad?" I asked.

"Depends how you receive it. A Big Pharma company has made an offer for our little company."

Our little company, known as TMS Inc., was named after my father, Thomas Mark Spencer. It was based in Montreal where Rufus oversaw day-to-day operations with a primary mandate to develop the technology that originated from my dad's research work before he passed away late last year. Technology that could potentially lead to a cure for Covid and many other types of viral infections.

"Wow. That was fast. TMS isn't even a year old," I commented. "We are barely up and running. How would a Big Pharma company even know what we are doing or how far along we are?"

"That's the bad news. I really don't know."

"You don't think we have a spy or something like that, do you? Corporate espionage?"

Unlike Rufus, who had left medicine many years ago to pursue a variety of very lucrative business opportunities and knew everything about the world of business and corporate finance, I could barely balance my checkbook and, like most physicians, relied heavily upon advice from experts.

"I'm doubtful we have a spy, but we may have a worker in our midst with a loose tongue. The company was formed very quickly, and, while we did our best to vet everyone, it's certainly possible we missed something."

"How much money are we talking here?"

"An obscenely large amount," Rufus replied. "This also worries me. We are at the very early stages of development. It makes no sense that someone would offer us that kind of money unless they were worried we might succeed."

"How do you mean? Wouldn't that be exactly why they would want our company?"

"You are naïve in the ways of business, my friend. There is far more money to be made with preventative measures like vaccines or symptomatic treatments than there is with cures."

"Are you saying someone would pay exorbitant amounts of money for our company only to destroy it?"

"This is the way of the business world and has been going on since the invention of money."

"That's ..." I had no words to convey my feelings to Rufus. I clenched my eyes tightly. At that moment, I was ashamed to be a part of any company that was in any way associated with this kind of business world. My gut churned at the idea.

"... unbelievable. I know." Rufus finished. "It is the stark reality of this world we live in." He let out a deep laugh. "Bah! It makes pirates of old look like Girl Guides, doesn't it?"

I took a deep breath and said, "You know I would never sell?"

"Of course, my friend. Neither would I. But you must also know, these Big Pharma people, they have deep pockets and don't play by the rules. Things could get very dirty for us."

10 DAYS EARLIER

November 28th, 2021

I had my suit jacket and Blundstones on and was heading to the door to clear off the truck when my smartphone played out the first notes of *Get Back* – my ringtone flavor of the day after watching the new Peter Jackson Beatles documentary. Good thing too, because I'd forgotten it on the kitchen counter, a regular habit.

I glanced at the screen for a moment before answering. It was the hospital. "Hello, Dr. Spencer here."

"Dr. Spencer, it's Sandra from occupational health. How are you this evening?"

A phone call from Occupational Health was never a good thing, but it was also a regular thing when you worked in the ER.

"Hi, Sandy. Doing well. Just heading out to dinner with Sarah and then a concert at the Loft. Our first date since June was born." Ours was a small enough town that everyone literally knew everyone. "What's up?"

"How are you feeling?"

"Feeling?"

"Yes. Are you feeling well? No symptoms or anything."

I rolled my eyes a little. Sandy began every phone conversation with, "How are you feeling?" It was a bit of an open-ended question primarily targeting your physical health but also leaving some room for mental health – burnout, in particular. "No, I feel great. Top shape. Why are you asking? Another high-risk exposure?"

At this point in the pandemic, three or four waves in, depending on how you used the terminology, a high-risk exposure was a routine thing in the ER, and I'd been getting this call at least once a week. The phone call from Occ Health was as much a part of our work week as donning PPE.

"Remember the ten-year-old from three days ago who ended up in the ICU?"

How could I forget. I drilled a hole in his head.

"Yes. I remember him very well. His swab was negative when he came in. I've been checking up on him here and there. Last I heard, he was on the pediatric ward and almost fully recovered."

Other than that hole in his head.

"You're right. The initial swab was negative. However, we just found out today that there was an outbreak at his school a few days prior to his admission. So, we did a routine recheck, and, unfortunately, he's now positive."

"Any symptoms?" I asked.

"According to his father, he wasn't displaying any symptoms before the accident, and he's had no symptoms while in hospital. At least, that we know of. He *was* intubated for two days."

"Alright," I summarized. "He's an asymptomatic carrier with high-risk contact who tested positive on a routine protocol test, and he's been in the hospital for three days exposing everyone. Hmm, must have created quite a commotion."

"Oh, yes. Everyone who was in contact is being tested. If they are double-vaxxed, boosted, and have no symptoms, then they keep working but self-quarantine until testing negative."

"So, I should be getting tested?" *Again.* Testing for me was as common as the phone call from Occ Health. The two ultimately went hand in hand.

"Yes. Of course. The usual."

"Is a rapid antigen test still sufficient from an Occ Health standpoint?"

"For those who are double-vaxxed and boosted with no symptoms and were wearing full PPE, it is."

"That would be me. Excellent. I have a stockpile of kits here. I'll test myself and text you the results in the next twenty minutes."

"Perfect. Assuming it's negative, you'll need to retest yourself again in ten days."

"Sandy. The way things are going, I'm sure you'll be calling me for something else long before that."

Sandy sighed. "Yes. I'm sure you're right. Assuming you're negative, have a good time tonight."

"You bet. Talk soon."

Hopefully not.

I hung up the phone and pondered the whole situation for a moment. Archie, our ginger-haired Golden Retriever, wandered over, his tail wagging. Talking on the phone was like a magnet for him. Or, more specifically, ending a conversation on the phone. He somehow knew there would be a head rub and a chin scratch once the call was done. I squatted and obliged him, ruffling his bangs, and letting him lick my face, still deep in thought.

I'd really had no symptoms whatsoever and felt great. The one good thing about the pandemic was, other than catching Covid twice, I'd never been healthier: no colds, no sinus infections, no other flus. And I knew what the prodrome felt like. Plus, I was double-vaxxed and boosted with a small bubble of friends and family. Not to mention, I wore full PPE at work from the moment I arrived until Mr. Slate pulled the whistle.

In fact, there was probably no one on the planet more protected than I was. At least from the known variants. There was the new Omicron variant that was building steam in Africa and now found throughout the world, even in Canada. It was highly mutated with potential to bypass the vaccine and wildtype immunity from earlier variants, including Delta. Truth is, regardless of all the protection, it was entirely possible to feel great and still be a deadly carrier.

"Well, Arch. I guess it's time for another test."

I stood, opened a cupboard over the kitchen counter, and admired my vast collection of rapid antigen tests before selecting one.

"Who called?"

I turned to face Sarah, who'd just emerged from the bedroom with a sleepy June slumped over her shoulder, her cherubic face drooling freely onto a towel that Sarah had draped under her chin. Her beautiful blues were only partially visible as her eyelids fluttered with post prandial fatigue. Sarah had a bounce in her step and looked like she was trying to elicit a burp or two before putting her to sleep. I was holding the testing kit in one hand, which she immediately noticed.

"Uh, oh. I'm guessing that was work."

"It was." I explained the phone call. All the while, Sarah kept her distance, bouncing from one foot to the other, a familiar scowl on her face. This wasn't her first rodeo.

***

I usually did my testing in the bathroom which, in my mind, I perceived as my small, makeshift laboratory. For some strange and repetitive reason, every time I tested myself, I was reminded of my deceased father, a world-famous English virologist. Maybe it was the fact that he spent his whole life working in a laboratory. Or maybe, it was the ironic fact that Covid had killed him. Regardless, as I stared into the mirror before testing, I always caught a fleeting glimpse of our two faces superimposed one over the other. When I was an early teen, living in England, my mum said I was the spitting image of him. As I grew older, and feelings of abandonment to his job flared and my anger towards him escalated, I convinced myself that I no more resembled my father than I resembled any workaholic stranger off the street. This was a lie, of course, we were like twins born a generation apart.

Like my father, and encouraged by my pre-med background in microbiology, I was methodical about anything done in a lab, even my imaginary bathroom lab. I opened the kit and removed the various pieces of plastic equipment and then placed them on the sink counter. While in principle these kits should've been idiot proof, designed for the average person whose closest other similar life experience was checking a pregnancy test or mixing a luxury cocktail, the fact was they were fairly complex, and I felt my background actually came in quite handy. It made me think the kits really weren't designed for the average person's use and had only been appropriated that way to fill a societal need. To further complicate things, the instruction pamphlet was written in minuscule type, and I wondered how an individual with more aged eyesight could possibly decipher the instructions. Add to this the many different companies cashing in on the Covid bonanza, making testing kits with unproven and questionable accuracy, and you had a surfeit of reasons why the rapid test could give a false reading. In general, testing results from the rapid antigen test were notoriously inaccurate compared to the PCR test, somewhere on the order of 70% (versus 95% accuracy with the PCR test), and I suspected it was quite possibly because of poor sampling technique, which ultimately came down to how much discomfort you were willing to put up with to get the most high-yield sample. And contrary to online propaganda, as well as some unfortunate nicknames for the test like *the brain tickler*, there was no danger to your brain, which was protected by a reasonably thick bony skull and several layers of tissue at the point of sampling.

There was also the option of taking the specimen from just inside the deep part of your nose, a much less uncomfortable technique, however, it was well known that a deeper sample from the back of the nasopharynx had a much better yield. It was completely understandable why someone would take the easier way out. Who would want to inflict any more pain on themselves than they had to? Particularly if the test was being done for routine purposes, and you had no symptoms, or worse yet, you were on the fence about the way society was managing Covid-19 and were essentially being forced to do it to: return to work, visit a loved one in a nursing home, cross a border, etcetera.

Regardless of how it was done, if the test was positive, it was highly likely you had Covid-19, with only a one-in-a-hundred chance of it being a mistake. The problem was only if the test was negative, then you couldn't really be sure you didn't have Covid-19.

I certainly wasn't taking any chances. With my potential impact on society, seeing scores of the sickest and weakest people in my day-to-day job, not to mention the prize of my life, our unvaccinated little June, the deep-dive technique was the only way to go. I heard a large burp from the bedroom that made me grin, followed by an incredibly contagious giggle as she began to doze off. That was her nighttime routine: feed, burp, giggle, sleep. I lived for it.

I placed the collection tube into a tube stand, and then added the extraction buffer to the tube. I closed my eyes and then plunged the tip of the nasal swab into my right nostril – my right nostril seemed to have a more direct line of sight than my left to my nasopharyngeal target. The hard cotton tip contacted a patch of mucosa not far from the inner aspect of my skull, and my eyes instantly began to water. They always did. This was followed by an intense and focused pain in my forehead, not unlike a brain freeze from a popsicle eaten too quickly. I left the swab in place for a count of ten, wanting to saturate the tip with secretions.

I removed the swab and placed it in the collection tube ensuring that it was fully submerged in the buffer solution. And then I swirled and stirred it, milking the walls of the tube in the process. I placed it back into the collection tube holder and let it stand for two minutes. I then drew the swab out, squeezing the tube in the process to release as much liquid as possible. I attached the nozzle to the collection tube, squeezed three drops into the well of the testing device, and then set the timer on my phone. As I waited, I replayed my conversation with Sandy, a variety of a conversation we'd had umpteen times before, like a little waltz. Something about it was bothering me, tickling my memories in a sour way, a misstep.

"For those who are double-vaxxed and boosted with no symptoms and were wearing full PPE ..."

I always wear full PPE. Always. Except ... I

suddenly had a flashback.

Except for that brief moment three days ago after I had finished drilling the burr hole. Fuck!

Sarah knocked gently at the bathroom door and whispered. "June's down and Jenna is here. Are you ready?"

Fifteen minutes of introspection had apparently drifted by. I checked the rapid test and smiled when the result showed negative. I was about to answer Sarah when I thought once again, *the mask and shield were off for just a brief moment.*

I grabbed another test kit from the medicine cabinet – I had them all over the house – and whispered to Sarah through the door. "Fifteen minutes, Hon."

***

I swept an inch of snow off my SUV with a favorite old broom that had unusually soft bristles and a wooden handle that had been glued and screwed at least twice. I was sure it was irreplaceable, but, then again, I generally felt that everything I owned that was old and of "high quality" was irreplaceable. I was only mid-forties but definitely had some old-guy thinking.

My second rapid antigen test was negative. As per the guidelines du jour, I was free to do whatever I wanted with no quarantine required. I had shaken off the feelings of dread that had resulted from my momentary lapse of reason leading to my maskless and shieldless situation at work. And, although I still felt a little guilty about going out, I felt even more guilty about cancelling our date night. It was to be an epic night and somewhere a line had to be drawn, and life had to go on.

I got in and started up my aging Highlander, making sure the seat warmer was set to max on Sarah's side, and then settled in. Sarah would be a bundle of nerves until she had a cocktail or two. I imagined she was going through in detail every aspect of June's routine with her sister, Aunty Jenna, who had agreed to babysit. Jenna said we should consider this an early Christmas present. I was quite sure that June would sleep through unless Aunty Jenna woke her niece for some playtime. But that was on her.

I checked some emails while waiting and came across one from Rufus.

"Damn."

I struck the steering wheel in frustration with a gloved hand. This time it was truly just bad news. My father's potential cure relied upon a rare and special ingredient. Thanks to my new friend, business associate, and rogue third member of our little TMS company who called himself simply Hitchhiker, we had found a very limited supply of this special ingredient in the US, through the Mayo clinic. They, in turn, had stockpiled it for research years earlier from a small factory near Wuhan. Yes, the same Wuhan where the virus was thought to have originated. As Hitchhiker liked to say, "The best ironies in life are the truest ones."

Hitchhiker, a self-proclaimed full-time intellect who owned no vehicle and travelled using whatever means was at hand, had proven very adept at working behind the scenes and obtaining whatever we needed to progress the research, be it: information, manpower, or, most importantly in the beginning, our special ingredient. He was our brainy *MacGyver*.

Thus far, our results had been impressive, and my father's theories had all proven correct. At least in mice. We had just moved up the ladder to chimps and, it seemed, according to Rufus' email, we were no longer able to source any more of the special ingredient: the Mayo clinic had run dry. He wanted to do a three-way conference call in the morning to sort things out.

The passenger door opened, and Sarah took her seat. I looked at her and imagined I had a certain frustrated look on my face, because she asked, "C'mon, I wasn't that long. I had to make sure Jenna was all good."

I sighed. "No. It's not you. Just an email. We can talk about it over dinner." Or maybe not. Really, I just wanted to forget about it and enjoy the night. Tackle it as a new problem fresh on the morrow. I would tell her after our conference call. Sarah always wanted to know about these potholes, and she had an intuitive problem-solving mind that often steered me around them. Tonight, though, was only for happy time. We'd earned it.

It was nearing five o'clock and the sun was just disappearing, leaving a faint spectrum of orangy colors in the clear sky. The temperature was hovering around the zero mark, and the thin layer of ice that was clinging to the windshield was slowly being eaten away by the steady heated blow of the fan. Perish the thought that I would get out of my car and use a scraper. When I could safely see through the windshield, I nosed up to the end of our driveway and was preparing to pull onto Queen Street, when I noticed our neighbour, George, bundled up and sitting at the end of his driveway in a portable camping-style chair with his wife in a second chair next to him and his daughter standing behind.

Sarah commented first. "That's an unusual sight. What could the neighbours possibly be doing?"

I was perplexed as well, until I looked down the street and noted the long line of cars approaching much slower than the speed limit. Some had ribbons on them, and others had multicolored balloons. They all began honking their horns.

"It's a drive-by!" Sarah suddenly exclaimed.

"A what?" I asked, dropping my side window to get a better view.

"It's George's 70th birthday. See the sign his daughter is holding. It's a drive-by birthday party. I've heard about them but never seen one."

Drive-by birthday parties were a product of lockdowns limiting indoor home gatherings to less than five or ten people, depending on the severity of the lockdown.

Sure enough, as the first cars passed, I could see signs in the windows wishing George "Happy birthday." George and his wife were now standing closer to the street, and each car slowed to a crawl, opened their windows, and shouted birthday wishes. Some reached out to hand George giftbags and wrapped presents. Others simply fist bumped, hooped, and hollered.

I looked at Sarah, smiled, and leaned on my horn to join in. It felt amazing, like the sound was a release of repressed tension giving us permission to have fun. Sarah dropped her window, and we both yelled out our happy birthday wishes.

When the last car finally passed, we could see George just standing there, his gloved hands wiping tears of joy from his eyes. His tears were contagious, and I could feel myself welling up. I looked to Sarah for emotional support, but hormone laden tears were already streaming down her cheeks. I wiped my own eyes and then passed her a surgical sponge that I kept in my jacket pocket for emergencies. We both smiled goofily at each other and then laughed hysterically. It was strange that such a simple thing could be so emotional, but, then again, these were Covid times, and strange things accompanied by strange emotions were now the norm.

***

We stood at the glass door of a brand-new Asian fusion styled restaurant called *Peace*, six feet behind another couple also waiting. A waft of garlic and spices permeated the air. The couple ahead of us advanced and, with masks in place, picture IDs in hand, and our phones displaying a vaccination QR code, we pushed through the inside door and into another world: A world where smell and taste stood out among all other senses. We were both giddy, almost floating, with delight, and this was before we'd had a single cocktail. I had my arm around Sarah's waist and was holding her close.

The hostess checked our "paperwork." We then signed a ledger leaving our contact info (I used my own pen) and disinfected our hands before being led to our table. The restaurant had a modern ambiance with a sleek and angular look, the tables far apart, clearly designed for modern Covid-19 times. As we removed our winter jackets, shedding a light dusting of fluffy snow on the floor, I scanned the room briefly and nodded to people I recognized. When my head swiveled back to Sarah, I noticed for the first time what she was wearing: an elegant red strapless dress that I recognized from a wedding we had attended years ago. She had straightened her hair and added a dash of makeup – something she never did. She could have easily passed for a model.

"Sarah, you look absolutely stunning."

She returned a coy smile, and I suddenly felt like every eye in the room must be drawn to our table. We sat down and removed our masks. She was wearing matching red lipstick and a diamond necklace I had given her for our 10th anniversary. She was an absolute smoldering sex bomb, and I wanted everyone to look away because she was all mine.

Sarah interrupted my leering. "Don't you start with the 'why do we have to wear masks when we are *standing* in a restaurant and not when we are *sitting*' routine."

I grinned slyly. "To be honest, I was thinking about something else altogether ..." And then what she said registered and prickled my scientific survival instincts. "But seriously, who's idea was it to allow people to congregate in one large room and arbitrarily base mask usage on appetite and thirst, like the virus cares how hungry or thirsty you are?"

While I understood it was a government policy and restaurants had little input, it had never made sense to me. Did restaurants have access to some kind of anti-Covid forcefield device for each table that I didn't know about? Perhaps in the candle holder?

"That's enough, Mark. Be grateful we're going out to dinner at all."

"You're right. I've had enough take-out food to last a lifetime."

"And let's make a rule for tonight. No talking about Covid."

"Ouch. That could be challenging."

I mean, what else is there to talk about?

"Okay. How about no Covid talk until we at least have a few courses under our belts." Sarah offered.

"Deal." *And a few cocktails*, I thought.

Our waitress accepted our drink orders and delivered them quickly to get the evening started. For me: a Whisky Sour topped with sage and orange that found taste buds I never knew I had. For Sarah: a Tanqueray Martini which provoked a luscious smile with the first sip. Sarah had planned accordingly and pumped enough milk for a full night on the town.

A song from the playlist on the overhead speaker system caught my ear – Fleetwood Macs' *Dreams* – and dissolved away a stubborn knot that had taken up residence in my lower back.

This was indeed promising to be a dreamy night.

The head chef, Matty, wearing an obligatory black apron with a few floury type cooking smudges, wandered over to our table for a little chit-chat. He spoke of his training in Toronto, explained that the menu tonight was of the pre-set tasting variety, and then moved on to another table. A fixed menu was perfect since I'd already reached my daily decision-making quota, and I knew my life choices would all be downhill from here. Always best to leave it in the hands of experts, especially late in the day.

"So ... what non Covid thing do you want to talk about?" I asked.

"Well, we are out and about, getting a small taste of travel life once again. When it's all over, where do you want to go first?"

And so, we danced pleasantly through the evening alternating through a myriad of recurring non Covid conversational topics that had become routine to any lockdown dinner table – apparently at home, or in a restaurant. Each topic paired nicely with an exquisite creation: Places and people we wanted to visit? Meet Fanny Bay oysters from British Columbia with mignonette and a dash of horseradish; Broadway shows and sporting events we wanted to see? Say Hello Dolly to a crispy daikon and vermicelli slaw; dream renos to be started or finished? Hammer home the delightful tuna tataki; gossip about who was separating and who was sleeping with whom? Enjoy a tasty and sexy Peace Maki. All of these topics and dishes paired with a perfectly chosen transformational glass of wine and delivered by a host of exceptional servers dressed in black that hovered at the periphery, like bees circling their nest waiting on the queen.

Of course, interweaved in all of this, was the recurring non Covid subject of our little baby June which ultimately brought us full circle back to our current reality. June was a Covid baby and would likely suffer the long and short-term consequences more than anyone else. We feared greatly for her and all children born and raised during this pandemic. What a different and shitty world they were inheriting.

"What if she's like me and tends to look more at people's mouths when they're talking?" I asked.

"I guess the face masks will quickly cure her of that habit, and she'll look people in the eye as you're supposed to, like me." Sarah gave me a smiling, wide-eyed ogle to prove her point.

"Humph," I responded, and chopsticked a beautiful morsel of tuna into my mouth.

"More importantly," Sarah retorted, "if this pandemic continues on and on, she won't know how to interact with other kids properly."

"I suspect that ability is ingrained in our genes as a survival mechanism, and no amount of pandemic can remove it. Evolutionarily speaking, I've read that humanity's greatest survival strategy is the ability to work together and form communities."

"And gossip is a powerful tool for exchanging the information that brings a community together," Sarah added.

"Yes, well, I think Covid has allowed us to fine-tune that tool even more."

"Yeah, actually, did you hear about ..."

We were about halfway through the menu when *that* sound started. The one that pushes your body in an equal and opposite direction, like Newton's third law.

A *cough*.

From the table next to us.

Building in intensity with tremendous cringe-factor.

A crescendo of cacophonic expectorations.

I could practically feel the droplets raining down upon us.

The elderly man tried desperately to stifle it, however, that just seemed to make it worse. His wife tried to put his mask on for him, but he would have none of it. It was likely just a chunk of food that found its way down the wrong pipe, but that didn't matter to everyone around us. A hush descended over the crowd as patrons reached for their masks. The holiday season was fast approaching, and the government was already warning about rising Covid numbers, minimizing gatherings, and cancelling travel plans. We'd heard it all before, but it still injected us with a slow-release guilt when we were living on the fringe of those recommendations, like going to a restaurant.

I looked at Sarah, and she checked her phone.

"Mark! The time. The concert starts in fifteen minutes."

Thank you, thank you, Sarah. Saved by the clock.

While it would have felt terribly awkward to leave a fancy restaurant simply because someone was coughing, we now had a legitimate excuse.

Sarah waved our waitress over, and we explained that the food was so amazing we lost track of time, and we had another engagement at 8 PM. Nothing about the tornado of aerosolized viral particles assaulting us from the next table.

She understood completely and mentioned that she had wanted to attend the concert also but had to work. Sarah picked up the tab, leaving a generous tip, and then we rushed outside. I removed my mask and breathed deeply from an easterly air current wisping down Queen Street, almost like I'd been holding my breath.

***

It felt like we were Trekkian planet

hoppers, moving from one exotic culture to another. Whereas the restaurant, Peace, was all about the nose and the taste (and some great oldies), The Loft concert hall was about the sights and the sounds. Leaving only *touch* absent in our evening's sensory tour, and this, I hoped, would be covered when we got home – say no more!

The Loft was housed on the upper fourth floor of the historic Algoma Conservatory Building. A gigantic stone structure built in 1901, it was once the home office of Francis Clergue, an American businessman who was the founding father of the paper and steel industries in our town.

The building was now the home of The Algoma Conservatory of Music and was an absolute cultural landfall for the community. Previously an attic storage space containing wall to wall filing cabinets, the concert hall had been renovated up from the studs, and now, staying true to its heritage, sported a vaulted arched ceiling of steel trusses separating burnished copper panels. The walls were stacked with white roughened stone bricks, and the floors were layered with sanded hardwood that may have come from the original paper mill itself. From an acoustics perspective, it was truly the perfect venue to see a concert.

After checking in with the usual ID presentation, QR code and contact info, we took the stairs up, working off our sumptuous dinner while admiring the colorful paintings that adorned almost every square inch of the oak paneled walls. We found a pair of lounge style seats situated to our liking – to the left to see the pianist's hands at work – and then kicked back to catch our breath. Judging from the number of people still filtering in, we had a few moments before the inaugural concert that would christen The Loft open for business began.

"This place is stunning," Sarah whispered, her head swiveling side to side and up and down.

"Yes. It's absolutely amazing. If this is what a Boring Apocalypse looks like, sign me up."

"How do you mean?"

"Oh, you didn't see that article in the New York Times written by Adam Grant?"

"Must've missed that gem."

"He compares the pandemic to a horror movie we've all seen before where the killer jumps out over and over again brandishing a weapon and then killing someone. Because it happens repeatedly, and you've been desensitized by seeing it in countless other horror movies, it just doesn't scare you the same way anymore. The pandemic is like that same horror movie playing over and over, wave after wave, surge after surge, lockdown after lockdown. It becomes boring, and people become complacent, sloppy. Hence the Boring Apocalypse."

"Well, he can speak for himself. You know I hate horror movies. There's enough horror in the world as it is."

I laughed and nodded my head at the truth of that statement. The lights clicked on and off a few times and then dimmed. I melted even further into my seat as the outside world disappeared. The steam of multiple lockdowns and almost two years of pandemic frustration and misery evaporating into the stratosphere to be diluted by thousands of years of every other human calamity. For all humanity was going through, we forget how bad it could really get.

Applause filled the room as David Jalbert took the stage and adjusted his seat before the elegant nine-foot Yamaha grand piano. I'd seen him perform Bach's Goldberg Variations once before, and it was extraordinary. He sat with perfect posture as his hands performed miracles at the keyboard. He worked his way through a brand-new contemporary composition, *Smoke Darkened Sky* by Kelly-Marie Murphy, which required him to do something I'd never seen before. He suddenly stood in the middle of the performance and strummed the strings of the piano directly with his fingers, somewhat like playing a horizontal harp, if a harp had strings the thickness of a pencil. It was a mesmerizing effect. From there he moved to Debussy's *Images* with the opening piece, *Reflets dans L'eau,* interpreting the reflection of light on water that left me completely entranced and spellbound, so much so that I didn't feel the text vibration inside the breast pocket of my jacket until the very last wave rippled through my chest.

I was suddenly and solemnly jerked from my happy place back to the real world. I stealthily snuck a peak at my phone. Sarah noticed and was staring at me, frowning. As the text hit home, my stomach went queasy.

I leaned into Sarah's ear and whispered, "It's June. She's sick with a fever. We have to go."

9 MONTHS EARLIER

March 8th, 2021

Without a doubt, I was vaccine hesitant. How could I not be? Typical vaccines took five years to develop, and this one was on our doorsteps in less time than a full-term pregnancy. How was that possible? A little digging revealed three important realizations: One, there is an insane amount of red tape and administrative document inertia when bringing a vaccine to market; two, the scientific community can be a remarkably powerful machine when working towards a single, common focus; and three, *there's gold in them thar hills* to the tune of billions of dollars for the pharmaceutical company, or companies, that capture the market. The gold rush was on, Moderna and Pfizer had reaped the motherload in North America, and I had decided it was time to check out their glitter.

I wasn't going to be the first in line, though. Despite the rest of the world being submerged in a nightmare of Covid lockdown and hospitals busting at the seams, we remained in our little storm's eye with a few scattered cases here and there. There was no hurry, particularly since I'd had Covid twice and probably had some degree of wildtype immunity.

At the hospital, the problem was that almost every symptom and sign of Covid-19 was also a symptom and sign of every other disease. As a result, we were naturally suspicious of almost everyone that walked through the ER doors (or came by ambulance), but they invariably tested negative. In some ways, our little community was incredibly lucky. We were given a chance to fortify our defenses before the real war came to town.

However, this was new technology: A vaccine based on messenger RNA (mRNA). Unlike Polio, Measles, Mumps, Rubella, and every other vaccine that used a neutralized form of the actual virus (either inactivated or live-attenuated), this new mRNA vaccine contained no live virus whatsoever. Just a piece of messenger RNA wrapped in a lipid envelope that could enter a human cell and produce a copy of a part of the Covid-19 virus known as the *spike protein*. This copy could stimulate and build an immune response led by antibodies that would attack the virus if and when it attacked you. In fact, the mRNA vaccine wasn't so new, with human trials being conducted as early as 2013 for other viruses like Rabies.

Our Covid-19 hospital vaccination

program had begun four weeks earlier. I was purposefully slow and hesitant to book my appointment. It couldn't hurt to see up close and friendly how people were reacting to the vaccine. Right? Was that cowardly? Maybe a little, letting others lead the charge. Or maybe, I was just doing my own due diligence and what was right for me at that time since the psychological aspects of the vaccine were as great as the physical ones.

So far, everyone who'd had the vaccine had been fine: an achy shoulder, an occasional fainting episode, a few hours of feeling flu-like. All normal, expected side effects of any vaccine. No one died on the spot, no one grew a third eye in their foreheads, no one turned permanently green, and, to my knowledge, no one had been turned into a zombie under remote control of the government.

I escaped from my shift in the emergency and ran up the stairs to a meeting room that had been converted to an in-house vaccination center. I entered the registration area and immediately recognized the young woman with long black hair behind the desk. It was the same woman who had been a screener at one of the entrances to the hospital where they asked a series of questions designed to detect people at high-risk for carrying Covid-19: "Have you travelled outside the region, the province, the country? (This changed according to world Covid numbers); "Have you been exposed to anyone with Covid?"; "Are you waiting for a Covid test to come back?"; "Have you had any fevers or coughs?" Etcetera. On a day-to-day basis, the routine of this interaction with hospital staff mostly became a grunt with some form of words to the effect of, "I'm all good."

"You seem to be everywhere these days?" I commented.

"You bet, Doc. Wherever they need me, I'm there. I even do some work at the community test center across the street."

"Lucrative?" I asked, winking.

She hushed her voice and leaned in. "Very. And easy work, too. This will cover a good chunk of my university tuition."

Yup, there's gold in them thar Covid hills, and it's not just Big Pharma doing the prospecting.

"That's terrific. I'm sure they're desperate for bodies also."

"Yeah, there's no lack of shifts, that's for sure." She scanned some papers, found my name, and crossed me off. "Okay, read and sign this, please."

I scanned the consent document and signed on the bottom line. She looked it over and then handed back the paper. "Good to go."

"Thanks. See you where I see you."

Her eyes smiled at me. "For sure."

I walked out one door and into the next where a number of stations were set up to administer the vaccine. I recognized a lot of the nurses, many of whom had been retired for years. I was waved over to a chair, where I handed my paperwork to a nurse I didn't recognize and sat down.

"Good morning," I said. She was busy tapping away on her keyboard, and there was a momentary silence before she said, "And good morning to you, Dr. Spencer. How are we today?"

"Pretty good. This is a nice little break from my shift in the ER."

"Excellent. So ..." She quickly got down to business and read through a litany of questions to obtain further consent for what she was about to do: "Have you had any reactions to a vaccine before? Do you have any issues with needles?" Etcetera.

I listened, but by the third question had tuned her out. The whole idea of people repeatedly firing questions at you day in and day out, even if it was for your own good, grew tedious early on in the pandemic. My mind drifted away and, being a doctor who constantly thinks about everything that can go wrong with every patient I see, I involuntarily began to do just that, but for myself. The truth was, although this new vaccine had been tested on a large scale and had been found 95% effective in preventing Covid-19 with very few short-term side effects, no one really had any idea about mid or long-term side effects. It was comforting to know that reactions and side effects to vaccines generally showed up in the short term, but there was always that "What if?" question bouncing around my brain, a brain that was conditioned to always look for the bad side of life. It's what I was paid to do.

However, before I could spiral any further down the Covid rabbit hole, I heard, "All done."

I was startled. "All done?" I repeated meekly.

I hadn't felt a thing. Nothing except the coolness of the alcohol swab. No jab. Nothing.

"Yes," she repeated, her attention once again turned back to her keyboard. "All done. You can have a seat over there. You have to wait fifteen minutes and then you can go." She reached for her printer and then handed me a paper. "Here's your proof of vaccination, and I'll have it emailed to you as well. Okay?"

I accepted the paper. "Yes. Yes, of course. You know ... you're very good. I didn't feel a thing."

"Not my first circus. And trust me, this is a circus. Okay. Run along, Dr. Spencer. We must keep the revolving door revolving." She looked at me. "Feel okay?"

Actually, I felt better than okay. I felt like someone had removed a spiny thorn from my foot that had been there since the vaccine program had been announced.

"Feel fine." I got up and walked to a chair at the back of the room. "Thanks again."

She nodded her head, politely dismissing me.

There were three other people sitting in chairs six feet or more apart. Everyone had their heads down, tapping away at their phones. Some taking pics of their new *proof of vaccination* paper, no doubt posting it on social media. It had become all the rage to post this on Facebook or Instagram. A symbol of doing what's right to protect your community. A badge of honour, like a Cross of Valour in this war against Covid.

I sat back in my chair and slouched a little, processing the whole experience, trying to remember *why* I had been so hesitant, even a little scared. I realized, as always, that it was the unknown that was scary. The not knowing. Well, now I knew. And there was nothing to it. If the vaccine did have some untoward side effect months or years from now, then I would deal with it then. For now, I had a new and powerful weapon added to my arsenal, and I felt almost invincible.

10 DAYS EARLIER

November 28th, 2021

Continued

Sarah and I bounded up the steps to our house, panicky first-time parents returning guiltily from our first night out, hearts pounding with concern for our little baby June, the product of five years of in vitro fertilization: our miracle child.

After awkwardly disrupting the concert by leaving halfway through Debussy – there was no way Sarah was waiting until the intermission, which was only fifteen minutes later – we sped home with a corner skid here and a locked brake slide there as I negotiated the glistening fresh snowy roads. Sarah remained on the phone with Jenna the whole time, relaying info to me, the doctor, from which I was supposed to arrive at a diagnosis and a treatment plan on the fly.

June awoke coughing and sniffly, which probably wouldn't have worried Jenna, however, the fever of 104 tipped the scales, prompting the phone call. And rightly so. That temperature was dangerously high. Jenna gave her Tylenol, which helped a little, and then noted June was struggling to catch her breath. This prompted an evil stare from Sarah and a litany of questions while she held the palm of her hand over her phone:

"Can kids get Covid? I thought it was super rare?"

It's very rare, but it does happen. The last I checked there were fifty pediatric deaths in the US.

"You're sure your rapid test was negative?"

I did it twice. For whatever a rapid test is worth.

"She doesn't have the vaccine." Sarah's inside brain was processing on the outside.

She's too young to have the vaccine.

"Dammit! What if she really has Covid, Mark? What the hell are we going to do?"

It was time to speak. Time to offer some reassurance. "Sarah, common things being common, it's probably just a bad cold. You know that."

"Nobody around us has had a regular cold for a year and a half. Where would she get it from?"

"And because of that," I said, "she hasn't had a chance to develop her immune system yet. Maybe you or I brought something innocuous home from work that might be a bigger deal for her to fight off."

Sarah sighed deeply and sank into her seat.

Jenna met us at the door with June draped

over her shoulder. Jenna looked scared and June looked lethargic, pale, and was struggling to breathe.

This is bad. It sure as hell isn't a regular cold.

I looked quickly at Sarah and made a command decision. "Bundle her up, we're going straight to the hospital.

***

It was far quicker to drive her to the hospital in our SUV rather than call an ambulance, although I would have donated a lung for a face mask and some oxygen. She was struggling so hard to catch her breath.

Reminder: burr hole set for ER and oxygen for home.

Sarah had called ahead to the ER, and they were waiting for us. We burst through the sliding doors of the main ER and walked directly to the trauma bay, where a nurse in full PPE grabbed June from Sarah's arms and placed her directly on her stomach in a pediatric crib they had prepared. She applied a tiny face mask and pumped oxygen into her while another nurse, who had come down from the pediatric unit, started an IV: no easy task in a feverish, dehydrated four-month-old. Someone did a quick swab for Covid while someone else drew several vials of blood after a successful IV was placed. I was incredibly grateful for how efficient my colleagues were.

June quickly disappeared from view as the cluster of medical professionals around her grew. We were forced away by the tide, much to Sarah's chagrin. I knew we needed to let them do their job. I was on the other side of the fence now, a parent who could be an obstacle to my child's recovery. The charge nurse approached us and gently escorted us from the room. I had my arm around Sarah's waist and pulled her along. When we were just outside of the trauma bay, she turned and buried her head in my shoulder, sobbing wildly, like a mother wolf in the dead of night standing over a slain cub. I was torn between my professional self in my own work environment, where everything was nicely compartmentalized, and my human fatherhood where the world was crashing down upon us. The flood came, and it was all I could do to keep us afloat.

***

Ultimately, we weren't just escorted from the trauma bay but were placed in an isolation room. Despite the rarity, June had Covid until proven otherwise, and that meant we probably had it also.

Swabs were taken from both of us – my third of the evening – and were sent off emergently to the hospital lab, which had a much quicker turn-round time then the community testing center. Ours would be run with the same batch as June's. I was scheduled for a shift in the morning, so there was some ulterior motive urgency to determining my status.

We sat patiently waiting, not allowed to leave the room until our results were back. The circumstances were somewhat unusual. Even though we weren't considered patients – since we were not sick in any way – we were still considered potentially hot cases.

I couldn't help but wallow in guilt as I sat there thinking about June. If she had Covid, the chances were high that it came from me since I was exposed daily. And given the incubation time of three to five days, it coincided with my unintentional break in PPE protocol after drilling the burr hole in the ten-year-old's head.

I thought about tonight's date night. If Sarah and I tested positive, we unwittingly exposed a ton of people to some variant of the virus: Delta? Or the new Omicron we'd been hearing about which was supposedly twice as contagious? I tried to take some comfort in knowing that I had done everything by the book, even testing myself twice. Or had I? What about my breach in PPE protocol? Maybe I purposefully buried the importance of that event, so desperate was I to go out tonight.

I was having flashbacks once again to my disastrous flight back from Florida at the beginning of the pandemic, when I exposed an entire plane full of passengers to the original virus, several of whom probably died. I hung my head dolefully.

"Thinking about the plane ride from Florida again, aren't you?"

I looked up at Sarah and let out a deep sigh, "You know me all too well, Sarah."

"It wasn't your fault then, and this is not your fault now."

She doesn't know about my PPE breach. Do I tell her? Would that make anything better? At least she would know that it wasn't her.

"Sarah, there's something I need to tell you ..."

I explained in detail what had happened, that I had to take my shield off and the N95 came with it. It had only been for a few minutes, and I had everything back in place before I spoke to the child's father (after being reminded by one of the nurses that I looked way too happy with far too many teeth showing).

Sarah was not pleased. "Why didn't you tell me?"

"Well. There was no reason to. The child's initial Covid test was negative. And I didn't think anything more of it at the time and completely forgot. It's not like these minor breaches don't happen all the time, accidentally, or sometimes, even on purpose. Have you tried wearing an N95 mask for a full eight or twelve-hour shift? It's brutal."

We both heard a brief *here-I-come* kind of rap on the closed door, and then Dr. Patterson, one of my junior colleagues, walked in. With the mask and shield, it was impossible to read her.

She cleared her throat. "Mark. Sarah. I won't beat around the bush. June tested positive. Your daughter has a severe case of Covid. I'm very sorry."

We were both facing Dr. Patterson when we received the news. Sarah skipped denial completely and bolted straight to anger. She pivoted towards me and slammed her open hands into my chest, pushing me back, away from her. She cried out through tears, "Mark! How could you? You should have told me sooner?"

"Whoa, whoa," Dr. Patterson said, stepping forward, between us. "I'm not sure what this is all about, but, if it's a blame thing, you can both rest easy. At least for the moment."

Sarah and I stared at her with open mouths, waiting for her next words.

"You both tested negative."

8 DAYS EARLIER

November 30th, 2021

Human beings, for whatever reason – simplicity being the most obvious – tend to think of science in black/white, yes/no, zero/one terms. It's much easier for our minds to process. From a medical perspective, this would translate to either having a disease or not having a disease. You would think this was obvious for something like cancer: either you have it or you don't. In fact, as we age, we all have mutagenic or cancerous cells: cells that grow out of control. But in low numbers, our body's defenses can handle it. So really, as we age, we all have cancer. It only becomes a problem when they overrun our biological defenses. That's when we *have* cancer.

From an infection perspective, we would like to think that we either have something like Covid-19, or we don't. Yes or no. Unfortunately, like cancer, infectious problems are often part of a spectrum of disease and dose related. You can have just a little bit of the SARS CoV-2 virus in your body and have minimal or no symptoms, or you can be flooded with it and die. It all depends how big a dose you received (how large the host of your enemy is), and how well your immune system is working (how big your defenses are). Luckily, we have weapons – vaccines – to boost our defenses by making more antibodies (soldiers), and PPE – masks, shields, and sanitizers – to protect us (the castle walls).

This was the theory, anyway. The reality was that the variables were so numerous and the disease so complex, you could dance through the Covid raindrops for years without getting sick and then suddenly, without rhyme or reason, *you were*. Such were the mysteries of medicine.

In any case, this was how our hospital's infectious disease specialist explained June's predicament to Sarah and I: "You were both previously infected, vaccinated and boosted and therefore have a strong defense system, but you could still be infected with Covid-19. It's just that you are able to keep it under control such that you don't have symptoms. In fact, you were able to keep the viral numbers in your bodies so low they didn't even register on rapid antigen or PCR testing."

Imagine that the constant war going on in your body is fought via many battles. In between battles, when the immediate threat is low, the soldiers may go on furlough or be deployed elsewhere. It's only when the fighting begins that your soldiers come back to the front lines to defend. That's when a PCR or rapid test will be positive. Hence the need to repeat the tests over several days.

Poor June, though, had very limited defenses; she was not vaccinated or protected in any way from Covid. Her shields were never up, and her phasers were barely working. If Sarah and I were subclinically infected because we had so much contact with her, we may have progressively increased the viral enemy in her system to the point that she could no longer fight it. As the specialist explained, "Remember the Italian health care workers, doctors, and nurses, who dropped like flies? Unprotected in any way, their bodies were overwhelmed by the sheer volume of virus they were exposed to. Or, closer to home, the healthy, young personal support worker in his twenties who died while working in a Toronto nursing home that had a full on outbreak of Covid? Every other client was infected, and the sheer amount of viral exposure overwhelmed him."

Sarah had asked, "But I'm still breast feeding. Wouldn't I be transmitting some of my antibodies to her?"

The specialist answered, "Certainly. But apparently not enough. Also, there's the matter that this is likely the new variant, Omicron, which is much more transmissible and for which neither of you would have developed any specific immunity. Although, you still have the global immunity from the vaccines to the other variants that will minimize or eliminate your disease severity."

I should have told Sarah from the beginning about my PPE breech. Now, after the fact, I looked guilty, and I felt guilty. A guilt that crushed me from the moment I awoke. Squeezing the life from me, just as Covid was doing to June. Did I give my poor child Covid? Was this all my fault?

As it turned out, further testing did confirm that she had the Omicron variant. A variant that we knew very little about at this stage, other than it did have an affinity for children and, in particular, infants. This worried me. The devil you knew was one thing ....

I was fully garbed, coming off shift, and making my way to the Neonatal Intensive Care Unit (NICU). Technically speaking, June didn't belong in the NICU, which was designed for newborns, but there was nowhere else for her to go. Our hospital was too small to have a pediatric ICU, and she certainly didn't belong in the main ICU, where the sickest of the sick adults were kept, even though she was *really* sick. We had discussed the benefits of transferring her to the world renown Toronto Sick Kids Hospital where they had a true pediatric ICU, but they were filled up with other things, and the truth was, pediatric Covid was so rare that nobody had a particular handle on it, and thus far, the available and accepted treatment options were limited to oxygen, positioning, hydration, and ventilatory support. All things that could be done in our hometown. Everything else was off label and case by case. And whatever Toronto had off label, I was assured we had it here also or could get it. Just like in adults, at the end of the day, treatment was largely supportive while the patient fought back. It was like sneaking onions and turnips into a castle under siege when what they really needed was more soldiers with longer spears.

I paused at the double doors and ran my ID over the scanner. Trepidation always filled my gut as I passed through these doors. On the other side, my little girl was fighting for her life, and my contribution to her welfare was limited. I no longer was in control, and nor should I be. This was where I parked my level of expertise and needed to trust in the pediatrician and infectious disease specialist to bring my daughter back to health. Trust was a ten-gallon word, though, and when it was your own flesh and blood, it came with difficulty. If push came to shove, I knew I trusted my instincts more than anything or anybody else, and my instincts weren't always right.

This was my third visit of the day. I'd snuck away twice during my shift at the urging of my colleagues. It was clear that my mind wasn't entirely on my work, and they knew it comforted me to see her even for just a minute and made me a more focused ER doc. Even experienced compartmentalization had its limits. I'd been strongly advised to take time off, but I was the head of the department, stubborn, and I preferred to be in the hospital, closer to June in case she needed me. And I needed to keep busy.

Given the situation, and despite multiple negative swabs, I was still on work isolation protocol. This meant nothing more than wearing full PPE all the time (which I was already doing) with no removal of gear around other workers, i.e., no eating or drinking in the vicinity of others. My situation was unique and didn't fall into the playbook, so there was a lot of hour-by-hour decision making going on.

I nodded to the two NICU nurses at the desk, who were charting. I didn't need to ask how June was doing. I could tell by their eyes that she certainly hadn't improved. I had them both on speed dial and was starting to feel a little sheepish. They did have three other neonates to take care of. Technically, we weren't allowed to visit with current Covid restrictions. Being on staff had its privileges, though.

Because of her Covid status, June had her own isolation room within the NICU. I stood in front of a big heavy door and peered through the glass window. Sarah was already inside dressed in full PPE. She was here even more than I was. I quietly opened the door and tip-toed in, trying not to disturb her. She was sitting on a stool next to the incubator with one gloved hand reaching through a porthole holding a small nippled glass bottle containing breast milk she'd pumped earlier in the morning. June was on her back, and Sarah was trying desperately to negotiate the nipple between her lips with little success.

"Dammit!" Sarah whispered harshly. "C'mon, Juuuune. Take the nipple. Pleeeeease."

I stood behind Sarah, placed my hands on her shoulders, and kneaded muscles taught with anxiety. She pulled her arm out of the porthole and, with one hand still holding the bottle, rested both arms on her laps.

"Not happening?" I asked needlessly.

Sarah turned and looked at me with wet, sad eyes. "No. She won't take anything anymore."

I visually examined June, an involuntary and inescapable habit coming off a work shift. It had only been three days, and she already appeared to have lost weight. Her eyes were sunken and glazed, staring emptily at the reflective inner surface of the incubator. Her cheeks were saggy and drawn, dragging the corners of her lips down, giving her a look of total despair. Typically, when June was awake, she fidgeted. Her hands and feet continuously squirming. Now they lay dormant, as if she were a floppy doll left abandoned at the bottom of a child's closet. Only her chest moved continuously, straining and creaking with every inhalation, accessory muscles taught like the stays of a tall ship, struggling to suck the oxygenated wind from the incubator through Covid laden lungs to supply her bloodstream, the rest of her body, and, most importantly, her brain.

She suddenly went rigid and then hacked and wheezed, spittle dribbling over her cheeks. An alarm sounded. I eyeballed her monitor and noted her oxygen saturations had fallen into the eighties. Not good. I reached in, one hand through a porthole on each side, and gently flipped her into prone. As with adult Covid patients, lying on her stomach seemed to allow her to breathe more easily. Her saturations improved above ninety, and the coughing stopped.

The door behind us opened, and I turned to see our pediatrician, Dr. Bouliane, enter. He had a grim look on his face that told me everything I didn't want to know.

"Mark. Sarah."

"Isaac," I responded, half-heartedly.

In a strange reversal of roles, I had been his preceptor at one point in time while he was still in med school. He had done an elective in the ER for four weeks, thinking that it might be his future career, however, he had been so enthralled by the pediatric cases we had seen on that rotation that he quickly gravitated toward that specialty. This was a fairly common phenomenon in the ER from a teaching perspective, where every age and walk of life limped through the door. Students were drawn to the emergency room by the glamour of TV shows like *Grey's Anatomy* and *ER* only to find that they were not heroically saving a life every time the doors to the ER swung open, and that work in the ER was more about paper cuts and gucky throats than AK-47 wounds and open cardiac massage.

After a pediatric residency in Toronto, Dr. Bouliane upped the ante with two years of fellowship training in the US. As with most every northern kid, though, he ultimately returned to his roots and, after five years working in San Francisco, brought his bountiful knowledge home with him along with his partner. It was impossible to tell given the surgical gown he was wearing, but, underneath, I was sure he was dressed in chic, big-city clothes. Like the straight cut of his accoutrement, Isaac was always direct and to the point, which was good for me but not so much for Sarah, who needed the blows cushioned.

"Look," Isaac said to both of us but mostly making eye contact with me. "I think you can both see that June is struggling. Her little lungs are full of Covid, and every breath is an effort. We are giving her the maximum amount of oxygen that's safe via the incubator, but we may have to do something more ...."

That something more was placing a tube

through her mouth or nose and into her trachea – intubation – and then putting her on a ventilator to give her breathing muscles a rest. This was the final movement of the symphony with no encore in reserve.

"You want to intubate her?" Sarah cried out, tears flowing freely now.

I stepped away abruptly from everyone, from June, and felt my back up against a literal wall. Logically, I justified this by telling myself I needed a more objective viewpoint to think and get a grip on the big picture. Realistically, I just needed space to build a wall between my spiralling feelings and the event that was unravelling in front of me.

And then my phone buzzed. A text message.

Grateful for the distraction, I glanced at it. It was from Hitchhiker, and it said, "Check your email."

And so, I did.

As I read it, relief enveloped me like a warm blanket on a sub-zero night.

"Mark!!" Sarah yelled. "What the hell? Where are you right now? We're talking about intubating your daughter who's dying from Covid. Don't you have anything to say about that?"

I looked up from my phone and blustered, "Hyperbaric incubator."

***

"Sorry?" Isaac responded.

"We have an idea that may buy her some time. Enough time to avoid intubation while she eradicates the virus from her system."

Sarah eyed me suspiciously, one eyebrow raised to the ceiling. "Who's *we*?"

I held my phone in the air like a torch, and said, "Hitchhiker and I. He sent me a link to a paper from the India Institute of Medical Sciences published online in the *Reader's Forum of Acta Paediatrica*. They discuss how a regular incubator can be turned into a negative pressure incubator to minimize aerosolization in infant patients with Covid."

"Yes," Isaac said, "but hyperbaric chambers used to treat adult Covid patients are positive pressure environments. It's the opposite."

"Agreed," I replied. "However, my friend talked to a biomed engineer, and they feel the incubator could easily be modified into a positive pressure environment."

"STOP!" Sarah yelled. "Can someone please explain what the hell you are talking about?"

I turned to Sarah and placed a hand on her shoulder. "Remember that documentary I made you watch a few years ago about Connor McDavid – the superstar hockey player for the Edmonton Oilers – when he injured his knee, and they put him into this chamber to quicken the healing?"

"Sort of," she replied.

"Well, it turns out that a high pressure oxygenated environment is good for healing many other things also. In particular, there have been several studies looking at its use in Covid patients."

"Mark's right," Isaac continued. "Studies have come out from all over the world demonstrating three-fold faster recovery times by placing Covid patients in hyperbaric oxygen chambers for ninety minutes per day, where they breathe oxygen at a higher atmospheric pressure."

"Don't they need those special coffin-looking glass chambers to make it work?" Sarah asked.

"As it happens, after we watched the documentary, I looked into it. There are some companies making portable machines now," I replied.

"How does that help June, though? She's stuck in this incubator." Sarah waved her hand over it.

The fact that June was in an incubator at all was something novel. Normally, incubators were meant for newborns. It took some novel thinking and discussion to negotiate the idea that June would benefit from it. Given that she was only four months old, and perhaps a little small for her age, she just fit the largest one we had. Everyone agreed, though, that it was the best way to maximize the delivery of oxygen to her lungs. It also had the added bonus of being equipped with multiple sensors, allowing us to closely monitor all her vital signs.

"Can I see your phone, Mark?" Isaac asked.

I opened my phone to the study that Hitchhiker had sent and passed it to him. While he read it, Sarah reached over and held my hand. Her palm was clammy and tense.

"You know, Mark, I think this could work. Your friend might be onto something. Let me give biomed a call and see if we can modify June's incubator, jury-rig something. It might be just the thing we need to prevent intubation."

I clasped my other hand around Sarah's and let out a whispered, "Yes."

"Oh, and what kind of name is Hitchhiker, anyway?"

I waved him off and said, "Long story."

Dr. Bouliane handed back my phone and looked very excited as he turned to step out of the room, pulling his own phone out of his trouser pocket. He looked back and said, "Mark, send me the link to that paper. You know, if this works, it will make a great case report study."

I frowned.

It's rarely a good thing when a physician tells you they are going to write a scientific paper about your loved one.

6 DAYS EARLIER
December 2nd, 2021

I was dicing garlic and onions while Sarah slept. The last five days had been brutal. The plan was to freshen up, have some real food – something different than Timmy's – and then head back to the hospital. Dr. Bouliane had to threaten Sarah before she would acquiesce to leave June's side. "Sarah," he had said," you're officially not even allowed to be here, remember? The current hospital policy is no visitors. Don't make me enforce it. Go home. Eat some real food and have a nap. June is stable and isn't going anywhere."

We were following our doctor's orders to the letter. I could hear a gentle snore coming from the bedroom as I was putting together a pasta comfort-dish. Unlike Sarah, I had been catnapping for the last five days, a skill I had learned in residency and maintained daily, willfully, or not. If my brain was tired, no matter what my body was feeling, it would shut down for a few minutes. Sarah thought it bordered on narcolepsy. I thought I was just being efficient, like when the display on your laptop goes blank to conserve battery power. After all, our bodies are really just one great big ATP battery recharged by sleep and food.

I tossed spaghetti into a pot of gently boiling water and then inserted a set of ear buds. It was time to call my mother in England to let her know what was going on. She had no idea, and June *was* her only grandchild. I dialed her number and slipped my phone into a pocket. As the line was connecting, I filled Archie's bowl with dried food, topping it with some cooked ground beef I was using for the meatballs. Poor Archie had been alone for most of the last five days and, apparently, according to the neighbors who were checking on him, had been barking up a storm. I ruffled his bangs and gave him a forced smile as I placed his bowl on the floor. The line connected.

"Hello. This is Frances," an energetic and elderly female voice answered.

"Hi, Mum ... It's Mark."

"I gathered that since you're my only son. Not to mention call display."

I rolled my eyes. Strangely, sometimes my mother reminded me of my new friend, the Hitchhiker: minimal filter with maximal pragmatism. Although their accents couldn't be more different: he from Kentucky, and she born and raised in England.

"What's wrong, Mark?" She asked softly. "I can tell by the tone that something's bothering you."

Mother radar. Yeah, there's definitely something bothering me.

I blurted it out, or, perhaps, unloaded was a better word. Five days of pent-up guilt and despair.

"Mum. It's June. She's sick."

"Covid?"

"Well ... yes."

"The new strain they're talking about? That *Omicron*?"

"Yes, it is."

My mother had lived with my virologist father for more than fifty years. She knew the lingo.

"How sick is she?"

"Very," I croaked. "She's in a modified incubator receiving high-flow oxygen. There's talk that she may need to be intubated."

There was a long pause, and, for a moment, I was reliving the reverse of a conversation we'd had almost a year ago to the day, when my mother phoned me up out of the blue to inform me that my father had Covid: but that he had possibly discovered a cure ... that was locked in a safe in his laboratory basement ... that only I could open. I shuddered when I thought back to everything that happened afterwards: the good and the bad. Unfortunately, there would be no silver lining in this conversation she and I were having now.

"Mum. She's only four months old. I can't ... I can't lose her. We ... can't lose her." Try as I might to be stoic and in control, a sniffle escaped.

She whispered something bizarre, almost unintelligible, that sounded like, "*Abigail.*"

"Sorry, Mum. What? What did you say?"

Silence, save for a low-grade overseas buzzing noise.

"Mum? Are you still there?"

She let out a low, hurtful groan and then said, "It was nothing, Mark. Just an old memory that surfaced unexpectedly. Forget it."

"Is it something to do with June? Tell me, Mum. You have to tell me."

She seemed to be thinking hard and then released a long sigh. "I'm an old woman now, Mark. I've lived a long life. Your father and I swore we'd take this to the grave. But he's gone, and I'm tired of keeping secrets. Except for June, you're the only blood I have left."

"What is it, Mum? Tell me."

"Abigail was your sister, Mark. She died before you were born and was only four months old. It was wrong, but we never told you."

***

If my phone had been in my hand, it would have dropped to the floor and splattered. I began walking slowly, aimlessly through all the rooms on the main floor, a slow march through fog. "I had a ... a sister?"

"You did. We named her Abigail after your father's mother."

"What .... What happened?" My tongue was thick with a hundred questions, but I found myself struggling to get anything out.

"Your father was working at the university, then. Some classroom teaching and some lab work. Abigail was born healthy. She was the cutest, perfect baby. And then one day, when she was four months old, she developed a fever and then a brain infection."

"Meningitis?" I asked.

"Yes. That was it. Meningitis."

The doctor in me had to know more. Always more. "From what? Why did she have meningitis? Was it from the lab?"

"It was the mumps. There was an outbreak in the neighborhood."

And then it hit me. The conversation Sarah had with my father not long before he passed. When his dementia was progressing, and he was suffering from Covid induced delirium and was trying to repair a decade old broken father-son relationship, trying to explain why he missed our wedding because of a local outbreak of Mumps in the UK when he was working at the level four Porton Down Containment Labs. It made no sense to us at the time. Mumps was usually a benign disease. Apparently, there were underlying currents I was not aware of.

Archie suddenly began barking and jumping at a side window. Something he never did. I was still marching solemnly from one room to another as we talked, processing everything my mother was saying, working off nervous energy. I passed by the window and, for a fleeting moment, thought I saw a shadow move just outside of my basement office window. Archie settled down, and I scratched him under the chin and whispered, "Good guard dog, Archie, Good boy."

"Mum, I'm so sorry."

"No. It's me who's sorry, Son. I should have told you long ago. I know your father was a workaholic and a hard man, but deep down he meant well. I wish he were alive. He would know how to help June."

A sparkle of hope suddenly erupted in my chest.

Dad may not be alive anymore, but he had left me a legacy. Something that could potentially help June. Even from the grave.

5 DAYS EARLIER

December 3rd, 2021

Limbo is the first circle of Dante's hell. But for an ER doc, it may as well be the ninth and last. We don't do well in limbo. We need to act, do something, make a difference, prescribe or change a medication, adjust an IV, get another opinion. Something. Anything. Waiting around feeling useless does have a medical term, it's called: *expectant observation*. It's what we tell patients when we have nothing to make them better right now, but we hope time and Mother Nature will do the job for us at some point in the future.

Equally appropriate, the ninth circle of hell is called betrayal. Had I betrayed June, my own flesh and blood? Given her Covid? Although my swabs were negative thus far, the incubation period could be up to fourteen days. It was why Sarah and I were still testing daily. I had the exposure in the ER with the burr hole kid. The timing was right: three days after. My day-to-day life was now carried out under the smothering weight of this contrition, and I was suffocating.

The hyperbaric incubator had been a

brilliant idea, and it was allowing June to hold her own. She was maintaining the oxygen in her blood above 90% and had not required intubation ... yet. The problem was that she hadn't progressed beyond that. It was a stalemate, which is a great option in chess if you're losing, but an unacceptable one in life when you're fighting a deadly disease.

By day's end, the biomed team had converted June's incubator into a hyperbaric incubator, attaching hoses here and there, blocking the access portholes with little air-tight doors to seal it off, and then raising the pressure inside her little world to one-and-a-half times normal atmospheric pressure, while continuing to deliver high-dose oxygen. At two hours per day (the maximum allowable time), we had done it for the past two days, and she had indeed perked up. Her skin looked less grey, and she seemed to have more energy, fidgeting like her old self. She was taking some of Sarah's breast milk, and this had a tremendous effect on Sarah's morale. She got that much better and then just stopped, like the virus had mounted a counterattack, and she regressed back to where she was two days earlier, except now she required the hyperbaric oxygen therapy to keep pace with the virus. It seemed we had reached a balancing act, where everything we threw at the virus was thrown back at us – more of Newton's third law at play.

In between treatment sessions, the incubator returned to its normal self, and we were able to touch her and feed her. I rubbed her back, and it felt like my fingers were running down a washboard. In six days, she had already lost ten percent of her body weight. Her metabolism was through the roof trying to run neck and neck with the virus.

"Why haven't they given her monoclonal antibody therapy?" Hitchhiker asked.

"They're considering it, but it's off label for pediatric cases and they're having trouble getting approval," I replied.

I was at home on a three-way evening Zoom call with Hitchhiker and Rufus. Monoclonal antibody therapy was already being used throughout the world to treat the sickest patients with Covid. Antibodies specific to the spike protein on the Covid virus' outer shell were mass produced in a laboratory and then infused into the patient intravenously. The antibodies, once attached to the virus, interfered with the virus' ability to enter human cells and replicate, slowing down the attack and allowing the body's immune system a chance to counterattack.

There were, however, many problems with the therapy. Most notably, the antibodies grown in the laboratory were harvested from people recovering from Covid infections. Which meant they were based on a *specific* Covid variant, like Alpha, Beta, or Delta. June had the new

Omicron variant, which had appeared only in the last few weeks, and it was doubtful the labs were fast enough to develop updated and appropriate monoclonal antibodies. Also, in Canada, unlike the US, there were strict criteria for administration, and June did not meet any of them. In particular, her young age, since the guidelines only permitted monoclonal antibody use in patients over the age of twelve.

"Ridiculous," Hitchhiker retorted. "Seventy percent of all medications used in pediatrics are off label."

"Like I said, we've got a good team in our corner, and they're fighting for us."

"Humph," Hitchhiker snorted. He clearly wasn't impressed with my team, which realistically only consisted of one pediatrician and one infectious disease specialist. "At the Mayo clinic, there would be a dozen specialists involved."

I didn't need to be reminded that my hospital was not the Mayo clinic.

"Everyone's doing the best they can," was all I could mutter back.

I could see Rufus' lips moving, but there was no sound.

Hitchhiker sighed and then said, "Please unmute yourself, Rufus. We can't hear whatever crucial comment you have to add to this conversation."

Rufus shook his head, paused, and then we

could finally hear his voice. "Sorry, mon. Damn technology gets the best of me sometimes. I was saying, 'look at the bright side, at least you have Hitchhiker and myself to help.' You know, like *The Three Musketeers.*"

Hitchhiker and Rufus had never met in person, only through Zoom meetings and telephone conferences. Although neither had said anything specific, they each felt the other had certain personality flaws that warranted improvement. That was not entirely true. Hitchhiker, in his typical closed mouth fashion had said nothing about Rufus – although his mannerisms said everything. Rufus, on the other hand, was very vocal about every one of Hitchhiker's eccentricities. And there were many. Essentially, I was friends with both, but, at best, they were business partners with each other.

"The three who?" Hitchhiker asked.

"*The Three Musketeers,*" Rufus replied. "From the novel by Alexander Dumas. And from the many movies. Have you not heard of them?"

"Of course, I've heard of *The Three Musketeers*. But these days, who has time for make-believe?"

"Perhaps you should make time, my friend. It is a classic –"

"Alright. Let's stay on task," I interrupted. "First, Hitchhiker, I want to thank you again for the hyperbaric incubator idea. It was brilliant and innovative and has definitely kept June one step ahead of the virus."

"Of course," Hitchhiker replied.

"Rufus, any more news about that buyout offer?"

"Nothing more. I've been snooping around the lab a little more, talking to the scientists and technicians. There is one fellow I'm curious about, a scientist from Brussels. Constantly asking why we aren't expanding more quickly. He's convinced we have a workable cure, and that we are doing the world a disservice by not bringing in bigger companies to develop it sooner."

"Yes, bigger companies who want to either maximize profits by charging outrageous amounts of money for it, or squash it completely to keep the vaccine business going strong," Hitchhiker said dryly.

"In any case, I'll look into it further. There's nothing worse than someone who thinks he's doing it for all the right reasons."

"Agreed," I said. "And listen. My dog's been acting strange, barking a lot. I noticed –"

"Archie?" Rufus asked. "How's the pup doing?"

Rufus had met Archie when he had come for a visit after the second lockdown, while he was still recovering from his frostbite wounds after our transatlantic adventure to recover my father's research in England. He ended up losing a couple of toes on each foot and considered himself fortunate since he could have lost so much more.

"Good as ever and not a pup anymore," I continued. "But, as I was saying, he's been barking more than usual, and the other night I noticed something peculiar. It was like a fleeting shadow in the backyard and, when I checked the next morning, there were multiple sets of footprints in the snow outside my office window. And they weren't *my* footprints. Could someone from Big Pharma be watching me?"

"It's possible, my friend. With this much money in the pot, these people are capable of anything."

"I agree," Hitchhiker added. "It might be wise for you to keep your laptop with you at all times, or at least in a safe when it's not with you. Also, please ensure it's well encrypted. Am I wrong in thinking that all your father's original work is still on there?"

"Yes. As well as on my backup."

"You should check all your security systems. Video cameras, locks, etcetera."

Now I was getting creeped out. The idea that people were potentially spying on me. Maybe even listening in?

"Wait. You guys don't think I'm in any danger, do you? I mean, they wouldn't break in, would they? Whoever *they* is?"

"Yes. Of course, you are," Hitchhiker said

flatly. "Did you think Big Pharma was going to sit around while you manufacture a gigantic dent in their investor's income stream? Don't be foolish."

Count on Hitchhiker to sugar-coat it.

"So … what do I do? I have a wife and child at home."

Well, there was supposed to be a child at home. Terrific news. If the virus doesn't get June, saboteurs might. Maybe she was safer at the hospital. I really was foolish. How was this the first time the potential for foul play had crossed my mind?

"Mark, mon, don't let him get you all riled up. We are still a fledgling company in the early stages of development. No one wants to harm you, my friend. They just want to keep an eye on you."

My partners were like Yin and Yang: two completely opposite sides of a coin. Somewhere in the middle of this road was the truth. Which meant at the very least I had to be more careful.

"Okay. Thank you, both. Message received. And you should probably take precautions also."

"I've anticipated all of this," Hitchhiker said coolly. "I am … well protected."

I had no idea what that meant, but also knew Hitchhiker would share nothing further.

Rufus added, "And I have an elaborate security system at home as well as at the lab. Money can buy those kinds of things."

Outstanding. I'm the variable in this

equation.

"Okay. I'll beef up my 'security' and keep my laptop locked away or with me. Let's assume bad guys are watching us at all times."

Suddenly, I felt like I was the bad actor in a John Le Carré novel. And how the hell do I tell Sarah this delightful bit of news? She has enough to deal with.

It was interesting that early on, in November of 2020, when I retrieved my father's research and presented it to colleagues, drug companies, and venture capitalists that Rufus worked with, none of them wanted any part of it, saying it was: "Too out there," and "Unlikely to work," and even "Completely impossible." And it was never money that was the issue. I would have given everything for free to any group that was able to turn his research into a clinically working drug. But, in reality, money *was* the issue. Everyone said it would cost too much to develop a working prototype, and they already had their research fingers dipped into other more promising pies. In the end, Rufus and I took matters into our own hands and formed the company. It was that or let my father's research sink into oblivion at a time when the world really needed it. Rufus had the financial know-how, and I had the rights to my dad's research, as well as at least some background in microbiology from my undergrad days. Now that we had our own company, it seemed like everyone wanted a piece of the action but maybe for all the wrong reasons.

"Any progress on sourcing our special ingredient?" I asked, changing topics, and working my way through a mental agenda.

The *special ingredient* had a complicated chemical name that was difficult to pronounce, and so we continued to call it simply, the "special ingredient." This also aligned well with our evolving policy of keeping everything hush-hush as we made progress since, to someone on the outside looking in, the special ingredient could be anything. It was kind of like hiding something in plain sight, "Our potential cure for Covid required a special ingredient, and it's called the *Special Ingredient*."

As to the cure itself, in a nutshell, my father had worked out a way to harvest antibodies from patients infected with SARS-CoV-2, reverse engineer the genetic code that produced those antibodies, meld that genetic code into a non-Covid type, deactivated virus (much like those used in cancer gene therapy) and then inject the new, genetically modified virus into the muscle of a sick patient, where that virus' modified DNA would combine with the patient's native muscle cell DNA and, in a factory like way, quickly produce the new anti-Covid antibodies necessary to fight off the illness. It was like arming your knights with AK-47s during the Middle Ages, allowing your white cells to spit out a million times more Covid-fighting antibodies than normal. And the beauty of this "cure" was that it could be used with any viral infection, not just SARS-CoV-2.

The trick was incorporating the gene modified viral vector into the patient's muscle. This is where the special ingredient came in. Typically, this ingredient would be used in garden variety gene therapy studies and would be available in abundance, sourced from Asia. Unfortunately, because of the large numbers of Covid studies being carried out across the world since the beginning of the pandemic requiring this same "ingredient," the demand outstripped supply, and it was near impossible to find. With the help of Hitchhiker, though, we were able to source some from the Mayo Clinic. It seemed, however, as the email from Rufus had alluded to, this well had run dry as well, and with Covid causing global disruption in supplies chains, we were unlikely to find any in the near future, which completely ground our progress to a halt. This meant that very sick patients, like my June, were resigned to fate and what little medical technology we had to throw at the virus. My poor June.

And then, for no reason I could imagine, yesterday's conversation with my mother squirmed into my head, and an imagined image of what my sister from forty or more years ago might have looked like hung there, floating. Did she look like –

"In fact," Hitchhiker said, interrupting my spiralling thoughts, "I have a lead."

It took me a moment to realign with the conversation, re-establish my walls. "That's … that's excellent news, Hitchhiker."

"Perhaps not as excellent as you think. As you know, the original and only source for our secret ingredient was from some unknown plant grown in a small town near Wuhan. My connections at the Mayo Clinic tell me that, in fact, Wuhan is not the only place that has this plant. There is a place in Central America where a similar plant grows."

"Damn. Central America," I muttered. "That's good news but not exactly next door."

"No, it isn't."

"Do you know exactly where in Central America?" Rufus asked.

"Yes, of course. I'm heading there tomorrow," Hitchhiker stated bluntly, like it was a given.

"Wait. What?" I asked. I could see Rufus' eyes go wide with surprise. "How –"

"The how is irrelevant. The point is that I believe I can have it in my hands and be back within the week."

"That's … amazing." It was best never to ask how Hitchhiker was going to accomplish something. You just let him do it, and it would get done."

"Rufus," I asked, "Once you have it in the lab in Montreal, how fast can you synthesize it and begin testing?"

"Oh, we are ready to go. It would take no more than a few hours."

"Excellent news all around. Great job everyone."

It was more than excellent news, much more. It was potential salvation for my little girl, if modern medicine and her own immune system didn't come through ... and if she survived long enough. The ethics of using a barely tested drug trotted through my mind fleetingly. However, if it came to that point, it was because we were looking for a Hail Mary anyway.

We said our goodbyes, and I imagine by that point it should have crossed my mind that, with current technology, anyone could have been listening in on our Zoom call.

4 DAYS EARLIER

December 4th, 2021

"What are the numbers like today?" I asked. *The Daily Question.*

Sarah replied without looking at her phone, "Fifty-one new cases and rising."

There wasn't much else for her to do when she was sitting at June's side but peruse the news. She didn't have the concentration to lose herself in a book. In fact, she told me she didn't want to lose herself in anything, lest she not be there for her daughter when she was needed. As a result, she was an encyclopedia of news knowledge.

We slept at home the previous night for the first time since June was admitted to hospital and were sitting down to a sparse breakfast. Neither of us had much in the way of appetites, which was good since there wasn't much food in the house.

"Damn, Shelley wins the pool."

"Excuse me?"

"Shelley, one of the ER nurses I work with. About two weeks ago they started a betting pool. A dollar a day. Closest guess to the daily Algoma

Public Health number wins."

"You're kidding me? The nurses are betting on the number of new Covid cases?"

I suddenly regretted opening my mouth. While I was able to – had to! – tuck work and Covid into a little impenetrable steel box in my head, Sarah was not so fortunate.

"Forget I said anything," I backpedalled. "The nurses are all burnt out. They're grasping at anything to lighten the day. Even the most morbid ideas."

"I thought you said it was quiet in the ER these days? You've been able to spend lots of time with June."

"You're right. It has been quiet. But, Sarah, it's been almost two years of this ...."

Sarah knew exactly what *this* was.

"They're just human beings, and, like I said, it's just the same horror movie over and over with no end in sight. Plus, they're starting to hear buzz about another lockdown as cases rise with this new Omicron variant. And there's a boredom factor setting in –"

"*They* don't have a daughter in the NICU, Mark."

"This is completely true."

My phone sang out the first few bars of *The Logical Song*, an oldie by *Supertramp*, and a reminder to keep my analytical mind on the front lines during our family crisis.

"Hi, it's Mark Spencer."

"Hi Mark, it's Isaac. Just wanted to update date you and Sarah. June spiked a temperature overnight." He followed this with all the specifics of her other vital signs and blood work that he knew I would want to hear, and then continued, "I suspect it's a secondary bacterial infection, possibly nosocomial (acquired in hospital), maybe from her central line. Blood cultures are pending." It was one thing to have a viral infection, but infinitely worse to add a bacterial infection to the mix since her immune system was already busy fighting SARS-CoV-2.

"We've started her on high dose Cefepime, but her breathing is becoming labored again. We're going to give the antibiotics a chance to work, however …."

I bloody well hated "howevers."

"Okay. That's shitty news. Thanks for keeping us in the loop. We'll be coming in shortly. Just having a quick bite and getting freshened up."

"Take your time. I don't expect any rapid changes."

I hoped there would be no "rapid changes." Typically, rapid changes in our world were always of the negative kind.

"And Mark, the way things are going with June, we might have to start thinking even more outside the box than your hyperbaric incubator. I've been in touch with all my colleagues down south in the big centers and, as you know, there's very little precedence to work from here. There are, however, some experimental protocols in play. Pharma studies looking for subjects. Anyway, we can discuss when you come in this morning."

"Thanks, Isaac. Talk soon."

I eyed Sarah as I put my phone on the kitchen island. I would have thought the little cisterns that produced her tears would be all dried up by now, but no, tears flowed freely once again. The desperate look of concern and sadness on her face was like a vise around my heart. I pushed my plate away, stood, and pulled her in for a hug. She had heard the conversation and knew June was slowly losing another battle ... and the war.

It came from nowhere, really. Although obviously it had been simmering for at least a little while. Still, I really didn't expect it when she whispered into my ear, "Mark, what about your father's cure?"

I gently pushed her to arm's length such that I could see her face. "What about it?"

"How far along are you? How close is it to being phase one trial ready?" A phase one trial is the first time a drug is used in humans, and its primary purpose is to assess the safety of the drug.

"I've told you all of this before. We had just begun tests in chimps when we ran out of our special ingredient. Why? What are you thinking?"

I know what you're thinking. The same thing I am.

She bowed her head like she was about to pray and then mumbled something in a low voice.

"Pardon?"

I need to hear you say it.

She suddenly stood tall, eased her shoulders back, looked me square in the eyes and said, "June is going to die unless we take drastic measures. It's time to take drastic measures."

Normally, these were the kind of careless words that would come out of my mouth, not Sarah's. I felt a strange combination of relief and guilt, knowing that I had already put a plan in play, but not shared it with her. The last thing I wanted to give her was false hope. I had planned to discuss it with her only as a last resort, if Hitchhiker and Rufus came through, and it was time to throw the Hail Mary.

I have to be one hundred percent sure you're onboard.

"Sarah, the drug we are making is still highly experimental. Untested –"

"But so far," she interjected, "there have been no reactions, severe side effects, or deaths in the animal studies. Correct?"

"That's true, but –"

"And all the animals that had Covid were cured and cured quickly. Right?"

"Also true, but –"

"Mark." She gazed deep into my eyes as if she were searching for my soul. "You know I'm right. June will die if we don't do something different."

Giving my baby an experimental, barely tested drug that was concocted in my own mad laboratory was certainly something different. It was also reckless, irresponsible, insane, and a dozen other adjectives consistent with the craziness of what she was suggesting. But she had independently arrived at the same conclusion I had. The way things were going, June was as good as dead if we didn't take a chance.

"I trust your father's work," she added softly. "More than I trust any other experimental treatment option."

I pulled away from her and moved slowly to the other side of the kitchen island. In some ways, I knew I was putting distance between myself and Sarah and the *idea.* Creating some space to think objectively. Emotions were running so high that it was easy for me to be convinced.

The drug I was creating with Rufus and Hitchhiker was my other baby. It had occupied every waking and sleeping moment since I arrived home that fateful November morning last year, with the document outlining my father's work tucked tightly under my arm. The truth of it was, that, as soon as June was diagnosed with Covid, somewhere in the depths of my mind, I had held onto the notion of my drug as a life preserver for her. If all else failed, if the ship was sinking, her daddy had something tucked up his sleeve to rescue her. And the second I recognized this thought, I buried it like a pirate's treasure. It was one thing for June to die, and another for my other baby to kill her. How could I live with myself? How could Sarah ever stand being around me again. Even though it was her suggestion, every time she looked at me, she couldn't help but lay blame, no matter the logic that June would have died anyway. Because that's what humans are: emotionally fickle entities with no control over their deepest inner feelings.

And yet, maybe I could save her ...

I came back around the island and planted my feet square in front of Sarah, gave her a crooked, unsure smile, and said, "Okay."

"Okay?" She repeated. It was just one word, but it said everything, and the most important thing: hope.

"Yes ... okay," I whispered. "But there's something I have to tell you."

I quickly brought her up to speed on my conversation yesterday with Rufus and Hitchhiker. At first, when she realized that what she had suggested was a plan that was already germinating behind the scenes, she gave me a brief look-to-kill. It only took her seconds, though, to reframe everything and say, "Well, that's just *you,* isn't it? I should have known."

I smiled dolefully as she washed away my little guilty secret.

She continued, a look of determination on her face, "But, I'm sorry. You can't leave your daughter's life in the hands of someone you barely know. You've done all you can do here. You need to go."

Just like that, one of the many niggling doubts circling my star system evaporated.

I do need to go.

I picked up my phone, scrolled through my contacts and texted.

"Hitchhiker? Where are you? I'm coming along."

ACT II

A Voyage of Alternatives

3 Days Earlier

Sunday, December 5th, 2021

Crossing the International Bridge that joined Ontario to Michigan, I felt like I had come full circle. This is where it had begun almost two years earlier, in March of 2020, at the very beginning of the pandemic. Since then, it was like living in a washing machine stuck on repeat, going round and round, wave after wave, the same cycle over and over, getting jostled, drenched, and rinsed. Yet still damp. Always damp. What we needed was that final trip to the dryer to reset a new day, and that always seemed to be around another distant corner.

Unlike the last time I crossed, there was traffic on the bridge – commuters interspersed with transport trucks. To the east, the dawn sun slowly erased the darkness and already its heat was working at the random clumps of snow still stubbornly frozen to my Highlander. To the west, a sliver of moon gently faded behind the wispy billowings from the tall stacks of the steel mill. In different circumstances, like our yearly weekend getaway to Bay Harbor, it would be picturesque and a good omen of a romantic weekend to come. Today, well, it was anything but that. Today, it all seemed different, somehow changed. But the reality was, the bridge and everything else around it was no different from the last time I was here. It was just that everything *felt* different because I had changed so much. As I dove deeper into this thought, I decided that I wasn't alone. The last two years of pandemia had likely resulted in the most rapid changes to humanity the world had ever seen. The literature was replete with the resultant psychological and physical changes caused directly and indirectly by the SARS-CoV-2 virus: isolation, depression, and increased rates of suicide and drug overdose; lockdown alcoholism – particularly in women in their 40s and 50s; obesity – the Covid paunch from overeating and under exercising; relationship breakdowns – maybe we weren't meant to spend all our time together. And then, of course, there were the economic implications ….

Not to say that everything that came out of the pandemic was bad. There were also silver linings, such as: the slowing down of life enough to take notice of it, bringing families closer together and spending more time with loved ones; money saved from not travelling and not eating out (with the potential corollary of eating healthier foods and adopting healthier lifestyles); new hobbies, tapping into creativity normally suppressed by the speed of modern life, like writing the book that's been sitting in the brain rafters for years, waiting for the moment to see the light, or picking up a new musical instrument and exploring that same part of the brain that's laid dormant since grade school piano lessons; the emergence and discovery of an inner resilience – for the luckier ones! – that could move future life to a higher level of confidence and happiness.

I approached the US border and lined up in the one open lane with a dozen other vehicles in front of me. Every time we inched forward in stop and go fashion, my anxiety ratcheted up a notch. I played with the satellite radio looking for a station but couldn't settle on one. Even though I didn't need them, I pulled my vaccination documents out of their envelope at least five times and fiddled with my passport in a similar fashion, flipping it open to stare at the expiry date over and over. I scrolled my phone, blinking in and out of the wallet app where my vaccination QR code was kept, a backup in case my paperwork was stolen (because certainly my vaccination papers would be of vital value to someone else), making sure the magic of technology hadn't caused it to disappear. I did some deep breathing exercises, until I became lightheaded and had to crack the window. I really had nothing to be nervous about, but I was. My last encounter two years earlier did not go well and involved three customs officers with automatic weapons. I also had this lousy feeling that they might have blacklisted me after my kayak escapades across their watery borderline – an event I had to come clean about when I returned to Canada, and the customs officers had no record of my leaving the country. I'd called ahead, but, apparently, blacklisting isn't the type of information they gave out to a rando over the phone.

I felt terrible leaving Sarah behind on her own to tend to June, but, at the same time, I was elated to be doing something, anything, that might contribute to the cause. I was also still in shock that Sarah had permitted, nay, suggested this trip. This ... time-crunched rescue mission to find the cure for our dying baby that sounded exactly like a piece of Hollywood fiction. And yet, here I was. I consoled myself by remembering that the child never died in these movies; there was always a happy ending. I could only hope.

One crack in the pot was that I still didn't really know anything about the trip. Only that we were going south to Central America. Hitchhiker wouldn't say more, fearing Big Pharma would somehow get wind and ... what? Intercept us? Stop us? Kill us? More Hollywood again, but Rufus assured me that this kind of stuff happened in real life. Just not usually *my* real life.

Hitchhiker had instructed me to pack for tropical, no easy feat when you're coming from minus five degrees Celsius. My plan was to ditch all my winter gear in my Highlander before we boarded the plane that would fly us from Pellston to Detroit. After much discussion – read, argument – Hitchhiker and I chose Pellston as a reasonable rendez-vous point. It was an eight-hour trek for him from the Mayo Clinic and had numerous flights daily to Detroit. For stealth reasons, Hitchhiker had insisted we purchase our tickets directly at the counter and not in advance.

Truth be told, it wasn't easy convincing Hitchhiker to bring me along. He clearly had a plan in mind – that he wouldn't share – and I was nothing more than a squeaky wheel. As the supreme loner, he preferred travelling by himself. Ultimately, I stood my ground. It was my daughter that was sick, and I wasn't going to leave it in the hands of one man. A man I'd only met once before and, realistically, as Sarah pointed out, didn't know much about.

Our destination beyond Detroit – i.e., where in Central America – was, apparently, on a need-to-know basis, and I still didn't need to know, I just needed to go. At least, that's how Hitchhiker put it. Well, it would certainly make for some lively discussion with the Customs

Officer:

Customs Officer: "Where are you headed?"

Me: "I'm really not sure. Somewhere in Central America where all the drug cartels live. My handler hasn't told me yet."

Customs Officer: "Wait. You're not a spy or a drug mule, are you?"

Me: "Dammit, Man. Can't you see I'm a doctor on a super-secret mission to save my child and possibly humanity as we know it?"

Customs Officer: "Right. Sir. Why don't you just pull in over there and step out of your vehicle ..."

I sucked in a deep breath of cool air. The window was still partly rolled down because I didn't want to make the officer wait any longer than necessary when it was my turn. I mean, what if my window got stuck and wouldn't open? I leaned my forehead into the steering wheel and closed my eyes. My thoughts right now were patently absurd, and my imagination was running wild.

Is this what one of my drug addled ER patients feels like when they're on speed?

Clearly, I was more nervous about crossing this border than I thought. Forget that I was possibly a persona non grata because of past idiocies. There was also the element of the different philosophical approaches our respective countries were taking in the handling of the Pandemic, particularly at this time of the progressing fourth wave.

If China was the North Pole in their approach, enforcing a complete "No-Covid" policy with aggressive mandatory vaccination and repeated lockdowns at the slightest cough, the US was the South Pole, with a Wild Wild West approach and different Covid strategies in every state, city, and borough. Hell, they still had football stadiums with eighty thousand unmasked people in them, more than the entire population of my little Northern Ontario town. I was comforted to know that Canada fell somewhere in the middle of these two polar opposites. At least it gave our more limited healthcare system a fighting chance.

I had some understanding of China's No-Covid approach; they were planning to host the Beijing Olympics. What I couldn't understand was the US strategy. They had the highest Covid numbers and death rate in the world. Did they care more about their economy than about their people? "Land of the Free" seemed meaningless if you were dead.

I drove into the booth and my adrenaline spiked. I toggled my window all the way down and tried to look as nonchalant as possible. Before the Customs Officer said anything, I thrust my hand and documents out the window and yelled, "Good morning."

He gave me a slight nod, and said, "What's your license number?"

My license number. He's trying to trip me up.

I yelled out in almost military fashion, "JKWG 979." *Sir! Yes, Sir!*

"Thanks," he replied. "I can't read it with all the damn snow plastered on."

Okay. Not trying to trip me up.

He took my documents and scanned them briefly. He handed back my vaccine papers and said, "You don't need this. At least not yet."

"Oh," I said. I already knew that but was trying to be as complete as possible. It still amazed me that we needed a vaccine passport to go to a restaurant in Ontario but not to enter a completely different country.

"How long are you staying in the US?"

"A week," I answered warily since I had no idea how long I was really going to be there. "Business." I added.

"All right. Have a safe trip. Don't forget to check the Covid re-entry regulations when you return. They change as often as I change underwear."

"Daily?" I smiled under my mask hesitantly.

"Damn near." He laughed.

And with the simple ease that follows some lucky people around like an aura – not usually me – I was through and on my way. My heartbeat regulated. My back and shoulder muscles unwound. I sank into my seat and relaxed my hands on the steering wheel. I turned on my satellite radio and found a good travelling tune: *On the Road Again,* by Willie Nelson. It was one of Rufus' favorite travelling songs, mostly because it reminded him of his Jamaican born father who would say, "Willie had smoked more weed than all of Jamaica combined."

My father, a staunch Brit who never travelled, said different, more practical things like: *Plan for the worst and hope for the best.*

My mission had just begun, and this was by far the *best* it would get.

***

The drive from my house to the Pellston Airport was a breezy one hour and thirty, and I was making great time, until I hit an unexpected blizzard blanket that was nowhere in the forecast. It was as if I'd taken a wrong turn and found myself negotiating a desolate road on the Arctic Coastal Plains. Visibility was near zero, and I slowed to a crawl with my eyes glued to the striped centerline separating the two lanes. If it hadn't been for the vibration from the rumble strips, I wouldn't have known I was nearly on top of the Mackinac Bridge. More memories of my last visit here two years ago surfaced, and I glanced to the median area between the north and southbound highways just in front of the tollbooth. From what I could see through the whiteout, there was no police car this time.

Winds were howling as I approached the tollbooth, and I could just make out a large electronic billboard sign that read, "Severe weather warning in effect. Escort required."

I paid my toll and lined up with several trucks and other vehicles on a side lane. My timing was perfect, and, just as I arrived, the convoy departed, led by a Bridge Authority patrol vehicle sporting flashing yellow lights on its cab. At over eight kilometers long, Big Mac, as it was known, was the longest anchored suspension bridge in the Western Hemisphere. We advanced at a snail's pace, which was frustrating at first, until we hit the midspan and felt a heavy jolt of wind that slid my whole Highlander sideways an inch, reminding me of the many stories of cars being blown off and into the icy waters of The Straits of Mackinac, two hundred feet below. It also reminded me of an event that happened many years ago, when I arrived at the other end of the bridge minus the top of my Thule rooftop ski carrier. This was not a bridge to be trifled with. My eyes remained stubbornly fixed to the red glow of the taillights in front of me as we inched along. The normally spectacular view of the waterway from the side window remained obliterated by the white sheet of snow.

I regained the I-75 on the other side of the bridge without incident and, a few minutes later, exited on the US 31. The snowfall had finally tapered to a steady stream that my wipers were able to manage, and the driving improved dramatically. Before long, the sign for the small Pellston Regional Airport came into view, and I pulled off. Plows were hard at work on the airfields, and I had no doubt there would be delays. The parking lot, in as much as I could see of it, was buried in a solid foot of fluff. Those few vehicles already in the lot were aligned in the row directly in front of the airport. I spied a parking spot right next to the entrance and pulled in, quite pleased with myself. It was perfect.

I tapped out a quick text to Sarah and checked for messages from Hitchhiker. Nothing. I shot a text off to him indicating I'd arrived, and then donned hat, gloves, mask, zipped up my parka, and made my way through the long timber-truss roofed entranceway of the airport.

I stood for a moment, stamping my boots, and shaking off snow, like Archie coming in from a winter's hike, and then scanned the terminal. I hadn't used this airport in many years, and it had apparently enjoyed a substantial facelift. It was a little like walking into a themed Disney restaurant. There were full scale stuffed animals – deers, bears, and a cougar – scattered throughout the airport consistent with the comfortable, rustic, northern motif, including varnished, roughened log interior supporting structures, furniture, and staircase. Along with stone walls, flagstone floors, and a large stone fireplace in the waiting area surrounded by lounge chairs, not unlike the one I was sitting in at The Loft, the night June became sick. I couldn't help myself; I texted Sarah again, making sure there was no change in June's condition. She reassured me all was stable.

I was still staring at my phone when I felt a tap on my shoulder.

"I see you still have your head stuck down the rabbit hole of that little device," a deep voice said. "It will be the bane of you someday."

I turned to find Hitchhiker; his naked hand outstretched in salutation.

"Hitchhiker!" I yelled. I hesitated for only a moment before ungloving and reaching to return a vigorous greeting. It was so foreign to shake hands nowadays. It almost felt wrong. I would be spending the next several days with Hitchhiker, however, and the handshake was an indoctrination to my new travel bubble as much as anything else.

I hadn't seen Hitchhiker in person for two years, not since I'd picked him up on the side of the road in Kentucky on my way to Florida. We'd Zoomed numerous times coordinating business for our new company, but neither of us had crossed the border since the pandemic had begun. Remarkably, he hadn't changed all that much. He was still wearing a black business suit over a white collared shirt, but this time with a long, black winter trench coat overtop. His bushy beard was covered by a black N-95 mask, and his black hair was longer, now touching his shoulders. He was sporting a classic black tuque and carrying a large black briefcase in his left hand. Were the lights to dim, he would very quickly disappear from sight, a phenomenon I was sure he very much counted on.

"How the hell are you?" I asked.

"No doubt much better than you," he replied. "Any change in your daughter's condition?"

"No. She's stable for now. Partly thanks to you and your hyperbaric incubator idea."

"Good. Then we may still have time. Shall we purchase our flights?"

Hitchhiker was never one for small talk. He was always direct, to the point, and answered questions only when he was ready. This could be incredibly annoying, particularly on occasions like this where some degree of social decorum and catch up was required – we hadn't seen each other in two years! – as always, he was right, though. Time was of the essence, and we'd have plenty of time to catch up on the plane to wherever we were going.

I led the way to the Delta ticket counter and said to Hitchhiker, "Still Detroit, right?"

"Correct."

There was no line up, and I walked directly to the large wood slab that was the counter and pushed my passport and vaccine papers across to a young man dressed in a Delta uniform. He wore a lime green mask, had spiked orange hair pointing straight to the ceiling, and his eyes bulged just enough to make me think of hyperthyroidism and Grave's disease. He was the antithesis of what you would expect for a northern rustic theme and reminded me of the character Beaker from the Muppet show.

"Hi, "I said. "Next flight to Detroit please. Two tickets."

"Reservations?" He asked.

"No. We're being spontaneous."

He turned and glanced out the large snowswept windows overlooking the runways, shook his head, and mumbled, "Hmm, let's see what we can do."

There was a lengthy silence punctuated by the sound of fingers tapping away on a keyboard until he said, "Huh. You're in luck. There's been some cancellations. I have two tickets on the early afternoon flight."

"Perfect," I said. "We'll take'em. No checked luggage. Just carry-on." I confirmed this statement with a questioning look at Hitchhiker, who made a small lifting movement with his briefcase as he nodded his head.

"Wait," I whispered to him. "Is that all you have?"

He nodded once again.

"Wow. You travel light." My carry-on was still in my Highlander.

The agent continued to dabble away at his keyboard, shuffling my papers around, while I slid a corporate credit card from my wallet. Suddenly, there was a long pause, and he stepped away from the terminal for a moment into a back room. Shortly after, he emerged with an older, meek looking gentleman who seemed to be taking over.

"Um, Sir." He looked at my passport. "I'm afraid we have a bit of a problem."

"How so?" I asked, a feeling of dread creeping from the counter through my fingers – which were drumming rhythmically on the counter – and up my arm.

"Well. I'm afraid the *Mark Spencer* on this passport is on our No Fly List."

"Wait. Isn't that the list they put terrorists on?"

"Um, yes, indeed. The very same list." He spoke in an irritatingly calm voice. Slow and steady. "Of course, it's also used to keep other types of undesirables off our airplanes such as people who've had … um, perhaps some issues with alcohol in the past, or … um, violent tendencies, or, these days, Covid-19 related infractions?"

He tilted his head subtly, as if waiting for an answer.

"Well," I stammered, "I … I did have an *issue* two years ago, at the start of the pandemic, when no one knew any better. But no one ever told me anything about being blacklisted because of it."

"Have you attempted to fly since then?"

"Well ... Well no. I mean, there was no reason to. But now ... my daughter's very sick, and I need to get to Detroit. You have to help me. Please." I looked at him with large, pitiful eyes.

"Sir. I'm so sorry about your daughter. There's really nothing we can do. This list is produced by Homeland Security and is strictly enforced. It would mean my job."

My knees buckled a little as I bowed my head, my mission discombobulating before my very eyes. I looked up at him again, "Does this list apply to all airlines?"

"I'm afraid so."

"Is there someone higher up I can talk to? To get this overturned? I'm a doctor in good standing. I'm no threat to anyone."

I wanted to get angry. To stomp my feet and slam my fists on the desk, however, I knew there was nothing he could do. And deep down, somewhere, even two years later, and even though it wasn't my fault, I somehow felt like I deserved it: punishment for exposing a plane full of people to a new virus on my flight home from Florida with Sarah.

"It is easy to get on the list, but a long and complicated affair to be taken off it. Something that often requires lawyers and ... um, money."

I bowed my head again, capitulating, and

mumbled, "Thank you. Sorry for wasting your time." The battle felt lost before the first shot was ever fired.

Hitchhiker had been watching this whole sordid conversation in silence. He tugged at my elbow and said loudly to no one in particular, "There's obviously been a mistake here. People aren't blacklisted for getting sick. Come. We will find other means of getting to where we are going."

He dragged me towards the parking lot. "You have a car, don't you?"

We were out of earshot of the Delta agents who were watching us leave, "Yes. But so what? How will we get to wherever it is we are going without a plane?"

He turned me around, placed one hand on my shoulder and fixed me with a piercing stare. "There's always a way. Trust me."

He continued, "But first, wait here a minute."

He walked back to the counter, had some words with the older agent, and then walked purposefully towards the exit. He had a confident look in his eyes, as if he'd just solved a riddle. I followed him, the automatic doors sliding aside as we emerged under the covered walkway. The snow had finally stopped, and the parking lot sparkled glistening crystals as the sun crept from behind a large grey cloud moving to the east.

"Now," Hitchhiker asked, "where is your vehicle?"

I looked to the left of the entrance and found my Highlander parked where I'd left it, buried under another couple of inches of snow. My stomach lurched as I got closer. There were fresh boot marks in the snow all around it that did not belong to me, and on the left front wheel was a large yellow contraption I hadn't seen since my days in Montreal: a Denver Boot?

***

I squatted directly in front of the tire clamp and stared at it for a moment before unleashing a torrent of expletives, which culminated when I stood and kicked the Denver Boot with my ... boot. My big toe throbbed enough afterwards to dissipate some of the anger. I looked towards Hitchhiker, who still hadn't said a word, and yelled, "Why would someone do this? I couldn't have been in there more than a half hour."

He walked over to a thin metal post standing at the head of the parking space, placed a hand around it and shook. Snow feathered to the ground revealing a sign showing a stick figure in profile sitting in a wheelchair. The sign read: "Reserved Parking."

My eyes must have looked like little white saucers, blending nicely with the surrounding snowy landscape. My hands flew to each side of my head in exasperation. "But … it was snowing so hard. Everything was covered. How could I possibly have known that sign was there?"

"Bad luck. Come. Let's go inside and see if we can't get this device removed."

So much for my perfect parking spot.

I followed him into the building and directly to the security desk. The security guard was dusting a few flecks of snow from the shoulders of his overcoat as he hung it up on a rack. There was a set of greasy work gloves thrown onto a chair next to it. He looked like every airport security guard I'd ever seen. It was like they were cut from a particular mold: medium height, thick neck, stocky build with a good-sized belly, a sharply pressed uniform, and an air of authoritarian power that far exceeded any possible level of education and training they might have. In short, they irritated me to no end. Even the black mask he wore seemed to have been ironed tight and sharp. His name tag read: "Mike."

Hitchhiker stepped aside allowing me to approach the desk.

"How may I be of service today?" Mike, the security guard, asked in a neutral voice.

Since there was virtually no one else in the airport, I was reasonably sure he knew exactly *how* he could be of service.

"Why did you boot my Highlander?" I

blurted. "I wasn't even parked for twenty minutes, and the sign wasn't visible with all the snow.

"Mmm. Tough break. Unfortunately, I make parking rounds on the hour, which, I guess, happened to be while you were in the airport. In keeping with Emmett County's protocols, this airport has very strict enforcement rules for illegal parking."

"Okay. No harm, no foul. Right? Mike. Just a harmless mistake. Can you please remove it?"

"Well. There's the rub. Only Clint, who runs the towing company, has the key, and he's an absolute stickler for the rules, particularly since his son was in that car accident and is completely wheelchair-bound now."

"Sorry to hear that. No problem, though. Just ring him up. Happy to pay, so I can get back on the road."

"Yeah. Big problem. He doesn't work on Sundays and is quite religious about taking the sabbath off. He won't be available until tomorrow morning."

"What? That makes no sense. Now my car will be blocking a handicap parking spot for the next 24 hours, or more."

"Well. I appreciate your concern, but we have a work-around. I'll just grab this temporary sign right here," – he pointed to a three-foot-tall self-standing handicap parking sign – "and place it in front of the parking spot next to yours until your car is moved."

"Moved?" I said, my voice rising a few decibels. "Moved where?"

"To Clint's garage on the edge of town," he stated, like I should already know that.

I took a deep breath. "But normally, from what I remember in Montreal, you just dial a number and pay over the phone with a credit card."

"Mmm. I've heard that. Unfortunately, we aren't quite that advanced yet. Cash only, for now, although I hear that technology is coming."

That technology is coming? What year is it here?

Hitchhiker interrupted, "Sir. Am I to understand that there is no way to get access to my friend's vehicle until tomorrow?"

"That's what I'm trying to say."

Hitchhiker looked at me and then tilted his head in the direction of the Avis car rental desk. "So be it. We will rent a car."

I stepped back from the desk and yelled, "Whoa. Hang on a second. What about my bloody Highlander? I'm just going to leave it here? Nuh-uh. No way."

Hitchhiker stepped close and fixed me with another one of his piercing stares. "DO you want to save your daughter?"

"Of course, but ..."

"Then we don't have time for your temper tantrum."

I sulked like a kid caught with his hand in the cookie jar, my head falling forward off my shoulders and staring at my snow speckled boots. “You’re … right. Of course, you’re right.”

Hitchhiker made to move towards the Avis counter, and I followed. The security guard slowly released a long, “Ahemmm.”

Hitchhiker and I both froze and turned.

“Janey couldn’t make it in today ‘cos of the storm. She asked me to cover.”

“Okay,” I stepped back and placed both hands firmly on the security desk. “Would you like us to move over there to do the paperwork.” I thrust my chin towards the rental car counter, all the while pondering how I was going to get my Highlander back, if we ever left this purgatorial place.

“Um. Not really necessary. We have no vehicles left to rent.”

I heard a “tsk” escape from Hitchhiker. It seemed even he had had enough of the Pellston Airport antics. I peered over the guard’s shoulder and out a window overlooking the parking lot. Already, the sun was melting away the light cotton candy snow, revealing a fleet of rental vehicles.

I pointed in that direction. “And all those cars?”

“I’m afraid they’re all spoken for. On reserve.”

“Can’t you check for cancellations, or

something?"

"I'm afraid not. Since I'm only covering, I only have limited access to their computer system."

I was beginning to think the No Fly List also included a No-Nothing-For-You-Ever-Again component.

"However, ..." he continued, scratching his chin through his mask, "as it happens, my brother, Ike, is heading to Detroit this afternoon. I'm sure, if the price was right, he'd be happy to take you along. Plus, you wouldn't be stuck with a rental at the other end."

I couldn't tell if this fellow was truly being a good Samaritan and helping us out, or if this was just some old-fashioned scam.

"How did you know we were heading to Detroit?" I asked, glaring at him.

He shrugged his shoulders. "It's a small airport. Word gets around pretty quick."

"Yeah," I said flatly. "It sure does."

***

We had three hours to kill before Ike picked us up. I transferred my hiking shoes, a light waterproof jacket, underwear, clothing, and toiletries, including sunscreen from my carry-on luggage, to my trusty backpack. If Hitchhiker could pack super light, so could I. The heavy winter boots, parka, hat, and gloves would be a problem as we moved further south, but Hitchhiker already had a solution in mind. Since I wouldn't be getting on a plane anytime soon, I grabbed my Rambo survival knife from under the front seat and stuffed it deep in my pack. Sarah hated this knife, but I loved it and always kept it under my driver's seat. It had a waterproof compartment in the handle that held all kinds of goodies, including matches. It was always best to be prepared for anything. The last thing I packed was some Covid rapid tests. Day ten was the day after tomorrow, and I still needed to be one hundred percent certain I hadn't given June the virus. Not that it really mattered at this point; her die was cast. Still, for peace of mind, I needed to know.

As for my Highlander, the security guard explained that Clint would come by tomorrow and tow it to his garage, where I could pick it up anytime. He assured me the cost wouldn't be any different. "Once you're booted, it's the same price to unboot today as it will be next week, as per county rules. Just don't leave it longer than a few weeks." I tucked my car keys into a deep pocket in my backpack and then tried to forget about my Highlander. Getting it back to Canada would be something I'd have to coordinate with Sarah another point in time. It truly was the least of my worries.

I'd already talked to Sarah and explained the situation. I called it a minor setback, which she interpreted as a full-on death sentence for June. It took a considerable amount of reassurance to bring her back to ground zero. It helped that Hitchhiker was with me. She had never met him other than on a Zoom call, but, somehow, he inspired confidence, or at least filled the gap where my normal level of confidence usually resided, particularly since he was responsible for the hyperbaric incubator that was giving June a fighting chance.

Second on my call list was Rufus: our plan A was, thus far, failing miserably. What would we do when we arrived in Detroit? I filled him in on the situation, in as much as I could. Hitchhiker was still tight-lipped about our destination. More so because I was talking to Rufus over an open cell phone line. Rufus said we could bypass the whole No Fly List policy by using his private Gulfstream jet. This seemed a perfect solution that in retrospect should have been our plan from the start. This was Hitchhiker's gig, though, and he wasn't thrilled about using a private jet to fly directly to our destination. He said it was like pointing a spotlight on our objective, something we wanted to avoid at all costs. We needed to work in the shadows. Still, he appreciated that there was no other option at this point and that time was of the essence. Rufus said he thought he could have it gassed up, on the tarmac, and ready to go by the time we got to Detroit. I felt a change of momentum in our favor, like we had a shot again.

We enjoyed a full lunch, not knowing when we'd get a chance to eat again. There was a lull in our conversation that, up until that point, mostly revolved around just how crooked Mike the security guard was. He was certainly a little trigger happy with the Denver Boot. It seemed to me it would have been a simple thing to walk into the almost empty airport and yell a little warning first. Like, "Hey everyone. There's a burgundy Highlander parked in the handicap zone. Move it or get booted."

Also, he clearly had many vehicles still in stock he could have rented us. He was right, though. It would be easier and probably cheaper to be dropped off at Detroit Airport and not have to worry about returning a rental.

As to the No Fly List, well, that seemed beyond his reach. And then Hitchhiker revealed a card he'd been holding.

"Mark, I need to tell you something. The older man in charge at Delta was kind enough to share with me that you were only placed on the No Fly List earlier this morning."

"Wait. That's what you went back to the desk to ask him?"

"Yes. It didn't make sense that they would put you on the list for something entirely beyond your control that happened two years ago."

"So . . . ?"

"Remember, Rufus said Big Pharma was in the game and they had deep pockets and long tendrils?"

I remembered.

And the little nerve endings in my gut tied themselves into even tighter knots.

***

"You boys keepin' them masks on the whole trip? It'll be a good four-hour drive."

It was midafternoon, and we were finally en route to Detroit. After a little bit of haggling, mostly initiated by the very thrifty Hitchhiker, we had agreed to fifty bucks each for the ride, which was likely substantially cheaper than a rental would have been with drop-off, and probably quicker since the storm had grounded all flights. I hated the concept of "it is what it is" and "go with the flow," but, realistically, we were on a good path.

I was sprawled out in the back row of a pick-up truck cab with Hitchhiker in the front passenger seat and our new friend, Ike, driving. Everyone was just settling in, getting to know each other. Ike and Hitchhiker had been chatting away, like old friends. Despite his unorthodox personality – I suspected he was very much on the spectrum – Hitchhiker had a chameleon like way of fitting in to almost any environment. An ability to connect with people in his own special way. I was sure this was a good survival trait for someone who travelled almost exclusively by means of his thumb.

"I'm only wearing my mask as a courtesy to protect you," Hitchhiker said, his voice muffled by his N95 mask. "If you're comfortable with us removing them, I would be most grateful."

The big, maskless Northern Michigander smiled widely, revealing a radiant gold front tooth and said, "Hell, yeah. You can remove them. Don't need to wear them on my account. I got Covid a month ago and recovered, no problems. That was my second time. Now I'm fit as a fiddle and fully protected with God-given, natural immunity. You boys safe?"

I spoke up from the rear, "I'm double-vaxxed, boosted and have had Covid-19 twice. Plus, I'm rapid tested pretty much every day as part of my job."

"Holy crap," he guffawed. "The only way Covid is crawling up your ass is if that commie bastard's got a new and improved bazooka."

I nodded my head, making brow raised eye contact through his rear view mirror. *A bazooka? Commie bastard?*

I had run this scenario through my mind the minute we agreed to riding with Ike and wasn't sure exactly what I was going to do when the time came. Well, now was the time. Whereas, not long ago, it was scientifically felt that a good three-ply scrub mask and six feet of distance was sufficient to protect the wearer and everyone around them, the CDC had come out with a statement in April of this year that there was a high probability the virus could be aerosolized and get through or around a standard mask. Ventilation and filters suddenly became more important in houses, schools, and business buildings, and HVAC was instantly a household acronym. The terrifying concept was that an asymptomatic individual could breathe out the virus in a normal exhalation, flooding a room, and a previously healthy individual might wander in and inhale the virus in that same room sometime later, long after the carrier had left the premises. Many months later, hospital organizations would enforce N95 mask use for caregivers looking after patients who were sick with Covid as well as those suspected of carrying the virus.

While it was quite feasible to wear an N95 for the four-hour drive to Detroit – we did it all the time in the ER for eight hour shifts or longer – it wasn't the most pleasant thing, and many workers were developing all sorts of irritating skin problems. In the end, since I was about as protected as I could possibly be, I had resolved to leave it to Hitchhiker to make the first move, and I would follow suit. I wasn't sure myself what his status was. It was entirely possible he'd had Covid already, maybe several times. This wasn't the kind of thing he would share openly. I stared at Hitchhiker, waiting ....

"I've probably had some degree of Covid on at least four occasions," he stated, as he removed his mask. "Once for each variant, I suspect, much like the common cold."

Probably?

"I'm not a big believer in the all-in testing process for the general public," he continued. "It mostly appears to be a moneymaker for Big Pharma and their ancillary companies. For healthcare professionals and more susceptible people, it's obviously a different story."

I still wasn't clear if Hitchhiker had been vaccinated, but it sounded like all of us had been infected with Covid more than once. That meant everyone at the very least had some form of wildtype immunity. There was, of course, the new and very contagious Omicron variant, that, to date, I hoped I hadn't gotten.

Hitchhiker turned to look at me in the back seat with his maskless face, and I felt the peer pressure radiating from his eyes, like I was at a house party in my early twenties on the losing end of a ridiculous bet. And then, I realized his entire face under the area of the mask was completely shaved, yet everywhere else was his burly, black ZZ top beard. It looked ridiculous, and I couldn't help but chuckle. I hadn't seen his face without a mask since he FaceTimed me outside of a bus stop over a year ago. He always wore a mask on Zoom calls because he was typically in a public setting – like a coffee shop, truck stop, or a diner – hijacking free internet. His lonely connection to the internet was an ancient iPad that only worked through Wi-Fi. He had never owned a smartphone and was adamant that he never would. These were just some of his many peculiarities.

He eyed me sternly, clearly unimpressed with my chuckling.

"Whoa!" Ike said before I could get a word out, his wide-eyed face whiplashing repeatedly from Hitchhiker to the road in front of him. "You got yourself a chin curtain, there. I thought you Amish types weren't allowed to ride in motor cars?"

It was all I could do to suppress a full on outburst of laughter.

"Humph. The Amish," Hitchhiker stated in restrained tone, his lips thinned and baring a few teeth, "are very much allowed to ride in motorized vehicles for the most part, but generally prefer horse and buggy. *I* am not Amish. *This* is a compromised strategic move to allow me to retain my beard – which I like very much – and still obtain maximum, airtight fit for my mask."

I stopped chuckling. As always, he was completely practical and completely right. Still, he did look a little funny.

"Yeah, man," Ike said, smiling and nodding

his head, "It's a good look on you. Really."

"Humph." Hitchhiker grunted and turned his head to look out his passenger window at nothing in particular.

I removed my mask. Not because of peer pressure but because of completely different reasons. I was back in high school again. This time in the cafeteria, sitting with one of the unpopular kids to make him feel less alienated. And, let's face it, the only way Covid-19 was going to infect me was if it crawled up my ass with a bazooka!

***

I was reluctant to speak aloud of our travel problems with Ike in the truck. Although I had no doubt his brother had filled him in on what had happened with the No Fly List since he never asked why we needed the ride. Nevertheless, I was sure Hitchhiker would not be happy if I got on the phone with Rufus and spoke about our situation out loud. So, I texted him:

Me: "Rufus, Gulfstream good to go?"

Rufus: "... ... ... There may be a problem. Looking into it. Where are you?"

Me: "Leaving Pellston, enroute to Detroit. Should be there in four hours. What kind of problem?"

Rufus: "Mechanical. Getting more details. Talk soon."

Me: "Okay. Keep me posted."

Rufus: Thumbs Up emoji.

A mechanical problem, I thought. *Another literal wrench in our proverbial machine.*

I texted Sarah quickly to let her know we were on the road and then tucked my phone away. Hitchhiker glanced back at me, and I gave him a neutral look. There was no sense in raising an alarm about the plane ... yet. Also, he seemed to be distracted, engaged in somewhat of a heated conversation with Ike, voices rising. And then I heard a word that I knew was bound to be controversial in this vehicle.

"There is no question," Hitchhiker lectured, "the science supports the efficacy of *vaccines,* both for preventing infection from the SARS CoV-2 virus and for decreasing the severity of illness if you do get infected."

In my mind, that statement at least answered the question as to whether Hitchhiker was vaccinated.

"Bah," Ike replied heatedly, "that's what they want you to believe, so you'll get the vaccine."

"Who are they?" Hitchhiker asked, his eyebrows peaked, like two unclimbable little mountains.

"They, of course, is *They*: the government, the deep state, the one-percenters."

Whenever someone talked about *They*, I was reminded of a Far Side cartoon, where a bland looking, portly fellow in a white cut-off tee-shirt was sitting at a desk in a basement with five phones in front of him all labelled *They*, his wife looking on incredulously. *They* was apparently some dude named Bernie Horowitz. Not an all-powerful round table of government bureaucrats, or a cabal of evil oil barons, or a faction of financial tycoons. Just ole Bernie in the basement. That's who *they* really was. I chuckled to myself.

Hitchhiker sighed deeply before asking, "Other than to achieve herd immunity, protect the less healthy, and maintain the economy, why do *they* care if you get a vaccine or not?"

"There's somethin' in those vaccines. I'm telling you. Something that will suck away your freewill. Maybe even some sort of nanobot tech that will allow them to track you."

Ah, it wasn't just *they*, but *them* also. A dynamic duo of malfeasant pronouns out to control the world.

Interestingly, there was a little bit of truth to what he was saying about freewill being sucked away. Or at least the illusion of freewill being sucked away. Using unfortunate words like "herd immunity" contributed to that. But the idea of being tracked through a vaccine ...?

"Seriously," Hitchhiker responded, "you think, even if the technology was available, that *they* – whomever *they* are – would be interested in knowing your whereabouts at all times? To what possible end? Why would anybody, like the government or wealthy billionaires, care where you are at any given moment?"

Ike turned his head to eyeball Hitchhiker for what seemed like a dangerously long time before putting eyes back on the road, "Does a Shepherd not want to know where his sheep are at any given moment?"

Another long sigh from Hitchhiker. "Okay. Let's say for some indecipherable reason you are right, and a nefarious organization wants to track everyone in the world for purposes we can't possibly imagine. Why bother? Everyone can already be tracked via their smartphones."

"I've read there's ways to cloak your phone, so no one can track it," he rebutted.

No doubt read on the website: *Bullshit Masquerading as Truth.*

This concept of research being equated to scrolling the internet for information purported as truth drove me insane. Just because you were well informed didn't mean that you were well-schooled. It was one thing to present to your doctor with a lengthy list of questions or even stacks of website print offs regarding a health problem in order to make an informed decision; it was another to use that unvetted, non-peer-reviewed information without guidance to treat yourself.

"Plus," Ike continued, "not everyone has a smartphone, especially in third-world countries."

Where they also have even less access to vaccines.

"I don't have a smartphone," Ike boasted proudly. "No one's tracking me. Your buddy in the back seat has been on his since we got in the truck, but I haven't seen you pull one out yet. I bet you and I are a lot alike."

Oh crap! What happens, I wondered, when two Hitchhiker-types meet in close proximity? Do they repel or attract?

"Ninety-two percent of the world population own a mobile phone," Hitchhiker stated.

"That leaves eight percent," Ike remarked.

"So?" Hitchhiker asked. "What problems could eight percent of the world population, mostly from impoverished countries, possibly cause?"

Ike's head swiveled to look at him again, his voice rising steadily. "That eight percent is where the Dark Horse or the Mule comes from, maybe causing a Black Swan event that takes *them* down. That's why they need the vaccines. To make sure they get everyone.

"Who knows? Maybe it's the vaccine that's really the contagious thing, using the Covid virus to infect others with its nanotech, allowing Big Brother to watch our every move."

I was shocked Ike had referenced *The Mule* from the Isaac Asimov sci-fi *Foundation* novels.

The Mule, in the novels, was a being possessing telepathic abilities that could influence people's emotions and consequently change the normal course of history. The wobbly gear in the wheel of time. I didn't think Hitchhiker read much fiction, so I wasn't sure he would get the reference.

"Despite your ridiculous animal imagery," Hitchhiker countered, his voice edgy, "it's all complete conjecture with absolutely no evidence. Imaginary conspiracies designed to keep the feeble minded distracted while self-serving policies are passed willy-nilly through the Senate by ignorant, power-hungry politicians."

"Feeble minded!" Ike yelled, his face beet red, as he slammed his brakes and pulled onto the shoulder.

Apparently, they repel.

***

"Well done, Hitchhiker," I said, kicking a blueish dirt covered ice ball off the shoulder and into a ditch. "Well done."

"Bah. I could never have lasted the entire trip to Detroit with that ignorant idiot. Next, he would have had us putting on tinfoil hats."

We were just outside Gaylord, not even an hour from the Pellston airport. This trip was slowing to a hippo's pace.

"Bugger didn't even give us our money back," I added.

"We're better off, anyway," he said, beginning to walk south. "I'm sure someone will pick us up before long. Winter is coming, after all. Someone will take pity on us."

I stared at him blankly, looking for a clue. I'd forgotten how difficult he was to read, and I couldn't tell if he was making a play on *Game of Thrones*.

He looked back. "Of course, I'm aware of the sigil of the House of Winterfell. I don't live my life under a rock ... and, yes, I recognized Ike's reference to Asimov's *Foundation* series. I was a great fan and an avid reader of science fiction as a teenager. *The Mule* was a favorite plot device."

Hmm. I wondered if Hitchhiker thought of himself as a little bit of a Mule. Someone who was outside the box and could change history simply by being himself and influencing people's emotions. He certainly influenced mine at times.

"You know," I commented, "some of what Ike said almost sounded believable."

"Ha. Don't tell me the great critically thinking doctor has fallen for the ruse of mock truth that is the internet. The internet is a tool, and, like any tool, it can be used properly or improperly. The vast majority of the world use it without adequate critical appraisal. They are sponges who absorb whatever information media savvy persons want to push."

"I know. I know. I was just saying that some of what he said *sounded* believable. It's easy to see where people fall into the trap of believing bullshit."

"Unfortunately," Hitchhiker said, releasing a frustrated sigh, "a lot of people want to believe what they read, particularly if it supports their view of something. The degree of confirmational bias on the internet is astounding. It's even designed into the search engines. The more you look for something, the more you are shown it."

"So, what is the great intellect's magic potion for finding the truth?" I asked.

He stopped dead in his tracks, whipped his head around and tapped me on the chest with his forefinger. "Always go to source."

"Always go to source," I repeated.

"Always," he said, "If it's science based, find the original paper, and review the references. If it's news based, find the original publication, and research the author. Never believe anything until you've dissected it down to the tiniest possible atom of knowledge."

"But that would take hours or even days, sometimes."

"And that's the problem with this fast-paced modern society we live in. No one really has time for the truth. So, they settle. Such will be the fall of our society."

"Wow. You are a bundle of joy to be

around."

"You asked the question."

"I suppose I did. I just didn't expect such a moribund reply."

A car finally approached. He stuck his thumb out and said, "If the truth was easy to discover then everyone would know it."

"Wouldn't that be nice."

The car zoomed by, followed by several others. It didn't look very hopeful.

"I'm curious. When were you vaccinated?" I asked. A random question to pass the time as we trudged along. It was midafternoon, and already I could feel the temperature drop as the sun slid toward the western horizon.

"Which vaccination?"

"Covid, of course."

"I've never been vaccinated for Covid," he replied.

"What?" I asked incredulously. "But you were all gung ho with Ike about the importance of vaccinations."

"Of course. The science is strongly in favor of their effectiveness."

"Why wouldn't you –"

He stopped again. "I first tested positive three days after travelling in your truck, the first time we met."

Ouch. That stung hard.

"I'm ... I'm sorry. I had no idea .... How do you know it was –"

"I went straight from your truck to my brother's house and didn't leave there for seven days."

My mind began to race. Trying to think back two years to when it all started. I'd always assumed I'd caught the virus on my travels through the US. But if I gave it to Hitchhiker, then I'd likely been exposed to the virus days before I ever left home on my quest to save Sarah. I'd been infected in my own hometown. Probably in my workplace. There was an irony here I was having difficulty putting my finger on.

"Wait. How did you end up where I picked you up in the first place, outside of Corbin? Someone must have dropped you off. Maybe they gave it to you. Maybe it wasn't me."

"As you know, I tend to keep to myself. In the five days prior to meeting you, I had contact with only one other person, the driver who dropped me off. He had tested positive for Covid by PCR four weeks earlier, so he was well beyond the contagion period of fourteen days."

"Damn," was all I could say. I thought back to my time in the diner, south of Knoxville, when they asked me – made me! – take my mask off. All the people I inadvertently exposed to Covid in the diner that didn't even believe in the virus. More irony, with a dusting of bad karma.

"After that," he continued, "I was infected three more times. Once for each strain that ran amok through the US. It's one of the perils of using public transportation and hitchhiking, which, as you know, is my preferred method of travel."

"Well, speaking of travel, how were you planning to get on the Delta flight in Pellston? They require proof of vaccination."

He looked at me strangely, like I was a child. "It is very easy to obtain the appropriate papers by alternate means."

"But ... but that's cheating and ... illegal."

"The point is to prove immunity for the safety of yourself and others. I am as immune as anyone. Perhaps more so since we are still using an original vaccine against a fourth generation or more strain of the virus. It is not my issue that the government and airlines are so naïve as to not recognize that.

"You could still have gotten the vaccine to boost your immunity even further," I argued.

"The timing would have been difficult and, quite honestly, I prefer natural immunity. While the science may not corroborate this, as I said, after four exposures, I feel I have at least a degree of immunity equal to or better than yours. I was never very sick and, each time, isolated myself accordingly to spare other less healthy people."

I thought hard about what he was saying but could not access any studies in my mental filing cabinet that addressed the idea of natural immunity versus vaccinated immunity. This was a topic that seemed Pubmed worthy. Also,

I needed to call Sarah and update her on our setback. I reached into my pocket for my phone and found ... nothing.

"Wait." I cried out.

I came to an abrupt halt and swung my backpack off my shoulder to the icy asphalt. I squatted and quickly unzipped every pocket, searching frantically. Nothing.

I looked up desperately at Hitchhiker. "My phone!"

***

"I must have left it in Ike's truck."

"Bad luck," Hitchhiker said, with not a shred of sorrow in his tone as he stood over me with his elongated shadow passing over my backpack. "You're better off without it. Your mind will be more focused on your surroundings and more opportunities will open up."

"What? That's pure mumbo jumbo bullshit. I need my phone to keep in touch with Sarah and with Rufus. Not to mention dealing with a hundred other obstacles I'm sure will come up."

"Mmm. You'll see. We'll get by. I have my iPad."

"But you have no cellular connection, right? It will only work with Wi-Fi."

"That's correct, but that's enough."

"Dammit!"

I was such an idiot. How could I forget my phone in Ike's truck? Ike, of all people. The guy who tossed us to the curb on a cold, wintery afternoon. I knew I would never see that phone again. I tried to think back to where I might have left it in Ike's truck and hit a wall. Perhaps it simply slipped out of my pocket at some point? I was wasting mental time. The phone was lost, and I had to move on.

Just off the highway, I spotted a Bob Evans family restaurant. There would be Wi-Fi there. Perhaps Hitchhiker was right. My observational skills and awareness of my surroundings were already improving.

We found a packed path in the snow that led directly from the highway to the restaurant. As we approached the entrance, a large sign came into view indicating that proof of vaccination was mandatory. I fumbled for my phone to find my vaccination QR code, and then remembered.

Damn! Did I transfer the paper version to my pack?

I dug through and found my passport. Tucked into the passport were my vaccine papers. A sigh of relief escaped. I donned my mask and showed my paperwork to the hostess, who barely glanced at it, and then watched Hitchhiker show her some sort of ID. She nodded her head, and then we followed her to our seats. I wondered what ID Hitchhiker had shown her since he wasn't vaccinated.

We took our seats, removed our masks, and the moment the hostess departed, I stuck my hand out and asked, “May I see that?

He had already slipped the ID back into an inside coat pocket. He shrugged, reached in, and handed me a plasticized ID card. I looked it over and then looked up at him,

“This is an old military ID.”

“It is.”

“What does this have to do with vaccination papers?”

“Nothing. But rarely does anyone turn away a vet.”

That made no sense to me and would never have passed muster in Canada. The US had strong ideals about their military history, though. I guess it didn’t matter since Hitchhiker was naturally immune at this point. Still, there was a fairness issue that was bugging me. I had to show my papers. My real papers. He should have to show his, shouldn’t he?”

“I didn’t know you were in the military,” I asked. “How long ago?”

He tucked his ID back into his inside pocket and brought his iPad from his briefcase. “Did you want to text Sarah?”

I guessed his military background was a conversation for another time. I was curious, though. His appearance certainly didn’t strike me as military. “Sure. Pass it over.”

We ordered dinner and, while we waited,

I brought Sarah up to speed on our predicament without going into too much detail. Suffice to say that she was not happy with our poor progress, nor with the loss of my phone and, more importantly, the loss of communication.

As we texted back and forth, I glanced intermittently at Hitchhiker. He sat rigid straight with perfect posture, his hands resting on the table with fingers interlaced. He seemed to be scanning the room, his eyes darting here and there. Suddenly, he stood and walked over to a young couple on the far side of the dining room. I decided to ignore his antics and focus on the limited time I had to communicate with the outside world before we would have to hit the road again.

While my texts with Sarah were sour at best, my exchange with Rufus was downright depressing. The mechanical problem his Gulfstream had was supposed to have been repaired yesterday. He had just received an email indicating that the part he required was on back order due to the nebulous "supply chain disruption" Covid excuse. The plane would not be serviceable for several days.

Disaster.

***

I had to hand it to Hitchhiker, he was resourceful and knew how to read a room. We were settled comfortably in the back seat of a white camper van en route to Detroit, both of us satiated by a grease pit of burgers and fries accompanied by two large glasses of chocolate milk. My stomach gurgled while my mind fought the flood of postprandial somnolence hormones. Greasy food was not something in our regular diet at home, particularly during Sarah's pregnancy.

The couple Hitchhiker had approached at the far side of the dining area was in the middle of a strange cross-country camper van trip that included multiple big city stops on the Eastern Seaboard of Canada and the US before heading south and crossing the US to the West Coast – "the actual camping part of the journey," they said. As of yet, because of December temperatures, the sleeping quarters in the camper van had seen little use, and they had stayed mostly in cheap motels.

The van had been purchased in Newfoundland, and from there, it had skipped, hopped, and jumped from one province to the next: Nova Scotia, New Brunswick, Prince Edward Island, and Québec. Logically, it would have made sense for them to go south from Montreal to New York City in their quest to experience the largest North American cities, however, they had some bizarre notion to dip a toe in each of the Great Lakes and ended up passing through Ottawa and Toronto (Lake Ontario) before ending up in, of all places, my hometown. They said it was a bit of a challenge to find open water that wasn't iced over on Lake Superior, but, ultimately, with the help of a small axe they were successful.

On their way south, they took small detours to see Lake Huron and Lake Michigan – no axe required. Now, they were en route to Detroit to wet their feet in Lake Erie and complete their tour of the five Great Lakes. From there, on to Boston and finally New York City before following the eastern coastline south to the Florida Keys and then west to California.

They were happy to give us a ride to Detroit for the price of dinner and a tank of gas. It was infinitely more comfortable than Ike's truck, and we were situated far enough in the back that Harold and Maude couldn't hear us talk. At least, that's the names they gave us: no doubt a reference to the fictional duo from the 1971 meaning-of-life rom-com travelogue film. The woman did appear to be a little older, in her thirties, while the man was likely in his early twenties. Both were attractive, full of boundless energy, completely British, and wielded the cameras on their phones like permanent extensions of their arms. Apparently, they were filming the trip and posting the videos on a YouTube channel to raise money for a charity back home. The title of their YouTube channel was *Harold and Maude's Camper Van Odyssey*, and recent episodes had reached over

1.2 million views, allowing them to rake in big advertising dollars. Suddenly, we found ourselves unexpected live guests on their "show." The pre-ride warning was more along the lines of "We might want to grab a few photos for our guest log."

So much for stealth and working in the shadows.

Hitchhiker hadn't flinched when he returned to our table inside the restaurant, and I told him about the problems with the Gulfstream. As always, he brushed it off like a mild inconvenience, a pebble in his shoe. Rufus said he would look into renting another jet, but this would be more complex, time consuming, and compounded by my No Fly List status.

Our plan at this point was to hitch a ride with our new camper van friends to the Detroit Metro Airport. Although it was highly unlikely Rufus would be able to organize a private jet for us by the time we arrived, at least we could rent a car and continue our journey south in the event a plane was never a possibility.

Realistically, though, if that were to occur, it made more sense for Hitchhiker to go on without me. Already, I felt like a heavy anchor weighing down any chances June had. If it became necessary, Hitchhiker would have to cut me loose and move on. It was one thing to be a part of the solution but another, altogether, to be a part of the problem. June had enough of those already, and I didn't need to be one of them. This was another reason why it made sense to go to the Detroit Airport. We could get Hitchhiker on a commercial flight to wherever his destination was, assuming his illegal vaccination paperwork was in order.

Maude was driving, her eyes darting intermittently to a mirror that looked towards the back of the camper. Harold unbuckled his seat belt and then moved to join us. He sat down on a small stool and then attached his smartphone to a tripod, which he placed on a counter near the sink facing us.

"Mark, right?" He asked with a thick accent.

"Yes," I replied, eyeing the camera wearily.

"How do you feel about a short interview for our show?"

I looked to Hitchhiker, who smiled as he dragged his black tuque down over his eyes to meet the top of his N95 mask. He then pulled the collar of his trench coat up around his ears and rested his head against the window.

Hmm. Looks like I'm flying solo.

"Well ... is it absolutely necessary? We're trying not to draw attention to ourselves."

"Necessary? No. But it would be bloody amazing if we had footage of someone who lived around Lake Superior."

That sounded innocent enough.

He apparently took my silence for

acquiescence and tapped a button on his phone. I took the opportunity to ask him something I'd been wondering about.

"Wherever did you come up with the idea of dipping your toes in each of the Great Lakes?"

Harold's maskless face lit up immediately, like he was a kid who just heard that a snow day had cancelled school. "That's a bloody great question, Mark."

He turned his phone to face himself and continued, "As I'm sure you already know, being a local, the five Great Lakes together represent the largest group of freshwater lakes on the planet. At least by total area, if not by volume. Maude and I strongly support climate change initiatives and felt it was imperative that we show our viewers these amazing bodies of water …"

Happily, I seemed to have been forgotten in the interview as Harold prattled on about a variety of statistics regarding the Great Lakes, some of which I wasn't aware of but had, indeed, experienced as a local. Namely, that climate change was causing the lakes' high water cycles to get higher and the low water cycles to get lower with these cycles occurring more rapidly. This certainly explained why my dock was sitting out of the water and surrounded by sand a few summers ago.

Harold seemed to be tapering off. He reached with a hand and turned the camera around, first showing Hitchhiker, before settling on me. He was about to ask a question when he did a double take. He leaned forward and seemed to be staring intently at my N95 mask. He returned to his phone and began fiddling with it.

"Mark, that's a most unusual emblem on your mask," he stated, still staring at the screen on his phone. "It looks like a peace sign."

Uh-oh. I had completely forgotten about the mishap at the diner. I had my mask off to eat and spilled a dollop of chocolate milk on it. I dried it off immediately and didn't think its effectiveness had been compromised, but it did leave a stain.

"A peace sign?" I repeated.

"Yes, it's definitely a peace sign, a fist with the second and third fingers shaped like a V."

I had no way of taking off my mask to confirm this and no phone to take a picture.

"Now, you are a Canadian physician, is that correct?"

We had exchanged brief introductions before climbing aboard. Hitchhiker felt it was important to share this particular piece of information since he felt it would add a certain amount of credibility and reassurance.

"Yes, I work in a small hospital near Lake Superior," I volunteered.

"Excellent. Excellent," he muttered. "I'm assuming you are strongly in favor of vaccinations then?"

"Well. I do interact with a lot of patients with Covid daily, and I do enjoy being alive," I answered, somewhat facetiously.

"Right, right," he said. "So, as we approach a potential inflection point where the pandemic becomes endemic, it will be important to bridge the gap between vaxxers and non-vaxxers, and the maskers and non-maskers, in order for life to return to some degree of normalcy. Wouldn't you say?"

Harold was proving to be much more informed than I anticipated. He was alluding to an analysis of the worldwide Covid infectivity where we were arriving at a point where infections would reach a steady state, indicating that the virus was here to stay, and would become a regular part of our lives, like a seasonal flu.

"Certainly," I responded, feeling like I was in familiar territory. "I think it will be very important that we put all our disagreements behind us and learn to live together in harmony once again. So many families have been torn apart by this pandemic."

"Right, right. And so, this 'peace sign' is meant to illustrate that and bridge the gap."

It was more of a statement than a question, but I saw no reason not to run with it. If it was going to help their show … what harm could there be?

"Um. Absolutely. Yes. Exactly that.

So many masks have sported aggressive or politically charged messages during this pandemic. Isn't it time we gave peace a chance?"

I hoped John Lennon wouldn't mind my borrowing one of his more radical song titles.

"Fantastic. Absolutely fantastic. And it isn't it a bit of fun that the peace sign is also a victory sign."

I was getting the feel for this interviewing thing. I said, "V for Victory ... over the pandemic."

"Spectacular," Harold said, "Victory and peace."

He turned the camera back towards himself. "Viewers. You heard it here first on Harold and Maude's Camper Van Odyssey. As our guest today, Dr. Mark, says, now that victory over the Coronavirus is imminent, let us all get along and, "Give peace a chance."

With that, he turned his phone to face me once more, raised his hand in a peace sign and pointed to me, waving it back and forth.

I got the message. I raised my hand in a victory/peace sign and placed it next to the chocolate milk stained emblem on my mask.

From the driver's seat, I could hear Maude yell, "Brilliant, Harold. Spot on brilliant, that should put us over the top."

Harold reached in to knuckle me. "Doc, thank you. That was incredible. We are going to be legends."

I wasn't quite sure which *We* he was talking about, but either way, I thought the message was a good one.

He went back to the front to debrief with Maude, and I could hear them planning out the video, "... and we'll close out with that Lennon song in the background ..."

I shook my head, not entirely certain what had just happened. Hitchhiker released a "Harumph," from under his mask and then said with a mocking British accent, "Bloody brilliant, Mark. You're definitely a pro at working in the shadows."

Who knew Hitchhiker had a sense of humour? And a sarcastic one, at that.

***

It felt late. Incredibly, with my phone MIA, I had no way to tell the actual time. My spine told me it was approaching 10 PM, though. A long day of sitting in cars, chairs, trucks, and vans, interspersed with minimal walking, was taking its toll. I was used to being on my feet and moving continuously, a little Energizer – What's up, Doc? – Bunny. Hitchhiker seemed to have the sense of it. He was out cold. A stone silent sleeper who could just as easily have been dead as alive. I needed to take a page out of his hitchhiking playbook.

I guessed it was about another hour until

we arrived at the airport. I shut my eyes and listened to Harold and Maude up front chattering about their day's adventures. They'd already released their end-of-day video and apparently were getting rave reviews, thanks, in part, to my "peace-mask" contributions. I stretched my legs, adjusted my head into the window and tried to dose off, absorbing the steady white noise of the van.

I was in that state of napping, somewhere between sleep and wakefulness, where moments of time go by that can't be accounted for, when images of my childhood in England began to surf my subconscious, no doubt stimulated by Harold and Maude's very British personalities. They were at once everyone I remembered in my environment as a child, and no one person in particular.

I could picture my Mum and Dad as clear as the Big Dipper on a moonless Lake District night, standing in front of our house in Netley Abbey, a house that had been in the family for generations. My mother was holding a baby. At first, I assumed it was me, but the baby was dressed in pink. As much as I resembled my father, the baby resembled a much younger version of my mother: a content, angelic face I didn't quite recognize with delicate, slumbering eyes.

My sister? Abigail?

As if it was made of Silly Putty, the four-month-old baby's face morphed and contorted.

June?

It then morphed again and became some weird combination of both faces. I stepped closer to get a better look, my parents fading away completely, until June/Abigail's face filled my entire field of vision.

The eyes suddenly snapped open, and a terrible look of accusing sadness radiated into me as she croaked, "Save me. Please, save me."

I jolted back to reality as if someone had kicked a chair out from under. Lingering images of the morphed face flashed before my eyes, rendering every fiber of my being fraught with anxiety and tension. I clenched forward with my elbows on my knees and rubbed my forehead relentlessly with both hands to rid myself of the desperate feelings. A single thought trampled over all others in the nightmarish menagerie.

I have to save them.

***

"You don't look well," Hitchhiker stated, our feet striking the airport floor in time as if we were soldiers doing drill.

"I dozed off and had a … a bad dream," I mumbled, cramped muscles just beginning to loosen up.

"Humph. It's never wise to deep sleep when you're travelling with someone you don't know."

"I don't know you?"

"I was referring to Harold and Maude."

The dream was still reverberating inside my skull, trying to pull me back inside. *Someone you don't know.* A sister I never knew. How was it possible that I grew up thinking I was an only child, with everything that implied in the day, and really, I wasn't? I had a sister that died at June's age. Damn! This happened over forty years ago and was completely messing with my head. How could a sister I never met so completely derail me?

A few steps went by as we made our way down a long tunnel bathed in multicolored lights, no doubt designed with artistic intentions but failing miserably for a single minded traveller on the go. "You didn't sleep in the van?" I asked.

"As I said, it's not good sense to deep sleep when travelling with strangers."

"So ... you heard everything?"

"You mean the interview?"

"Yeah, the interview ... was it alright?"

We arrived at the end of the tunnel and boarded an upbound escalator. We weren't half a dozen revolving steps up when a voice cried out from the downbound escalator adjacent to ours, "Hey, look! It's the "peace-mask" guy, Dr. Mark!! Duuuuuude. You rock. Give peace a chance, Man. Woooooooo."

The origin of this adoration looked to be in his mid-twenties with long brown hair tied back, a jet-black mask, and his fingers held out in a peace sign. Three other buddies above and below held one hand out in a similar fashion while their other hands worked their phones. A chorus of: "That's so cool. That's the guy from the video. He's the guy I was telling you about. That's the mask," could be heard echoing through the underground space fading away as the respective escalators marched on in opposite directions.

"Was it alright?" Hitchhiker asked. "Was that your question?"

"Yeah, yeah. I know. I didn't exactly stay in the shadows," I mumbled sheepishly.

"Mmm," was all Hitchhiker responded.

***

"Seriously. How could I possibly know they were so popular?"

We had found two airport style chairs away from any crowds with an electrical outlet nearby. The plan was to contact Rufus using Hitchhiker's ancient iPad that, not surprisingly, had a charge life measured in minutes. His defense was that "I rarely use this thing for more than a few moments at a time. Plus, there's always an outlet somewhere." He was busy fiddling with an equally ancient cable that he finally managed to plug in. And then we waited for the juice to flow and the little battery sign to turn green.

"They did say their last episode pulled in over a million views," he responded dryly.

"I thought they were bragging, Influencer style. You know?"

"Not really, but I'll take your word for it."

I made a halting grab for my phone to check the time, and then scanned the walls and ceiling of the airport looking for a clock of some sort. Regardless of the hour, Sarah would expect me to contact her. Hitchhiker obviously noticed my head movements.

"Stretching your neck or, perhaps, trying to figure out the time."

I rolled my eyes in his direction. "The time, obviously. Sarah will be expecting a call. Is your iPad relic fired up enough yet to tell the time?"

"Or," he said, "you could just look at your watch ... if you had one."

He pulled up his sleeve and revealed a large military grade timepiece.

Hmm, the military ID, the military watch ...

"It's 23:30 hours," he said, after a quick glance.

Uses the twenty-four-hour clock ...

My curiosity was peaked once again. I was about to ask him about his military connection when his iPad vibrated with an incoming call.

Sarah's face appeared on the screen. Some combined look of desperation, fear, and sadness that I'd never experienced. She looked horrible and pitiful in one breath. Hitchhiker immediately handed me the iPad, being careful not to unplug it, and then wandered off to give me privacy. For such an elusive and eccentric man, he always seemed to know exactly the right thing to do.

"Mark?" Sarah asked. "I've been trying forever to reach you."

Her face was drawn and caked with layers of dried tears. I couldn't believe I'd only been gone a day. She looked a thousand years older.

"We just arrived at the Detroit Airport. I was about to call you, but Hitchhiker's prehistoric iPad needed a charge first. You ... you don't look well, Honey. What's happened?

She blinked repeatedly, glanced down and to the right, and then pushed her phone away. There was a long moment of silence, and I could hear Archie whining in the background.

What the hell is happening?

"Sorry, Mark," she whispered solemnly. "I just needed a second to get my shit together."

"Tell me," I pleaded.

"They had to intubate June about an hour ago."

Intubation: The final straw. The last hope. The coda. There was only emptiness for an encore. Numbness spread through my body as each synapse shut down ... as each connection between every nerve in my body was guillotined.

"Okay," I rallied and compartmentalized. Walls falling from above protecting me from my emotions. "Okay. We knew that was probably going to happen –"

"MAYBE, you knew or expected it. You didn't see her struggling for every little breath, every little ounce of life she could reach for. It was horrible, Mark. Fucking horrible. Our daughter ..."

What could I say? She was right. There was nothing that could compare to seeing your own flesh and blood struggle for life. Teeter tottering on the abyss of this world and – maybe – the next?

"I'm so sorry I couldn't be there, Sarah."

"Yeah. Well, you should be sorry ..."

I could hear Archie whining again in the background. Mourning Sarah's pain? *Can dogs feel such things?*

I wanted – needed – to stand and walk and process. But I was tethered to the iPad by the electrical cord, my umbilical cord to Sarah.

"Where are you guys, Mark?"

She hadn't heard a word I'd said. "We made it to the Detroit Airport. We were charging Hitchhiker's iPad and were about to call Rufus to figure out our next step."

"Okay, Mark. Call Rufus and, for God's sake, if you can't be here then get to where you need to go and find what you need to find to save our daughter. Okay? Can you do that? For me? For us?

For June?"

"We're doing our best under the circumstances, Sarah."

"Well, you need to do better, Mark." She was yelling now, nursing a rage that only a mother can access. "*You* need to do better."

I had looked away from the iPad screen and her face much earlier. It hurt too much to see her this way. I realized I was staring at an empty grey airport wall. I looked back to the screen, and it was black. She'd hung up.

I needed to do better.

If my head was screwed up after my van dream, it was now a battlefield of unrecognizable emotions that I had no idea existed. I felt a hand on my shoulder.

"Mark. Your daughter's time is running out. We need to contact Rufus."

***

Hitchhiker had Rufus on FaceTime before I could remotely get a handle on my conversation with Sarah. Hitchhiker seemed to have the gist of it and quickly brought Rufus up to speed.

"Mark, mon. You know I love June like my own. Yes?"

My wallowing was abruptly dissipated as thicker walls pushed heavy feelings to the periphery. It was like the conversation with Sarah had happened, but without all the emotional baggage attached. June was sick. Now she was intubated. So, what do we do next?

"I know, Rufus. I know," I replied, holding the iPad at arm's length so that Rufus could see both of us. "Do you have a plane for us, old friend?"

"Bah. The Gulfstream is still under repair and, no matter how much money I offer, no one will rent us a plane."

"Is it the No Fly List thing?" I asked.

"Yes. Yes." A dejected Rufus replied. "That seems to be the barrier."

I took a very deep breath.

I need to do better.

Sometimes, doing better meant getting the hell out of my own way.

"Okay, Rufus. It's settled then. I can't be the anchor on this mission anymore. As much as I want to be a part of getting the cure, it's time to face reality. I'm an impediment to this journey."

Once again, I'm the parent in the ER with the best of intentions interfering with the welfare of my child.

"There's no reason why Hitchhiker can't go on without me. It's what he wanted from the beginning." I looked at him and then back to the iPad screen and Rufus. "We'll book Hitchhiker solo on the next plane to wherever he needs to go, and I'll find my way back home."

Back to June. If she – I couldn't say it. I couldn't even think it. I needed to be there with

Sarah. That was the right thing.

"In fact, there is a reason," Hitchhiker stated bluntly. "I am on the No Fly List, also."

***

"What? Why didn't you tell me? Did you find out when you went back to the Avis desk and spoke with the old man? Again, why wouldn't you tell me that? What the hell?"

Hitchhiker held the iPad directly in front of himself, ignoring me completely. "It is irrelevant. There has been a serious spike in Covid cases at our destination country. They've closed their borders to all air and land traffic."

"How could you know ...?" A large screen TV mounted on a column at the edge of a waiting area next door caught my attention, spitting out the news to anyone who would stand still long enough to watch.

"Ohh. This ... this is bad," Rufus mumbled. "Give me a moment." He disappeared from the screen leaving us staring at a gorgeous abstract painting that I recognized from his dining room in his mansion in Montreal. It was the kind of busy painting that frenetically drew your eye everywhere at once, and if you stalled on any one area for any length of time, whatever was going on inside your head magically coalesced with the painting. I had to look away.

We could hear the mutterings of Rufus

speaking to someone, presumably on his phone.

I stared at Hitchhiker, pissed off and frustrated. *He should have told me. That was my plan B.*

"You need to tell us where we are going," I said firmly and calmly. "The more minds working on this problem, the better chance we have of arriving at a solution."

Even with the mask and beard, I could see Hitchhiker's mouth was open, about to say something. And then he changed directions, like we were fencing, and he'd given me an opening to draw me in, and then stepped aside.

"Let's see what Rufus has to say, first. We are still on an open line." At this, he pointed to the iPad.

Rufus' face filled the screen again. This time he had a big toothy grin. "Okay, my friends. We are going to Central America. Yes?"

Hitchhiker nodded his head subtly. Even though we had already discussed this previously, it seemed to pain him to say it aloud.

"Alright. I have a floatplane that I keep in a hangar at the airport. It is stored for the winter, but my mechanic assures me he can have it ready for the morning."

"You called your mechanic at 11:30 PM? And he answered?" I asked, incredulously.

Rufus smiled an even wider grin. "He's an old friend and these are desperate times. Are they not?"

I didn't have to answer that question.

"How big is your floatplane, Rufus?" Hitchhiker asked, his voice hesitant. I noted he had turned a shade paler.

"More than big enough for the three of us."

"But," I said, "I thought the air and land borders were closed?"

Rufus asked, "I'm assuming the country we are going to abuts an ocean since all countries in Central America do?"

Hitchhiker, now with a bead of sweat forming on his temple, subtly nodded his head once again.

"Then we can land in the water and float to shore."

"That's legal?" I asked.

"Irrelevant," Hitchhiker said.

"Strictly speaking, probably not," Rufus added, "but it's enough in the grey zone that I think we can get away with it. Particularly, if they don't know we are there."

I turned this new plan over in my head. It seemed so incredibly desperate. Flying a small floatplane to Central America, landing on the ocean, sneaking into a country.

"How do we meet up?" I asked.

"Rent a car, drive south, and I will pick you up somewhere."

"That's it? That's the plan? Drive south?"

Hitchhiker had dropped his chin to his chest and was staring at the floor. He seemed to be in deep thought. When his head erected itself once again, the sweat was gone from his brow, and the color of his face had normalized. He seemed to have come to a decision. "This is a good plan."

What was good about this plan? The complete vagueness and spontaneity of it?

He placed a finger over his iPad mic and then turned to me.

"We can convene at some body of water in the southern states, an inland lake, that Rufus can plot out overnight. From there, once we meet, I can reveal our destination without prying eyes and ears. I think somewhere in Southern Florida should meet our needs. This way we will minimize our travelling time."

"Southern Florida?' I remarked. "Yes. That could work. Rufus has flown extensively in that area over the years."

I reflected on my previous journey to Florida eighteen months earlier. "That will take us at least 24 hours by car. More, since I'll need driving breaks because someone doesn't have his license. Unless something has changed?"

I looked at Hitchhiker, and he silently rotated his head from side to side. He then said, "Rufus needs to figure out a way to tell us exactly where to meet him, without actually telling us. We can't be too careful."

I thought about the No Fly List we were suddenly on, and, although it sounded like a crazy conspiracy plot, agreed.

"How –?" I asked.

He removed his finger from the mic, and Rufus immediately began talking, "My friends, I know where we can meet, it's –"

"– Somewhere we can discuss another time," Hitchhiker interjected as he put his forefinger to his lips.

Rufus nodded his head in understanding and said, "Yes. Yes. Hitchhiker. Another time."

There was an awkward minute of dead air before Rufus said, "I will send you something. A good book to read to pass the time since you won't be driving."

I didn't quite completely catch what was being exchanged between my two conspiracy minded friends, but I gathered they had somehow made a plan. Great. But I had other questions in mind.

"So, Rufus, it'll maybe take us thirty hours to get there, depending on where there ends up being. You'll arrive long before us. Why don't we pick somewhere closer to meet?"

"A floatplane is not a jet plane, Mark," Rufus responded. "By the time I get the plane ready tomorrow, file my flight plans, refuel, and take breaks along the way, thirty hours will be about right. If you leave tonight, we should be on schedule to rendez-vous Tuesday."

"Do think your Gulfstream will be ready to bring us back?"

"I hope so," was all he could promise.

I did some mental arithmetic and estimates. The floatplane ride from whatever lake Rufus chose to wherever our destination was in central America shouldn't take more than a half day. We could potentially arrive Tuesday evening, get what we needed, and then hop on Rufus' jet. Stopover in Montreal to synthesize the cure, which Rufus said should only take a few hours, and then be home by Wednesday evening, three days from now. Covid patients often spent weeks on ventilators. June could hold out for three more days.

Couldn't she?

2 DAYS EARLIER

December 6th, 2021

The digital clock behind the Avis counter read 12:05 AM. A sign posted on the wall read: "Hours 7 AM – 11 PM." We weren't even close. I scanned all the other rental agency counters and, other than a small cleaning crew mopping up, they were deserted.

I sighed and released a guttural groan. Fatigue was setting in. Despite doing nothing but sit all day, I felt like I needed to collapse into a comfy recliner chair.

"What now?"

There was only a momentary pause before Hitchhiker said, "We take the Greyhound."

"A bus? All the way to Florida?

"Why not? There's likely a red eye that leaves soon. You won't have to drive and will get a chance to rest and clear your mind for what's to come."

What's to come?

I didn't like the sound of that.

He was right, though. I wasn't relishing the idea of driving solo for the next thirty hours.

The temptation to push myself well beyond my capabilities would be high, with all sorts of potential for accidents.

"But wait. We don't have an exact destination yet. Do we?" I asked, wondering if perhaps I'd missed something in their conversation. Some secret lingo that explained everything.

"You're right. We don't know exactly where we are going to meet just yet, but we do know it's somewhere in Southern Florida. Let's pick a destination, and we can modify it as we get closer by transferring to different buses."

I shrugged my shoulders. "Alright, but it feels like we're flying by the seats of our pants.

"Yes," Hitchhiker said, his eyes smiling widely. "Sometimes you just have to release control and surrender to the flow."

I cocked my head, scrunched my eyebrows, and stared intently at him as I repeated, "Surrender to the flow?"

"Yes ... you know ... let the universe provide."

I shook my head in wonder.

Who is this guy?

***

When we arrived at the Greyhound Bus Terminal and I tried to settle our taxi fare unsuccessfully with my corporate Visa, I should have realized then and there that something was suspiciously wrong. Fortunately, I had enough US cash on hand to cover the fare. However, having already paid $100 to Ike, my wallet was now depleted. Presumably, there would be an ATM machine at the station.

We stood in front of yet another ticket counter, this time for a Greyhound bus ticket. Our perusal of the red electronic schedule board mounted on a large wall next to the ticket booths revealed, just as Hitchhiker surmised, a red-eye special leaving for Southern Florida: more specifically, West Palm Beach leaving at 12:50 AM and arriving at 10:25 AM on Tuesday. A 33-hour trip with multiple stops and transfers in Atlanta and Jacksonville. Not ideal, but, given the circumstances, an incredible stroke of luck. All the pieces of this journey jigsaw puzzle were slowing creeping into place.

The woman serving me was in her mid-thirties and looked as tired as I felt. The ticket booths were open 24/7, and I suspected she was just starting her midnight shift. She had an unusual droopy eye that very quickly reminded me that I was much more a doctor than I was an intrepid adventurer. And yet, here I was, once again, submerged in a would-be hero's journey. I could only hope, for my family's sake, that I *would be* the hero.

"Two tickets for West Palm Beach, please," I requested, presenting my driver's license along with Hitchhiker's military ID. His photo looked decades old; he was clean shaven with a buzz cut. He stood a few paces behind me, and I turned to look from his ID photo to his face. He was almost unrecognizable, but there was no mistaking his military bearing. He was standing like a cyborg from the Battlestar Galactica TV show, with that red blip doing its metronome thing from side to side, scanning everything in his environment. It made me feel safe to have someone watching my back, even a cyborg.

The eye-droop lady looked at me queerly for a moment and then began tapping away autonomously at her keyboard, like every other person behind a counter I'd met today. I couldn't help but think she would soon be replaced by some form of artificial intelligence, like bank tellers and ATM machines, and then she could at least get a good night's sleep.

"Two tickets to West Palm Beach? That will be $474. How would you like to pay?

I pulled my corporate Visa card from my wallet and waited for the banking machine, which she quickly slid under the plexiglass window. I inserted my card, entered my four digit password, and waited.

"DECLINED," appeared on the screen. I cancelled the transaction and then tried it a second time with similar results. I opened my wallet and retrieved my personal Visa and then a Mastercard. Both DECLINED. I tried my business and then personal debit cards: DECLINED.

I looked up from the machine and eyeballed her.

"Problem?" She asked.

"I don't think your machine is working. It won't accept any of my cards."

"It worked just fine for another customer a few minutes ago," she countered.

"Well ... it's not working for me. Can you hold those tickets for a moment while I confer with my friend?"

"Sure. Don't take too long, Dr. Mark. Your bus leaves in fifteen minutes and there won't be another until the morning."

I was taken aback. How did she know I was a –

She then made a subtle peace sign with her hand and touched her mask with her index and middle finger. It was like some secret society thing.

Having no idea what else I should do, I returned the greeting, which seemed to make her very happy. I stepped over to Hitchhiker, who was standing military rigid with his back against a nearby wall.

He said, "Working in the shadows, again, are we?"

"Hey, if it helps us along, where's the harm?"

"Look," I continued, "we've got a problem. None of my cards are working. My corporate Visa didn't work in the Taxi, either. It's like they've all been cancelled. I would call to sort it out but –"

"But you don't have a phone," he finished.

"Right. Can I use one of your cards?"

"I don't have any."

"What do you mean?"

"I don't have credit cards."

"None at all?"

He just shook his head.

"What about a debit card?"

He shook his head again.

"Wait! You travel all over and don't carry credit or debit cards? How do you pay for anything?"

He hoisted his briefcase ever so slightly.

I frowned and eyed it, wondering just how much money he carried around with him that he had to keep it in his briefcase.

"That sounds ... dangerous."

"There are stories abound of people losing their bank cards or having their cards stolen. Not once have I been robbed or misplaced my funds."

Why did this even remotely surprise me? This was Hitchhiker, after all.

"Alright," I said, "Any chance you have $474 in there? I'm tapped out."

He dropped his briefcase to the floor between his feet and then retrieved a money clip from his inside breast pocket over his heart. He leafed through, pulled five crisp hundred dollar bills, and passed them to me with no hesitation.

"Thanks," I said. "I'll pay you back when I can."

He shrugged his shoulders.

I returned to the ticket booth and exchanged the hundred-dollar bills for the tickets. She gave me the run down on the Covid protocols, which were only that we were recommended to wear masks as much as we could. Remarkably, no vaccine papers were required. Like restaurants, I had to assume Greyhound buses carried supersecret anti-viral technology the rest of the world wasn't yet aware of. Anyway, both Hitchhiker and I were fully protected, so my concerns about getting sick were minimal. It did make me wonder why Covid numbers in the US weren't even worse than reported, given a bus system carrying disease to every corner of the country on a daily basis.

We exchanged our "peace-mask" greeting again, I waved to Hitchhiker and began walking towards the depot; our bus was leaving on schedule. He caught up quickly.

I glanced at him sideways and whispered, "Think Big Pharma did it?

He shrugged his shoulders in what was now becoming a very familiar retort to my questions.

I asked, "Do you want your change back?"

"It looks like you need it more than I do."

***

Detroit, Michigan: 12:50 AM

As the bus pulled out and the brief smell of diesel washed over us before the ventilation system kicked in, we both settled into our seats, which were located towards the middle of the bus, Hitchhiker adamant about taking the window. He was a big man and occupied a lot of real estate. It was a little bit strange sitting so close to someone who wasn't Sarah. It had been a long time since I rode any significant distance on a bus, perhaps even since my teens. The bucket type seats were comfortable enough, certainly much improved from my last time on a bus. There was also a footrest and good leg room. All in all, definitely better than driving.

The N95 mask was a problem, though. They weren't meant to be worn for 24 hours, or more, at a time. The heavy elastics would leave dents in my head and the edges of the mask would dig into my face and leave marks that might take days to disappear. Fortunately, I was prepared.

I dug through my backpack and retrieved a standard surgical-type mask that tied up behind the head. While the N95 was much superior for aerosolized transmission, there was only four other people onboard, two in the forward seats, and two all the way in the rear. Every other row of seats was cordoned off such that, even if the bus were full, it would only be running at fifty percent capacity. Greyhound boasted a thorough cleaning of all high-touch areas as well as ozonation. The cabin air was exchanged with fresh outside air every five minutes. All things considered, it seemed more than safe enough to part with my N95 for the duration of the trip.

I nudged Hitchhiker with my elbow. "Here, it's a long trip to wear an N95, put this on instead."

I passed him a second surgical mask that I had packed. He looked at me like I'd grown a third eye in the middle of my forehead and raised both his eyebrows. "Do you think that is wise?"

"It's a risk versus benefit thing," I said. "This bus has amazing air circulation, and there's almost nobody on it. Plus, since we've both had Covid several times, we've both got natural immunity."

Not to mention, at least for me, added technological immunity from vaccines.

"The risks of getting a nasty rash are much greater than the likelihood of catching disease."

"I should think death outweighs a rash as a consequence, though."

"You probably have more risk of dying from this bus getting into an accident than from Covid."

"Hmm. That's reassuring," he said, strapping on his seatbelt, which reminded me to do the same. He then removed his N95 and donned the surgical mask I'd given him.

"You know," he said, "I haven't worn one of these since we first met in Kentucky."

I remembered it like it was yesterday.

"Do you mind giving me a hand?"

Just like the last time, two years ago, he was fumbling miserably with the ties behind his head. I gave him a hand, and he said, "That *is* much better. Thank you. If the bus fills up on the way, it would be prudent to use the N95 again."

"Agreed."

I continued, "There were a few things you were going to share with me once we got into a more private situation. It's fairly private here. Wouldn't you agree?"

"Mostly."

"So ... two things. The first is, where are we going? To which country?"

I waited patiently, but no answer came. Hitchhiker simply stared out the window. I was getting frustrated.

"Hello?" I said, more loudly. "Where the hell are we going?"

"Lower your voice."

I felt like I was being admonished by my father. Before I could get another word out, he whispered, "There's really nothing to be gained by answering that question at this moment in time, is there? I can tell both you and Rufus when we are safely onboard his plane tomorrow night in a truly private place."

"But I need to know," I pleaded.

"Really? Will it change anything for you?"

"It ... it will give me time to get mentally prepared," I argued.

"You're an emergency room physician," he countered. "You are always prepared."

"Well ... yes, but ... but –"

"Now get some sleep, and we'll discuss it tomorrow." He reclined his chair all the way back and, within a dozen heartbeats, was breathing deeply as sleep overtook him.

But ... what about my second question?

***

Dayton Trotwood, Ohio: 5 AM

There was a two and a half hour stretch between Toledo, Ohio and Dayton Trotwood, Ohio, where the bus didn't stop to let passengers on or off, and I was able to doze. Hitchhiker seemed impervious to disturbances and remained soundly asleep. I, on the other hand, being a shift worker with a tenuous sleep cycle at best, teetered erratically on the precipice of the real world, repeatedly falling into depths of unconsciousness, and then involuntarily being hauled out. Each time my eyes closed, and I fell, that same morphed image of June and Abigail – the sister I'd never met – would eventually etch itself on the inside of my eyelids and wake me from my brittle slumber. The more the cycle repeated itself, the more sleep deprived I became, and, for some reason, the angrier I was with my mother. How could she wait until now to tell me that I once had a baby sister? Now, of all times, when my four-month-old daughter was fighting for her life. I needed to speak with her again and talk it through.

The squeal of air brakes heralded our arrival to Dayton Trotwood just over four hours after our departure. My eyes popped opened, and, suddenly, I felt an urgent need to see a picture of June's face. I felt like I was losing her. I patted my coat pockets frantically, looking for a phone that had deserted me.

"Perhaps, your wallet?" Hitchhiker said in a soft voice. He was staring, watching my every move.

"My wallet?" I repeated hazily.

"I remember during one of our Zoom meetings shortly after June was born, you pulled a small photo from your wallet to show Rufus and I."

I remembered it also now. I fished through my otherwise useless wallet, bereft of financial worth, and retrieved a small artsy black and white photo of June taken on the day of her birth. I stared at it for what seemed like eternity, until my imaginary image of Abigail was pushed back over the precipice.

"She's quite cute," Hitchhiker remarked.

I smiled, as if she had been lost for ages and I had just found her. "Yes, she really is. She's everything."

***

Cincinnati, Ohio: 6:20 AM

In Cincinnati, we had a one-hour stop: time to pick up a breakfast sandwich along with some snacks and, for me, some reading material to pass the time. I took the opportunity to stretch and make a trip to the restroom to brush my teeth and splash water on my face, opening some of the crusty cobweb curtains dangling from my eyelashes.

We also took the opportunity to change out of our winter clothes. Or, at least, I did. Hitchhiker seemed quite happy to continue with his black trench coat, boots, and tuque, although I had no idea what he was going to do when we hit tropical temperatures. I changed into my hiking boots and lighter jacket and then stored my parka, gloves, hat, and winter boots in an overhead compartment on the bus.

We settled back into our seats as the bus left the station, storing our new travelling treasures in various pockets. The bus remained mostly empty and, despite our best intentions to switch our masks back to the N95 for our trip into the bus station, it seemed of little value given how sparse the crowds were. There was nobody around.

I dug into my breakfast sandwich – which

was horrible – and then attempted to drown it with a cup of hot chocolate – equally horrid. There was definitely no transformational pairing in this meal. I glanced at Hitchhiker, who was eating the same sandwich but drinking coffee.

"Pretty bad, isn't it?" I stated, placing the other half of my sandwich back in the bag for later disposal.

There was a short pause before he asked, "How is life without your phone?"

Here we go, I thought, *evasive question and answer time*. I wondered what path of controversial topics this would lead down.

I sighed. "Frankly, I miss my phone. The ability to catch up on the news; to look at my pics; to message and talk to Sarah, my friends, and colleagues; to listen to music and podcasts. Plus, all the more specialized apps that make day-to-day life fun."

He inhaled deeply. "Without looking, how many people are on this bus right now?"

It took only a moment for me to say, "Seven, plus the bus driver."

"How old would you estimate the bus driver is?"

"Mid-forties."

"Where is he from?"

"He has a very thick Bostonian accent …"

"Yes?" He prompted.

"But I heard him tell a passenger at the

front that he'd moved to Southern Michigan a few years ago."

"Without looking, what's the weather like outside right now?"

It was hard not to peek out the window, but I was able to keep my gaze fixed on Hitchhiker. "Blue skies but clouds rolling our way from the east. Temperature feels like around ten degrees Celsius."

A look of satisfaction overcame him as he formed his fingers into a steeple. "Do you think you would have noticed all of those details if you had been on your phone?"

"Probably not. But so, what? I could have looked up the weather on my phone as well as the forecast for the rest of the day. And who cares where the bus driver is from?"

"Being present and aware of your environment is a key survival trait, especially when you're travelling."

"Not sure how any of those things would influence my survival. Look," I said. "I'd be the first one to admit that I spend more time than necessary on my phone, and it has become a bit of a crutch to society and maybe even a wall to forming relationships. You just have to look at any elevator ride to confirm that: everyone's mind somewhere else, peering through their little looking glasses.

"But I still think the advantages outweigh the negatives. Why are you so against cell phones?"

We had had a very similar conversation two years earlier on our drive through Kentucky. It seemed he was still carrying the flag. He inhaled deeply again and brought his steepled index fingers to his lips.

"I'm not against cell phones. I have concerns about *smartphones*. When we had simple cell phones that had the simple and solitary function of contacting someone by voice, I didn't foresee any problems. The smartphone, however, is too powerful a tool for the average person. They get lost in it and lose their autonomy. Every move and behavior dictated by what their phone tells them. And the ability to wear a smartphone as a wristwatch has made it that much worse. Now, the watch monitors your internal vital signs and is slowly merging silicone and carbon. The next step will be even more disastrous."

I hesitated as I absorbed everything he was saying and wasn't sure I wanted to know.

"The next step?"

"Hmm. Have you heard of the *singularity*?

I thought for a moment. "Sure. That's when robots will become so smart that they can outwit humans."

"Not quite. Artificial intelligence outwitted the smartest humans at our most strategic games, like chess and Go, many years ago. There are several interpretations of what the singularity implies, but, essentially, it's when artificial intelligence can start improving upon itself without human involvement. That's when we will no longer be able to predict our technological future."

"Sounds like *Terminator* stuff to me."

"Not so far off. That's why people like Bill Gates, Stephen Hawking, and Elon Musk have all voiced concerns about runaway computer technology. An opinion I share."

"Seriously?" I countered. "I've read that we are many decades away from this kind of scenario even being a possibility."

"Are you so sure? Have you noticed how much your phone has improved in its ability to recognize what you say?"

"I have. Not to mention at work our EMR voice recognition transcription is eerily almost 99% accurate."

"That's called *deep learning.* It's the beginning of computers learning for themselves, and it's a runaway train."

"Perhaps. But isn't that a good thing? Look at all the progress being made. Even just from a medical perspective. All that deep learning will surely give rise to improved diagnostics and treatment pathways."

"It already has. IBM Watson is being used at Sloane Kettering Cancer Center in New York to help doctors treat cancer patients by forming and accessing a huge database of oncology studies and previous patient treatment experiences. Essentially, you plug in the symptoms and a host of other patient specific information, and the computer spits out potential treatment plans."

"Cool. A computer like that in the ER would be an amazing help. And that proves my point of how valuable the technology will be."

"Does it?" He said a little gruffly. "You're thinking too small and only about what matters to you. It's the big picture that is of issue."

He was, of course, completely right. My whole world, day in and day out, was my hospital emergency department, where people lived and died daily. It was hard to appreciate that there was something more important than that, a bigger picture. I stared at my lousy cup of tepid hot chocolate, deep in contemplation.

"So, you think robots will ultimately replace us?" I asked solemnly.

"Have you heard of Dr. David Gelernter?"

"No. I don't think so."

"Few people have. He is a pioneer of artificial intelligence, as was his father. Amongst other things, he's quite convinced that silicone will never be able to reproduce carbon consciousness mostly because of feelings."

"Feelings?"

"Most of the brilliant minds progressing the development of artificial intelligence are focused strictly on the mind, treating the brain as an operating system that just needs the right programs uploaded.

"Gelernter points out that we require our whole bodies to experience feelings, and these computer engineers are not focused on simulating our whole bodies, only our minds. The feelings we experience from things like art and music, which run through every part of our bodies before lodging themselves in our minds, are what make up a big part of our consciousness. Reproducing *artificial consciousness* is the real stumbling block. To paraphrase Dr. Gelernter, 'We can't reproduce a human mind until we can teach a computer to hallucinate.'"

"So ... *do* you think robots will replace us?"

"Maybe robots won't want to replace us, just control us. Think Matrix and not Terminator."

"In any case," he continued, "what I think is irrelevant. There's no doubt that we are headed towards a singularity. What happens next will be dependent on how careful humanity prepares for it. And right now, the average person isn't even aware that it's coming."

He turned in his seat and fixed me with that piercing, focused gaze of his. "If we can't control our own use of smartphones at the most basic level, how can we possibly control exponentially evolving supercomputers that can think for themselves?"

I could only shrug my shoulders helplessly in response.

"Oh, and there are eight passengers on the bus besides the bus driver," he added. "There's a small child sitting near the window with his mother up front."

***

London, Kentucky: 11:30 AM

The morning flew by quickly as I drifted in and out of sleep, processing the mind-bomb that Hitchhiker had dropped on me. If he was trying to distract me from the nightmarish visions of the morphed June/Abigail face –no doubt his intent, he was sneaky that way – he was entirely successful. Unfortunately, those faces were replaced by a convoluted tickertape of every sci-fi movie I'd ever seen, complete with the thumping background drums of the Terminator soundtrack. As if the pandemic wasn't enough and my daughter in dire straits, now I had to worry that she (and maybe me) would have to deal with some kind of potentially malevolent artificial intelligence beings somewhere in the future.

We were passing through Kentucky, where I first met Hitchhiker, and I decided, once and for all, it was time I learned a little more about him. The surest way to learn about him, though, was to ask him about something completely different. He was reading on his iPad and appeared to be quite engrossed. Perhaps, an opportunity to catch him off-guard.

"What is it, exactly, we are looking for in Central America? A plant? An insect? Bat dung? What is it we need as a substitute for our secret ingredient?"

Hitchhiker slowly turned his raised eyebrows to face me. A look that plainly said, *Just how stupid are you that you think I'm going to reveal this information in a crowded bus?*

The bus wasn't crowded, but there were twelve people on it as of the last stop in London, Kentucky. He placed his iPad into the pocket of the chair in front of him. "We are passing through Kentucky, where we first met, and you, the ever and always doctor, who pries into people's lives without shame, wants to know more about me. From whence did I come."

Busted!

"You know pretty much everything about me," I replied. "Sure, I'd like to know a little bit more about the guy I'm travelling 33 hours on a bus with."

"What's your second question?"

It took me a moment to realize he was referring to our conversation when we first boarded.

"My second question? Right. I wondered if you were in the military at some point. The way you stand, and, sometimes, the way you talk ..."

He turned his head to look out the window. Barren Kentucky fields whizzed by. We had left any snowy evidence of winter in our crumbly tire dust long ago.

"Do you like bourbon?"

I wasn't sure what this had to do with our conversation, but … "Sure, in a cocktail, occasionally. Honestly, I don't know much about it. I'm more of a rum guy."

"My family makes bourbon. Blunton's Bourbon, to be specific. Perhaps you've heard of it?"

I had. Even to a bourbon neophyte like myself, I knew that Bluntons was the mothership of Kentucky bourbons. "Yes. I've heard of it. Wait. Your family owns it?"

"Third generation. My grandfather won it in the late eighteen hundreds in a high-stakes poker game."

I thought about this for a moment, trying to figure out how it fit together with his apparent vagabond lifestyle … and I couldn't. It made no sense at all. If he was from that kind of wealth, he certainly didn't need to hitchhike. He could probably have a chauffeured limo, if he wanted.

"I'll bite. Your family owns Bluntons, one of the world's top producers of bourbon, and you galivant around the US hitchhiking from place to place, when it seems to me that you should probably be back on the ranch contributing to the family business. Why aren't you? Even more puzzling, why are you involved with our company, a company with little chance of any success, when you have all the money you'll ever need just by following in your families well-tracked footsteps?"

There is the pregnant pause, and there's the Hitchhiker pause that starts when it starts and ends when he's ready to talk. This current pause was of Moby Dick proportions. Finally, he spoke.

"You'll recall, when we last met in person two years ago on this very highway, I was going to visit my brother?"

"Of course."

"My brother was the CEO of Bluntons at the time. He passed away while I was with him, shortly after you dropped me off."

"I'm so sorry. That's terrible." And then it dawned on me. "Wait, did he ...? Did I give him Covid through you?"

"He did die of a Covid related illness. The timing was unclear, though. He may have been infected before I got there. He was still working at the distillery, overseeing production. He was a hands-on kind of guy, and there were outbreaks."

Unbelievable. With only a few degrees of separation, I may have been the modern day Typhoid Mary. Another notch in my Covid killer belt.

"I'm not sure what to say, Hitchhiker. If I had anything to do with it ... again, I'm so so sorry."

"Irrelevant. These things are beyond our control and not worth ruminating over. The point is, I was not the man to replace him. I never was. My dad passed away years ago and left my mother in charge. She was quite smart with numbers, and she knew the business inside and out. She had always assumed my brother and I would run the company together, someday. But I never had an interest. Frankly, it's boring work. Mostly running numbers, accounting. Very little to do with the actual making of Bourbon. At least there would be some art in that."

"So, you left the business?"

"I was never really a part of it other than in name."

At that moment in time, I had never wanted my phone so bad. A few taps and I could probably figure out Hitchhiker's real name.

He stared at me, like he was reading my mind. "Don't get your hopes up. I'm not listed anywhere online. I'm a ghost as far as the internet is concerned."

I sighed. I had no idea how that was possible, to ghost yourself in this day and age. Surely, one day I would find out his real name. Meet someone who knows him. Like his mother?

"If your brother passed, and you're not involved, is it just your mother running the business?"

"She passed from Covid as well, two weeks

after my brother did."

Holy shit! Now I was beginning to understand his commitment to our little company. His whole family was basically wiped out by the pandemic.

***

I gave Hitchhiker some "space" after he revealed his horrible family Covid woes. He became somewhat forlorn, staring out the window at a landscape that looked bland to me but likely held personal meaning for him.

I pulled my recent Cincinnati bus depot acquisition from the front seat pocket: a Rolling Stone Magazine. The cover was provocative, featuring a snarling Miley Cyrus mostly naked covering her breasts with her hands. I caught Hitchhiker glancing at it and felt like a teenager hiding a Playboy magazine, like I needed to defend it – "great interviews!" Rolling Stone had veered very much towards left-wing politics over the years, but it still featured solid investigative journalism along with the current state of the entertainment industry.

I reiterated these last thoughts to Hitchhiker, and he casually commented, "Left-wing, right-wing. Just like a bird, a country needs both wings to fly."

Well said, I thought. Typically vague, but well said.

I had picked up the magazine in particular because of an article on climate change. As I thought about it, it seemed that this would be a good topic to steer away from Covid.

"Yeah," I said, pointing to the article title on the cover, just below Miley's tattooed arm, "I'm curious what their latest thoughts are on climate change."

Hitchhiker rolled his eyes and smiled as he looked at the cover. "Nine months of pregnancy and four months of child rearing taking its toll, is it?"

"What? No. It's the article I'm interested in." I turned the slightest shade of teenage blushing red.

He raised his eyebrows.

I blustered. "You know. Where we are at in the world with the climate and all that."

He sat up a little straighter, turned his head to look back outside, and began, "Imagine you are a child at the end of a busy summer day, and your mother puts you in the bath and turns on the water. The doorbell rings and she leaves to answer it, getting distracted, and forgets about you and your filling tub in the process. That is what climate change is: A tub that is filling with water with no end in sight unless you do something about it. So, what are your options?"

He turned his inquiring eyes towards me.

I felt like a child being schooled. "Sorry?"

"What can you do about the situation?"

I thought for a second, assimilating the metaphor. "Turn off the water?"

"Yes, you could turn off the water and live with the water at whatever level it is, which in the case of planet earth is quite high, with a lot of imminent known and unknown disasters looming."

He waited.

"Slow down the water and give your mother some time to return."

"Something the world's been working at for a while with limited success because, even if you slow it down, the tub is still filling and will eventually overflow."

"How about if you pull the plug?" I asked.

"The best of ideas, however, technologically and psychologically, we simply aren't there yet. And so, the plug is stuck."

"Let if overflow, then. Your mother will come back and realize the mistake she made and won't do it again."

"That's the worst option since there are no do-overs. One planet and one shot at it. The water overflows and floods the downstairs. The house is a write off."

I'd run out of solutions for his metaphorical climate change thought experiment.

He smiled. "The last option is to get out of the tub and leave the house. Something Elon Musk and Jeff Bezos have been working towards with some success."

"Spaceships?" I asked incredulously. "That's your solution to melting ice caps, rising ocean water levels, crazy storms, and heat waves?"

I was reasonably happy with the direction the conversation was taking. His mind had clearly been drawn away from the Covid stuff.

"It's one solution." He frowned and looked to his feet.

"What if I like planet earth and want to stay here?" I asked.

"Do you want to live in a pandemic for the rest of your life? Do you want your kids to live in a permanent pandemic?"

"What? I'm not getting the connection."

"Most people don't. Look closer at the title of your article."

I drew my eyes away from Miley and read it out loud, "How the Climate Crisis is Creating a New Pandemic Era."

"Damn! That never occurred to me. How?"

"Think about it. Destruction of habitats from aggressive agricultural business and rising temperatures have caused every manner of species to migrate to more friendly environments. Suddenly, animals are meeting new animals and humans they've never come across before. Bring bats, ticks and mosquitoes into the equation carrying viruses to and fro, and you have the melting pot to create any number of viruses potentially far more deadly than SARS-CoV 2. Not to mention, thawing permafrost releasing deadly organisms from long ago that our current world has never seen."

So much for steering clear of the Covid topic. Why is it that every conversation seems to boomerang back to Covid? "You're saying, Covid-19 may just be the beginning?"

"It *is* just the beginning."

Bloody hell. Talking to Hitchhiker was often like chatting up the Grim Reaper.

"Does the full-time intellect foresee any solutions to this mess we are in?"

"Of course. Our conversation has come full circle. The answer is the great singularity we talked about earlier, if we allow it."

"How so?"

"In the same way that deep learning will save countless lives on highways with automated driverless cars, if we allow artificial intelligence to evolve to its natural heights and give it the necessary input into environmental decisions, then we could no doubt figure out a way to pull the plug. But we must get out of our own way, first."

"That sounds about as likely as gearheads and grandads giving up the stick shift and steering wheel to a robot."

Hitchhiker's face took on a dire note as he said, "It's up to every one of us. Each person must make their own decisions. If we don't make it work and marry climate change to the singularity, then, in addition to all the cataclysmic environmental events, we better get used to repeated and deadly pandemics."

***

Knoxville, Tennessee: 1 PM

I was finishing up the article as we cruised through Knoxville, Tennessee. Hitchhiker was bang-on correct about everything he said. We were potentially one mosquito bite away from a much greater catastrophe than Covid-19, and climate change was just making things worse.

It was a lot to take in, and, from my perspective, made our journey that much more crucial. A cure might be the thing we need to turn the tide, particularly if we were able to reconfigure it to other viruses. I took a moment to look past Hitchhiker, who was reading his iPad again, and watched the scenery whiz by. I recognized the area. It was the turn off that brought me to the diner two years ago, where I was forced to choose between much needed food and the protection of my mask. The mask won out, and I left with my stomach growling.

We pulled over for a thirty minute pitstop and grabbed a couple of ham sandwiches that we wolfed down. It was amazing how doing nothing for hours on end could make you hungry. Like our bodies knew to stockpile energy for some terrible thing to come.

1 DAY EARLIER

December 7th, 2021

Jacksonville, Florida: 12:15 AM

The journey became a bit of a geographical blur with stops in Athens, Atlanta, and Savannah. We slept on and off, read on and off, but there was not much more conversation until we hit the long stretch to Jacksonville, Florida. We were both restless and tired: tired of sleeping, tired of reading, tired of being tired. We both glanced at each other simultaneously, and I spoke first.

"What book are you working on?" I asked. Hitchhiker wrote books as fast as I read them, however, they were for his eyes only. His own personal canon closing on two hundred the last time I asked.

This question seemed to perk him up, and, as always, my question was answered with a question. "Hmm. It's been two years since the pandemic started. How do you think it will –?"

He stopped mid question and seemed to be rethinking what he was about to say.

In a very un-Hitchhiker like way, he

actually answered my question. "I'm researching and writing about what our new endemic world will look like. Everyone is focused on what our post pandemic world will be, thinking Covid-19 will be eradicated, but this is a false direction. The focus should be on what our *endemic* world will look like. A world where humanity and Covid-19 variants, or whatever virus comes next, coexist."

"And ... how's it coming along?"

"It's not." He became rigid in his seat. "I get blocked by the same thing over and over."

"By what?"

He pointed his index at me. "You."

"Me? How am I blocking your predictions of the future?"

"Well, not so much you. It's the variable you represent. You're very much like the Mule we spoke of from Asimov's *Foundation* books. You're the unknown."

"Still not following," I said, shaking my head.

"It's this cure your father designed, and you want to create. It will change everything. Vaccines have been around forever and have been studied ad nauseum. Sure, they've virtually eradicated or eliminated many diseases, including smallpox and Polio, by preventing the host from getting it, but eradicating an ongoing and world-wide established disease by curing the host has very little precedence. The invention of penicillin for bacterial infection would be the closest thing I can think of, and those effects worldwide, although substantial, would be trifle by comparison. If you are successful, for the first time in history, an entire family of pathogens potentially affecting every human on the planet will be treatable and potentially erasable, particularly when combined with vaccines. It is therefore impossible to predict what will happen."

"You keep saying 'you,' but it's we: you, me, and Rufus."

"Mark, *you* are the Mule. For some strange reason, the world has seen fit to provide you, and only you, with the tools and the connections to make this happen. And more importantly, only you have the motivational bond with a dying daughter that will push you to succeed no matter the cost."

***

In Jacksonville, we stopped for ninety minutes from 12:15 AM until 1:45 AM. Hitchhiker remained fast asleep as I left the bus to stretch my legs and pick-up more snacks with the cash that Hitchhiker had left me. My head was still reeling from our discussion. I was the Mule that could change the world? The unpredictable variable? C'mon. Get real. I was just an ER doc from Northern Ontario with a deathly sick daughter.

Several Greyhound buses were gathered here, and three more travellers recognized my "peace mask" from the video and gave me the peace sign to much fanfare, complete with selfies.

When I returned to the bus, I found Hitchhiker awake and chatting with Rufus on FaceTime with his iPad. Somehow it had never occurred to me that Hitchhiker's ancient iPad was hooked into the internet on the bus and capable of FaceTime calls. I needed to call Sarah.

I took my seat and squeezed next to Hitchhiker, such that Rufus could see my face. "Rufus. How's progress?"

He hesitated before speaking. "Progress?" He replied. "All good."

All good? Did that mean he was enroute to meet us tomorrow with his pontoon plane. "Does that mean –?"

Hitchhiker elbowed me aside and interrupted, "Well. Great catching up, Rufus. Talk soon." He then tapped out and turned to face me.

"Remember? Working in the shadows? Stealth?"

I had forgotten completely. This clearly wasn't natural to me. "Right. Sorry. Thanks for not letting me ... blow our cover." Whatever cover we had.

"So, what did you guys do? Speak in code?"

"Sort off. Rufus was able to communicate that he's enroute, and that he'll meet us."

"Great. Meet us where? We're almost in West Palm Beach."

Hitchhiker opened his Kindle app and said, "He finally sent me that book he promised."

Terrific. He's going to read.

He was scanning his selections from his downloaded library. He smiled and said, "Look. Alexander Dumas' *The Three Musketeers.* Brilliant."

From our Zoom conversation last week.

He then took a piece of paper from his briefcase along with a pencil and began flipping one page after another, marking down, what looked like, random letters on the paper as he did so. I looked over his shoulder and noticed that he was pausing at the capital letters that began sentences that were underlined. As I recalled, readers often underlined passages that they found meaningful and when more than ten people did this, it would appear in your book, if you had this feature turned on.

"Is it ... some kind of code?"

Hitchhiker had a gleam in his eyes and was sitting as straight as his pencil. He ignored me completely.

"Who knew your friend could be so ... stealthily creative," he whispered.

He put his iPad in the pocket of the seat in front of him and then showed me the paper.

"Pahokee Marina Lake Okeechobee"

***

"It's actually quite perfect," Hitchhiker remarked. "It's about forty miles northwest of West Palm Beach. A perfect place to land a seaplane."

"But ... how did you know to look for the letters in the book?" I asked.

"Why else would Rufus send me a book, if not to look for a message?"

That made sense, sort of. "And the letters?"

"I noticed the first underlined passage in the book really wasn't that remarkable and neither was the second. That's how I knew his cypher had something to do with the underlined passages. Then it was a matter of figuring out where he planted the key letter or word in each sentence."

"It takes ten people to underline one passage to be seen by anyone buying the book. How would Rufus have accomplished that?"

"He would have had to create ten kindle accounts or call on ten people with Kindle accounts to underline those same passages."

"Wow. No wonder it took him so long to get it to us."

"He also had to find a meaningful book without too many passages already highlighted."

Hitchhiker folded his fingers into a steeple

again and placed his index fingers over his lips. "Your friend is quite the cryptographer."

He seemed to have a newfound respect for Rufus. "Won't others be able to download the book also."

"They would have to know which book. This wasn't the only one he sent. There were a dozen others."

"How did you know to pick this one?"

He tilted his head ever so slightly. "*The Three Musketeers*? Fairly obvious, wouldn't you say? Given our previous conversation."

"Yes. But surely this isn't very sophisticated. Others will eventually figure it out?" If there are, indeed, "others" out there.

"Most certainly. But it will take them time. Time enough for us to get where we want to go without any further ... interruptions."

I contemplated Rufus' out of the box thinking and was quite proud of him. He even received a compliment from Hitchhiker, which was a rare achievement.

After a short while, I asked, "Hey. Is it okay if I talk to Sarah? I had no idea you were able to connect to the internet on the bus."

Hitchhiker looked at me strangely and then pointed a finger at *Free Wi-Fi* signs on the seats in front of us.

I rolled my eyes in disgust at myself. "I guess I haven't got the whole smartphone thing out of my system yet. My observational skills must still be in the toilet."

"Clearly," was all he said, as he hesitantly passed me his iPad.

"Do you think you can be … secretive? Otherwise, perhaps I should do it."

"No. Of course not. I've got this. Hey … do you really think all this stealth stuff will help us?"

"The last place we can be tracked to is the bus terminal where your credit cards failed. In our conversations, we gave away that we were heading to Central America via Southern Florida. Beyond that, there's no way they can know where we are. So … yes. I think it's important we stay a few steps ahead of whomever *they* are, if we can."

"Fair enough."

Hitchhiker really couldn't have known about all the "peace-mask" selfies being posted and going viral. Signposts to our every whereabouts.

***

I entered Sarah's phone number and FaceTimed her. Even though she must have been asleep, she picked up immediately. Her hair was pillow mangled, and her eyes were swollen and crusted.

"Mark! Where are you?" She said, her voice hoarse and scratchy.

I touched the side of my forefinger to my lips. "Oh. You know. On the road." I looked at

Hitchhiker, and he gave a thumbs up.

Her brows furrowed for a second before she caught on. She propped herself up in bed. "Right. On the road. How's the road … going?"

"Going well. Really well. Hoping to be home by the end of the week. How's June?"

"Same, no change. No better and no worse." I could tell she was holding back a lot, trying to maintain her composure. "Is Hitchhiker still with you?"

I glanced at him, and he gave me a nod. I turned the iPad camera in his direction. He smiled and said, "Hello, Sarah. Stay strong. This road trip will be done soon."

I turned the camera back towards me, and Sarah and I talked for a little while saying nothing in particular. It was really more just to look at each other and commiserate. This was the longest I'd been away from her since my adventures of last November, a year ago. The bus pulled out, and the picture began to freeze intermittently. Hitchhiker must have been jacked into the bus terminal's Wi-Fi.

"Sarah, I think I'm losing you."

"Mark. Don't forget your ten-day Covid test."

I'd completely forgotten. The picture was frozen now. I gave her a thumbs up and hoped she saw it. I tapped out and passed the iPad back to Hitchhiker.

I couldn't believe it had only been ten days

since June was hospitalized. It felt like months. It was time to find out if I really was in the clear. I'd heard numerous stories of patients and friends only testing positive at the ten-day mark after exposure and multiple negative rapid tests. I stood and pulled my backpack from the overhead bin, nodded to Hitchhiker, and walked to the rear of the bus to use the restroom. Once inside the cramped quarters, I lowered the toilet lid, sat, rustled through my backpack until I found my last two rapid tests, and began setting up the equipment on a very small counter space. This was no easy task, particularly when the bus hit a rough patch of road and began jostling all over the place. I decided to do both tests at once to put this question decidedly out of the picture for good. Once I had the three drops in the well of the testing devices, and the fifteen-minute waiting game began, I wrapped each one in a surgical sponge and placed them at the top of my backpack for easy access. There was no point in waiting the fifteen minutes in the restroom. In fact, I realized, I really had no way to determine when the fifteen minutes was up in any case. I would have to rely on Hitchhiker and his watch.

I exited and found my seat. "Can you tell me when fifteen minutes are up?"

Hitchhiker looked at his watch and nodded.

I picked up my Rolling Stone magazine and began leafing through, reading articles I'd already read twice. Finally, Hitchhiker elbowed me gently and tapped his watch. I put my magazine away, reached into my backpack and pulled out the tests. I unraveled the first sponge on my lap and looked at the testing device.

Only one purple line: a negative test. I smiled, showed it to Hitchhiker, and then wrapped the testing device back up in its sponge and returned it to my backpack for later disposal.

"That settles that," Hitchhiker said.

"Hang on. I've got a second test to look at."

"Why would you do two tests at once?"

"If one's good, two is better, right? I wanted to be one hundred percent certain the result was accurate.'

Hitchhiker looked at me dubiously.

I unravelled the second sponge. This time, there were two purple lines. A positive test.

"Fuuuck!" I exclaimed rather loudly.

"Still think two tests are better than one?" He said.

***

"One of them has to be from a bad batch," I said.

"Which one?"

That was the million-dollar question. Based on the science of rapid antigen tests, there was a far greater chance that the negative test was wrong. I felt fine, though. And for a million reasons, including having had Covid multiple times and being vaccinated and boosted, I felt sure the positive test was wrong. Although I recognized that my confirmational bias was front and center since I didn't want to be the one responsible for June getting deathly ill.

"Shit." I slowly and reluctantly put my N95 mask on. What else could I do? Run up to the bus driver while we were under full steam and say, "Hey, Mr. Bus Driver, I just tested positive for Covid. Can you let me off here?"

"Despite what the science says, Mark, given everything you've told me, it seems very unlikely that you actually have Covid. I'm inclined to believe the first test. You really shouldn't have done the second test. Two is not always better."

I certainly was agreeing with him at this point, but the deed was done. Still, I had to know, I had to be sure one way or another.

"I need a PCR test."

"Agreed. We can do one at a pharmacy once we arrive in West Palm Beach."

***

West Palm Beach, Florida: 10:25 AM

The bus squealed into the West Palm Beach terminal with the same flume of diesel smell that had washed over us as when we left Detroit, 33 hours earlier. I wrinkled my nose and stepped off the bus with one thought on my mind: find a pharmacy. First, though, we needed transportation.

We walked stiffly towards the taxi stand, trying to shake out over a thousand miles of cramped muscles. Even Hitchhiker wasn't walking with his usual bouncy stride. In fact, he almost reminded me of a walk-on zombie from a *Walking Dead* episode.

As we approached the taxi stand, in its own designated spot, we noted a most unusual looking vehicle with a paraphernalia of electronics on its roof, large windows, and no steering wheel. On the side of the car's sliding door was a big green and blue "W" with the word "Waymo" printed underneath.

Holy cow, I thought. *One of those driverless cars.*

I looked pointedly at Hitchhiker. "After our discussion, should we try it?"

His eyes widened and he gave me one of his patent "are-you-crazy?" looks before saying, "A very bad idea. It would be intimately hooked into the web and would telegraph our whereabouts to anyone looking for us. Not to mention we'd need a credit card."

"Right, stay in the shadows. I guess a regular taxi that takes cash should do the job. Too bad." I grouched over and snuck a peek inside the Waymo. "It would have been a nice finishing point to your argument."

The door to the Waymo suddenly opened,

and a disembodied voice invited us in. I backed away, replying, "No thanks."

I looked at Hitchhiker and said, "Spooky!"

"I guess the future is ... spooky," he commented wryly.

We moved on to the taxi stand and tried one cab after another with no success. At over an hour away, our destination of the Pahokee Marina and Campground on Lake Okeechobee was too far, and, I gathered, too inconvenient. It hadn't occurred to me that getting a cab ride would be difficult. Finally, fate and fame intervened.

"Hey," a cab driver in his thirties named Chad with a Fabio head of blond hair said, "I know you. You're the 'peace-mask' guy, Dr. Mark, and his sketchy sidekick in black, from the video. Damn right, I'll drive you. This is so cool."

I was back to wearing my N95 at this point, with the chocolate milk stain on it. Chad saddled up next to me and flashed a peace sign selfie before ushering us into his cab. When we were settled, he said, "So, Lake Okeechobee, here we come."

He stepped on the gas and started the meter.

"One stop first," I said. "I need a pharmacy for a quick PCR test."

It may not have been smart to tell him – he could have ditched us then and there – but it was ethically the right thing to do.

"No prob, Dr. Mark. I had Covid last month, so no concerns for me. I'll have to leave the meter running, though."

Hitchhiker slipped two one-hundred-dollar bills through the slot in the plexiglass window. "A little something extra for the inconvenience."

Chad's eyes widened, "Damn. You guys are even more awesome in person."

***

I slid back into the cab after getting the PCR done at a Walgreens nearby. I told them it was just a routine follow up test for work, which it was, sort of. They explained that the results would be in my inbox within 48 hours. This was irrelevant since I had no phone and no internet. I was hoping to at least get the results before I got home. In the meantime, when I was in public spaces, I resolved to do the right thing and keep my mask in place.

I would fail miserably at this.

Chad was a bit of a chatty ... Chad? He talked nonstop all the way to Lake Okeechobee covering his views on ... well, absolutely everything from Covid, medicine and world politics to sports, movies, and literature. By the time we reached the Pahokee Marina, it felt like someone had driven a fork deep into my brain through my eye socket. Of course, the minute Chad opened his mouth after we'd left the pharmacy, Hitchhiker pulled his black tuque down over his eyes and curled up to the window. I felt a little used, like I was a diversion. He was, however, funding the ride, so I guessed I owed him that much.

We were almost at our destination, when I realized I'd left all my winter gear on the bus. The disappointed look on my face was like a homing beacon for a Hitchhiker comment.

"No. We're not going back to get your stuff."

He's doing that freakin' mindreading thing again.

"But ... why didn't you remind me?"

"What were you going to do? Traipse all of it through the jungles?"

"I could have stored it on Rufus' plane," I countered.

"Unnecessary weight. Time is of the essence. Wouldn't you agree?

"Of course, but my stuff didn't weigh that –"

He eyed me sternly. "Everything you have right now is replaceable. Everything, except your daughter. Let it go. You're tired, and you're better off without anything that will weigh you down physically or mentally, so you can focus on the task at hand."

Damn him. He's completely right ... again.

After Hitchhiker settled our account with

a few more one-hundred-dollar bills, we bid farewell to Chad, exchanged peace signs, and entered the Pahokee Marina and Campground.

***

By Northern Ontario standards, the Campground aspect of the park was quite sparse. A single row of palm trees lined the shore of Lake Okeechobee, where 150 or so hookups for RVs were located. As a result, the view of the lake was perfect from every site. From the sky, the docks of Pahokee Marina, which occupied most of the shore of the campground, appeared to have the shape of a gigantic letter "G," with the opening of the "G" giving entrance to the marina and access to all its docks. This wasn't where we would find Rufus, though. A marina's docks were designed for boats. A seaplane had certain needs with regards to manoeuvring that typically would put it on the outer rims of the "G." That's where we would find Rufus, if he was here.

And he was!

On the northern aspect of the marina, just at the mouth where one of the length of docks on the perimeter of the "G" formed a 45 degree angle, the one and only seaplane in the Pahokee Marina was tied up, and, even from this distance, I could see Rufus standing next to his new Cessna Caravan, a purchase from this past summer. It had a blue fuselage and propeller with the wings painted traditional white. The cargo door on the starboard side was folded down and outwards revealing a set of inviting steps waiting to bring us skyward.

The joy in my heart at seeing my old friend put a tiny crack in a dam that had been holding back ten days of terror. A couple of tears escaped as I ran along the docks to greet him, and then we wrapped each other in a bearhug that stabilized the world.

Hitchhiker was a little slower to arrive, but when he did, he exchanged a smiling handshake with Rufus. Despite knowing each other for the past two years, this was the first time they'd met in person.

"Rufus," I said, "You are a sight for sore eyes. How was your trip?"

"Much better than I'd hoped, my friends. Strong tailwinds had me here hours ahead of schedule. So, my Little *Rumhawk* is refueled and ready to go."

"*Rumhawk*?" Hitchhiker asked. "A name not far removed from that of your sailboat that sank off the coast of England last year."

"I wanted to pay homage to it."

He looked skeptically at the seaplane, running his hands tentatively along the aileron and wing strut.

"Don't tell me you're superstitious? I asked.

"Only with things that fly," Hitchhiker

replied.

Rufus' "new" *Rumhawk* was from the late 80s but had been through many rebuilds. He was fond of saying that, like music, all the best planes were made in the 80s.

Hitchhiker sucked a deep breath, and said, "Okay. Let's get onboard." He threw his briefcase in first and had a foot on the first ladder rung when Rufus placed a hand on his shoulder.

"Hang on, mon. My *Rumhawk* is ready to go, however, she still has no idea where she's going."

Hitchhiker froze in place and looked to the sky, as if weighing the dangers that someone could be listening in.

"Set course for Nicaragua. I'll tell you more when we are in the air."

***

I sat comfortably in the co-pilot's chair, staring at a second control yoke and a confounding array of electronic instrumentation, while Hitchhiker was seated directly behind us in the first passenger row. After I explained the situation with the dueling rapid tests on the bus and the pending PCR test, Rufus convinced me to ditch my N95 mask, saying that he was fully protected and, like Hitchhiker and I, had already had Covid multiple times with no residual long-haul effects. Plus, he said, he really wanted to see the look on my face as we soared through the blue skies of another adventure. I reluctantly tucked the "peace mask" away in my backpack, all the while ruminating on Rufus' comment of "another adventure." Rufus naturally lived in the moment. For him, this really was another adventure, albeit for all the right reasons and with a specific purpose. For me, who also loved adventure, every time I felt a surge of happy adrenaline, it was steamrolled by the guilt of my dying daughter. I took a deep, meditative breath and vowed to be present in the moment. I knew intuitively that my mission to save June would stand a better chance of success if I did that.

Rufus was all smiles as we steered out to sea. Once we were far enough from the marina, he turned into the wind and yelled, "Ready for take-off."

I pointed with both fingers to my ears and asked, "Shouldn't you have your headset on?"

He shrugged his shoulders and replied, "Who would I talk to?"

He had a point. There was no tower, no mission control. And the Rumhawk was surprisingly quiet, with no need for headsets to muffle the noise. Not at all what I expected. Rufus explained that the new turboprop engines were generally very quiet compared to the standard piston engines.

With his left hand gripping the yoke and

gently pulling back, his right hand opened up the throttle. The nose of the Cessna lifted, and we inclined backwards as the floats plowed the water until Rufus eased the yoke forward a smidgeon, and we were hydroplaning. He glanced at the airspeed indicator and yelled, "Airspeed is alive." A few moments later, the floats broke free of the water's grip. He eased the yoke forward, this time to drop the nose, allowing us to fly parallel to the racing water. I marveled at the subtleties of his manoeuvres, and the dramatic effect they had on the Rumhawk. We continued gaining speed until Rufus turned his grinning face to me and yelled, "Liftoff!"

The Rumhawk climbed higher and higher until he pulled back on the throttle ever so slightly, sat back in his chair, and released a happy sigh. We were airborne.

I turned my head and glanced at Hitchhiker, expecting to see the same adventurous smile that I was wearing but, instead, saw a wide-eyed look of terror. Both of his hands white knuckled the armrests with a death grip, and both shoulders were hiked to his ears. His face had gone icy pale, and there was a gleaming sheen of sweat across his brow. I gave him a quizzical look, and he scrunched his eyes tight and then pulled his black tuque over his eyes.

He's afraid of flying!

Once we had leveled off at our flying altitude, and Rufus throttled back the engine, I yelled, “Hitchhiker. Are you okay?”

He grumbled, pausing unnaturally between every few words to gulp a breath, “I’m afraid … I have … an unusually … severe case … of aerophobia.”

“What? Why didn’t you say something before?”

“It wouldn’t have changed anything. We still must get to our destination, and this is the fastest way.”

Rufus offered, “I have some Lorazepam and Gravol in the first aid kit for exactly this occasion. Get it for him, Mark. It’s in a bag under your seat.”

He looked back at Hitchhiker and added, “Better give him two tablets of the Lorazepam.”

I found it quickly and poured two small one milligram tablets from the Lorazepam container and one fifty gram tablet from the Gravol container and then reached back to hand the lot to him. “Here. Take this concoction. It will help.”

Hitchhiker uttered no sound as he loosened his grip on the armrest and thrust a shaky hand forward, palm up. I deposited the pills, and he immediately dry-swallowed them.

“Wait,” Rufus said. “Hitchhiker, can you give me a more specific idea of where we are heading in Nicaragua?”

"Bilwi. Puerto Cabezas. Playa La Bocanita is a beach where we can land."

He slid his tuque down over his eyes, tightened his seat belt even further, and then crossed his trembling arms and legs vise-grip tight while he waited for the effects of the meds to kick in.

***

We flew predominantly south, passing directly through Cuban airspace, to which, when Rufus pointed out the landmass many miles below, I exclaimed, "Are we allowed? I thought Cuban airspace was restricted."

"Yes, my friend, it is. Not being sure exactly what our destination was beyond Central America, I obtained a Cuban Overflight Permit before leaving Montreal. Cuba is the one place that could have given us some serious problems."

"Brilliant foresight, Rufus. You still have some doctor in you, anticipating everything that can possibly go wrong."

This provoked a proud, toothy grin. Although Rufus hadn't practiced medicine in over a decade, he still enjoyed his title of Dr. Rufus Leandro and, every now and then, would swear that, if ever his business enterprises failed, he would return to practice medicine alongside me in the ER.

Before long, I felt the jostle of air

turbulence as we passed over another smaller landmass, and he said, “Look, mon. My homeland of Jamaica.”

Now it was my turn to smile. Rufus wasn’t actually from Jamaica, but his father was born and still resided there. He visited regularly and, somehow, had acquired dual citizenship. Here, we rounded from a southerly direction to southwest to take advantage of the easterly trade winds. Or so Rufus claimed. It seemed to me we could have taken a much more direct route, but he said it was more fuel efficient this way. I suspected it was as much for him to see his Jamaican “homeland,” even for just a little while from the sky.

The skies were a spectacular blue and seemed to transition seamlessly into the turquoise of the water on every horizon. I’d only flown commercially and never in a plane as small as this. Every moment exploded with new and unexpected sights and experiences. This was much closer to the true feeling of flying than I’d ever had, something akin to what birds must feel, that sense of being able to manoeuvre fluidly in three dimensions that can only exist in the sky or in the sea.

We were three hours into our flight and flying directly into a setting sun. Hitchhiker appeared to be comatose, his seat tilted all the way back and his jaw hanging slack. Rufus was still grinning behind a pair of aviator shades. He appeared to be enjoying every moment of this flight.

"Rufus," I asked, "what do we do when we get to this beach? Won't it be dark?"

Rufus responded, "Yes, the sun will be down by the time we get there, however, we are very lucky. It is la *luna llena*."

"Full moon?"

"Yes, and it will be at our backs illuminating everything we need to see. We will land a kilometer or so off this beach and taxi in, so no one will know of our arrival. It should be mostly sand, and I can drive the plane right up –"

A sputter interrupted our conversation. The kind of sputter that leads to more sputters and then, eventually, curses, as the propeller flails uselessly. I looked poignantly at Rufus.

"What's going on?"

He fiddled with levers and toggled switches until I heard the familiar sound of a starter trying desperately to turn over an engine, much like a stalled car. The propeller sparked a few times and then slowed and windmilled once again.

"Rufus?"

He tried the same manoeuvre a couple of more times before answering. "This is bad, my friend. The engine is either not getting fuel or something is wrong with the fuel it is getting."

Even though I knew very little about airplanes, I couldn't help myself from taking a history and running a differential diagnosis.

I asked, "What kind of fuel does a plane take? Is it the same as a car or a boat?"

"No. Cars and boats use unleaded fuel. This plane uses an old fashioned kerosene type fuel called Jet A."

I thought back to the marina. "I only saw boats at Pahokee. Where did you fill up the plane?"

"There used to be an aerodrome associated with the Marina. It's closed now, but the marina still has dedicated fuel tanks for the occasional plane that comes by."

Rufus tried the starter once more to no avail and released a nervous sigh of frustration.

I pushed further, hoping I might nudge a neuron into place that could help him solve the problem. "Could they have made a mistake and filled their aviation holding tank with regular unleaded boat fuel?"

"It's possible my friend or, more likely, the fuel was sitting for a long time or was contaminated."

"Contaminated? With what?"

"Water is most common."

"If it was the wrong fuel, or there was water in the fuel, wouldn't the engine have stopped a long time ago?"

"Not necessarily. My tank was still half full, and it is a very big tank. It could be the bad fuel is only just reaching the engine."

We were gliding now, yawing, and pitching a little more as Rufus worked the yoke to steady the *Rumhawk*. With the engine stopped, all we heard was the wind swishing past our windows, and I felt we were yet another step closer to what birds experienced … if they were on the verge of falling from the sky.

"What do we do?"

"Fortunately, we have good altitude and lots of room to manoeuvre …" Rufus' voice tapered off as he stared at the GPS map on his dashboard and then stretched his arm in front of my face, pointing his finger in the direction of the passenger side window. "Look. There."

He reached behind his seat, pulled out a set of binoculars, and passed them to me. "Scan over there for land."

I saw a land mass immediately. It seemed to be an island in the middle of nowhere.

"Yes. I see an island."

Rufus pointed to his GPS map. "It's Providencia, an island of Columbia, and –" he scrolled the GPS screen, "Yes! It has a small airstrip."

Rufus banked towards the island and smiled as he tapped the slowly decreasing numbers on the altimeter. "Twelve thousand feet is enough, Mark. Enough to glide there, land and check the plane. If it's water in the gas or the wrong fuel, we can drain it and refill. At the latest, we could leave very early tomorrow morning, before sunrise, and still arrive under cover of darkness."

Sure. Easy peasy, I thought. *The kind of thing we do every day.*

I was reminded once again that Hitchhiker had still not shared with us our specific destination, nor exactly what we had come all this way to find. I looked back at him, and he seemed to be fast asleep. I wondered if he was aware of our predicament and whether I should tell him? I decided against it. The last thing we needed was someone in full aerophobic panic mode as we attempted an emergency landing.

Rufus glided the plane onwards, as if he'd dealt with this kind of emergency on a routine basis. The wind continued to blow out of the east, and he explained there was only one airstrip, which ran from north to south, so they would have to turn the plane ninety degrees to align with it. Typically, he further explained, we would want to land into the wind to minimize turbulence and slow our landing speed. In this case, the wind would be hitting us from the side and, without an engine, would make it challenging. The runway itself was parallel to the east coast of Providencia, bordering the sandy shore of the Caribbean Sea.

Rufus radioed to anyone that might be listening at the airport, "Mayday, Mayday. We have a stalled engine and are attempting to land without power."

I didn't like the word, *attempting*.

Rufus turned to look at me, like it might be the last time he ever saw my face. "Here we go, my friend. We only have one chance at this. It must be perfect."

It would not be perfect. Not even close.

***

The wind was picking up fast as we lost altitude, and I could feel it pushing us hard on the port side of the plane. Rufus was struggling to keep us in line with the runway, constantly adjusting the yoke, and we were getting buffeted about as the wings tipped this way and that, as if we were waving at someone on the ground. I wondered what that someone on the ground might be thinking, looking up at us. *Holy shit, they're gonna crash!*

We were perhaps a few hundred feet off the tarmac, when a groggy voice erupted from behind. "What the hell is going on? Are we landing? Why can't I hear the engine?"

"Hitchhiker," I yelled, "tighten your seatbelt some more. We've lost the engine and we're coming in fast."

For a fraction of a moment, I thought Rufus would pull the rabbit out of the hat. We were perfectly lined up, and just as he pushed forward on the yoke to bring the wheels of the pontoons to the tarmac, a gust pushed us off course inland towards a row of tall trees. In response, Rufus pulled back on the yoke, the pontoons skimming over the foliage of palm leaves, and then swerved directly towards the easterly wind. This pointed us away from land and back towards open water. As we came into the wind, though, we quickly lost power and elevation. We were over water when the *Rumhawk* dove hard, nose down. Rufus pulled back on the yoke with all his strength and, at the last minute, managed to set both pontoons on the water.

Rufus had once explained to me that, while an amphibious plane has tremendous flexibility in terms of landing on water or on land, it has the distinct disadvantage of not being particularly good for either. The wheels were located on the front and towards the back of each pontoon. This meant that if the plane didn't come in with its nose up, there was a serious risk of the front wheels catching the water and summersaulting the plane end over end. A lousy way to die.

Our only saving grace was that, without our engine, and because we were heading straight into the wind, we had almost no forward velocity. As the *Rumhawk*'s pontoons contacted the water, the front wheels dug in deep, and the whole rear of the plane stood up on end, ninety degrees to the water. There, we perched for what seemed like eternity, hovering on the verge of a forward flip, until another wind gust came and pushed our tail back down.

We splashed and then bobbed around for a few seconds before we realized we were still alive. Rufus, his face ashen white and gleaming with sweat, let out a loud, "Whoop!" I echoed his "Whoop!" and then pumped a trembling, adrenaline energized fist into the air.

Hitchhiker's deep, throaty, terrified voice interrupted our jubilation.

"I really hate you guys."

***

The Pirate's Den was less than a kilometer from our crashlanding site, and was a popular local watering hole located on the eastern shore, where everyone gathered to celebrate the end of the workday. It was packed with all manner of locals who were mostly talking about our aeronautical acrobatics. Providencia was a small island, and word had spread faster than you could say, "I survived a plane crash."

Once our nerves had settled, we still had the matter of getting the plane to shore. Fortunately, being a floatplane, Rufus carried two canoe-type paddles. Hitchhiker was all too happy to get out of the cabin and take up a position opposite mine, straddling the front of a pontoon and digging in, while Rufus sat in the cockpit, working the two small rudders attached to the rear of the pontoons, steering us towards the beach less than a half-kilometer away. Paddling was good work to calm the nerves and release some of the travel kinks. Already, Hitchhiker had regained some color in his face. A few hundred feet from shore, when the water was waist-high, we all jumped in and pulled the *Rumhawk* the remainder of the way. The water was silky warm and sparkled with energy. We dragged the plane as high onto the beach as we could, and then Rufus rigged a long rope to a nearby tree to keep the plane from floating off when the tide came in.

Our little mishap had sparked more than a little attention, and we were quickly set upon by locals driving pickups with some of the biggest tires I'd ever seen. They came right onto the beach, helped us drag the plane up even further, and then gave us a lift to the Pirate's Den. Surprisingly, everyone spoke passable English, in addition to the more common native Creole. I asked if the police or customs would be looking for us, and this generated a round of uproarious laughter. I gave Rufus a sideways glance, and he shrugged his shoulders. He had never been here before and knew little of the place, but it seemed to have its own way of life.

Hitchhiker was still not even close to being himself. The cocktail of air sickness, sedative, and sudden awakening to a near-death experience, had left his bones rattled and his legs wobbly. When we arrived at the bar, I sat him down at a table on the outside deck overlooking the crashing surf. The fresh breeze of salted air coming off the water seemed like a good antidote to his ails. Rufus was still outside in the parking lot on his phone contacting locals, looking for anyone knowledgeable about airplane mechanics. Every now and then, he would wander back in to keep us appraised of his progress. Alternatively, if he couldn't get his plane fixed, he was looking to rent another plane, or possibly a boat.

On my way back to our table from the restroom, I was walking down the hallway where a large map was fixed to the wall with some geographical information in the margins. Providencia, in fact, consisted of two islands. The larger Providencia, where we almost landed, was seventeen square kilometers and connected to the smaller Santa Catalina Island by a quaint one hundred meter wooden footbridge. The total population of the two islands hovered around five thousand. Historically, in the sixteen hundreds, it was once the base of pirating operations for Henry Morgan and his raiding expeditions of the Spanish Empire. It took me a moment to make the connection, Henry Morgan … Captain Henry Morgan of Captain Morgan's Rum fame. I suspected he looked nothing like the picture on the bottle. Apparently, his treasures still remained hidden somewhere on the island.

We had literally crash landed on Treasure Island.

When I arrived at our table, there were three shot glasses sitting in front of a glassy-eyed Hitchhiker. The full moon was well up in the sky, and I could see its reflection in Hitchhiker's eyes. I sat down across from him and pointed to the shots.

"Are you sure that's a good idea?" I asked. "Given the sedative you took and the state of your insides?"

"Our friendly retired doctor and Captain thought it was," he answered sluggishly. "Initially, he sent over one shot to calm my stomach for air sickness. I told him it was more air *terror*, and he consequently sent over two more shots."

I sniffed one of them. "Bourbon?" I would have expected Captain Morgan's, given the history of the island.

"Bluntons, no less" he responded. "Did you know that John Wick drinks Bluntons? I love his movies." Hitchhiker was babbling, no doubt some residual effects from the sedatives. Sober, he could be difficult to follow. I could only imagine what he would be like intoxicated.

I was about to find out.

He continued, "I take it you two were catching up while I was passed out on the plane."

"We had a couple of hours to kill."

"Well. I suppose it couldn't make me feel much worse." He raised a glass to me and promptly downed all three shots, one after another, in rapid succession."

I was shocked. He licked his lips, gave me a crooked smile, and said, "Retired doctor's orders."

"Easy there, cowboy," I cautioned. "We *are* still on mission."

Out of the corner of my eye, I noticed Rufus was coming our way, but he stopped at the bar and was chatting with someone.

"I wouldn't worry about me," Hitchhiker slurred. "I grew up drinking this stuff like water. I'm practically immuuuuuune."

He stared at me for a second, and then said, "You're still wearing your mask. You stick out like a sore thumb in this place."

"I still don't have my PCR result yet. I'm not taking any chances. I may be killing everyone's vibe, but they'll thank me for it if it comes back positive."

"Mission, mission, mission," he repeated, now leaning back precariously on the two rear legs of his chair, rocking back and forth, until he suddenly slammed the four legs to the floor, propped his elbows on the table, folded both hands under his chin, and looked pointedly at me. "Your second question. You wanted to know if I was in the military? Didn't you?"

I was caught completely off guard. Right here and right now, this is what he wanted to talk about? I surmised that the anti-air-terror cocktail had dropped a few of his walls.

I fiddled with my fingers and would have beckoned for my own drink had it not meant I would have to remove my mask.

"Okay. Yeah. The way you stand sometimes ... the way you talk. Were you in the military at some point."

"Does it matter?" He countered.

"Not really. I was just trying to find out a little more about you. We spent 33 hours on a bus together and, other than your connection to the bourbon industry, I still know practically nothing."

"Again, does it matter? More important than my background, you know how I think, what I think about, and most importantly, what motivates me. Everything beyond that, including my background, is superfluous and irrelevant."

Some, but not all, of what he said was true. Background information – past medical history – was everything in medicine. And, of course, now I wondered if he was hiding something. Something he was embarrassed about. Something he did in his younger years for which he was ashamed. A military action gone wrong? Damn. I hated being a doctor sometimes. There was always a need to see behind the curtain that overwhelmed everything else, even at the risk of friendships.

I bowed my head and then looked up.

There was nothing that needed saying, because he knew me also.

He smiled, suddenly looking completely sober, and began, "After graduating college, I was unhappy with the state of the world. I had two close childhood friends who also graduated at the same time. We decided to join the marines. My father was not happy. Looking back, it was a patently stupid idea, but one I learned from. My buddies were successful, but I was not. I had a medical condition I wasn't aware of until the physical was completed. Yet, I was still unhappy with the state of the world and wanted to make a difference, so I joined another organization to fight another kind of enemy: Greenpeace."

"Greenpeace!" I repeated. I did not see that coming. It sort of made sense. He would want to diminish his carbon footprint as much as possible, hence not owing a car and the hitchhiking. All that talk about climate change ...

"Yes. As it turns out, I had a particular talent for information gathering that was of great value in those days, predating the internet and computers."

He suddenly launched an arm in the air with three fingers showing and looked hard in Rufus' direction. I saw Rufus smile and turn to the barkeep.

A thought occurred to me. "But what about that military ID you showed me at the diner?"

"A fake. Do you have any idea how easy it is to fake a military ID?"

I did not. And somehow that felt wrong. There are few professions that ask you to put your life on the line: firemen, police, and military being the big three. To take advantage of the perks without paying the dues didn't sit well. I didn't think Hitchhiker was in any condition to discuss my moral conflicts with his actions, though.

"Before we even did our physicals, the three of us had ID cards made so we could take advantage of the bar perks that came with being military before being shipped off for basic. It was virtually unheard of to be refused on medical grounds, especially at 21 years old."

And now, I couldn't help but wonder what medical condition kept him out.

"You know," he whisper-mumbled, "I had it all organized. It's a 63-hour drive. I could have been there and back with our WDO in five days. Completely off the grid. No one would've known. No planes."

WDO? What the hell is that?

"I didn't always have problems flying. And then the failed mission ... and the bodies, my friends ..."

Was his air-terror PTSD related?

Rufus interrupted our conversation with a clearing of the throat. I turned to greet him as he arrived at the table, carrying a tray of shots and someone in tow.

"Ha. Looks like I'm too late." Rufus laughed. "Let's see the great intellectual spout smartass remarks now."

Hitchhiker had passed out on the table with his face in the crook of his elbows. He released a loud snort that let us know he was still alive. I shook my head. There was still so much I wanted to know.

"What the hell are we going to do with him?"

Rufus sighed and responded, "This may be for the best."

He turned to introduce his companion. "My friend, I'd like you to meet a new acquaintance."

He stepped aside and a young woman with piercing hazel eyes looked me over, flashed a mile-wide grin, and gave me the peace sign. "Dr. Mark. Loved your video and love your mask."

Rufus laughed hesitantly. "Mark. Yara has an idea to get us to our destination, but it's a little crazy."

***

We were bouncing along a dirt road with Rufus' new friend at the wheel of a pickup truck that was even bigger than the ones on the beach. It had a reinforced metal grill on the front and should have come with a ladder to climb into it. It even had lights mounted on the roof. She didn't have the headlights on because she apparently knew the roads well and found it more enjoyable to drive by the light of the full moon.

Yara appeared to be in her mid-thirties and had black hair that was parted down the middle and fell straight to her shoulders where it became an entangled mess of curls. She said she was from Nicaragua originally but moved to Providencia as a child with her father, where she had lived ever since. When she smiled, I was struck by her prominent cheek bones, and the soft, sultry look of her eyes. She instantly reminded me of Marion, Indiana Jones' love interest from *Raiders of the Lost Ark*. I was almost certain she could have sat down at our table at The Pirate's Den and knocked back the entire tray of drinks without flinching.

With Yara standing there, Rufus had explained that all his phone calls had amounted to nothing. There were no other planes to rent on the island until the following week because they had all flown to Costa Rica for a weekend regatta. Anyone who knew anything about airplane mechanics had gone with them.

His plan B was a boat of some sort. However, Nicaragua had closed their borders with the recent new Covid Omicron wave, and no skippers wanted to tangle with the Nicaraguan military. Nor did they want to risk their fishing licenses to help a stranger, no matter how much money Rufus offered. That, and the forecast did not look favorable, with large waves anticipated over the next 24 hours.

Yara had struck up a conversation with Rufus at the bar, asking about our plane crash. Rufus had told her the story of how sick my baby daughter was with Covid, and how we needed to get to Nicaragua to find something that we required to make a cure that could help all of mankind – something that still only Hitchhiker knew about and was in no condition to tell us. When Rufus pointed to our table, Yara had immediately recognized me as "Dr. Mark and his peace mask" from Harold and Maude's video. She respected my words and wanted to help. This is when Yara suggested an unconventional alternate method of transportation. When I asked what method that might be, Rufus dodged the question and said we had to go quickly because it would be slower, and we wanted to land before daybreak to avoid attracting any attention.

We pushed three cups of robust Columbian coffee down Hitchhiker's gullet and were finally able to rouse him enough to hoist his awkward ass into the truck, where he promptly fell asleep again. I was beginning to think that two tablets of Lorazepam had been a little too much for him.

"Yet another adventure to tell our kids

about, eh? My friend?" Rufus yelled from the front seat.

I immediately thought, *Only if this adventure is successful ...*

"I'd prefer if you told me how we're getting there, Rufus. You know me. I need time to process things."

"Well, you also overthink too much, mon. And spend too much time anticipating the bad stuff when you should be thinking about the good stuff. Like in this case, when everything appears to be hopeless, an angel appears with a solution to our dilemma."

This elicited a flirty smile from Yara.

"You must keep an open mind," Rufus continued. "Plus, it's something I've always wanted to do."

Now, I was getting frustrated. If it wasn't a boat, what could it be? A helicopter? Or did Yara perchance own a submarine? This whole mission was diving down a rabbit hole of absurdity.

On the plus side, I was able to ditch my N95. Yara was vaccinated and boosted and had contracted Covid twice including the latest strain two months ago. She was like me: The virus would need a bazooka to get ... through her defenses.

After twenty kilometers or so, Yara pulled off the dirt road and into a clearing, a field of some sort. A large cloud had moved in, blocking the moonlight, and it was suddenly difficult to see, as if someone had turned out the lights. We passed what looked like a farmhouse, where Yara said she lived, and then kept driving for another couple of hundred meters before stopping.

"Alright, everyone. Time to get out." She looked into the back seat and saw Hitchhiker, dead to the world. "Maybe leave the man in black for now. We'll come back for him, later."

We all exited the truck and the sound of the surf crashing over rocks washed over me. Yara's farmhouse overlooked the water. I looked up to the night sky and saw the moon trying to ease through the large cloud that hung like a veil. Yara turned on a flashlight, and all my focus went to the circle of illumination that she directed in front of her.

"Come. This way."

She led us along a wide dirt path that ended at what looked from afar like a big rectangular straw-weaved basket. I had no idea what I was looking at. She turned her flashlight to the ground and then picked up a heavy extension cord that she plugged into a socket attached to the base of a post. Lights shone down from on high, as if we were in a baseball stadium for a night game. I was blinded momentarily and placed my hand over my eyes.

"So?" Yara yelled. "What do you think?"

My vision adjusted, and I could make out the basket again, and now I noticed ropes attached to it in the corners. I followed those ropes upwards to some sort of metallic awning. Beyond that, a copper colored inverted funnel expanded into the sky, and I finally realized what I was staring at. A little crazy didn't begin to describe it.

A hot air balloon.

***

"Are you fucking crazy, Rufus." I yelled. "You want to take a hot air balloon across the Caribbean Sea to Nicaragua in the middle of the night? Last year, I let you convince me to take the *Rumrunner* across the Atlantic in the middle of November, and we very nearly died. In fact, for the better part of a day, I thought you *were* dead. It was a miracle we both survived. And now, as if we hadn't tempted fate enough ..."

I went on for quite some time, working my way through both *denial* and *anger* at the same time, presumably to save time.

Then, I quickly slipped into bargaining. "A boat has to be a better and safer choice. Any boat, even a dinghy has to be better than a hot air balloon."

Rufus responded in a calm, steady voice, "Mark, there are wide shoals between here and the coast of Nicaragua. The same shoals that pirates once used to elude the Spanish Navy hundreds of years ago."

I pictured Captain Morgan standing at the bow of his galleon, a forty pounder of his own rum in one hand, while the other pointed here and there as they negotiated around an underwater ledge of rock that was only three feet under the surface, the Spanish fleet looking on from afar, afraid to venture any further.

"We have modern technology: GPS and radar."

"Maybe during the day with good light and a knowledgeable captain who knows the waters ... but at night? It would be suicide."

"And flying a hot air balloon at night is *not* suicide? Correct me if I'm wrong. You can't steer a hot air balloon. It goes wherever the wind takes you."

"Yara assures me that the wind direction is perfect. This time of year, the easterlies are as predictable as a good clock. She has been making this run for years, and it lands around Bilwi every time, which is exactly our destination."

Making this run. It sounded like he was describing Han Solo's twelve parsec Kessel Run with the Millennium Falcon. That was the fiction of George Lucas' mind at work. This was reality. And in reality, three average guys and a gal didn't make it across the Caribbean Sea by hot air balloon in the middle of the night.

Yara nodded her head slowly in agreement. "I started with my dad when I was a child. The trade winds from here take us directly to Bilwi. We did it together every year until he died last summer. This will be my first time flying without him." Her voice trailed off, the grief still palpable.

"There's no other way, Mark," Rufus said. "The clock is ticking. You know Sarah would have you do anything to save June. You know *you* would do anything to save your daughter."

How far would a father go to save his baby girl?

He would go all the way.

I know my decision-making abilities turn to shit as it gets later in the day. Decision exhaustion, I like to call it. I hadn't seen a bed or a pillow since Saturday, four nights ago. While this was clearly a bad decision, Rufus was correct, it was the only decision, and, by default, since no other option was available, that made it the right decision. This sounded, even to me, like the twisted logic of someone too tired to make *any* decision.

I plopped my ass onto the grass and stared up at the colossal balloon. I always thought hot air balloons were supposed to be painted bright colors: reds and oranges and yellows. Yara's balloon had a dull copper tinge to it, like a well circulated penny.

"Dammit. Yara. You sure you don't have a submarine?"

Yara looked to Rufus who simply shrugged his shoulders.

"No," she said. "Just *The Lofty Copper.*"

***

At midnight, as if inviting us skyward, the clouds parted, and we lifted off under a radiant full moon that brightened the night like a midday sun. If gliding engineless in Rufus' plane was like being a bird, Yara's hot air balloon was like being inside a warm soap bubble. She had the propane burners on full, and I could hear the hiss of the flames above my head and feel the heat pushing us upwards and upwards. The island of Providencia below was plush with mountains. We drifted above them to the west and they dwindled in size as we rose. Before long, the island was no bigger than the thumb of my outstretch hand.

We had spent an hour loading supplies onto the balloon and prepping it. Three large propane tanks, two canisters of water, a variety of local foods including a bag of patacones, a half-dozen chicken tamales and pork empanadas, a case of cerveza, and even a hot thermos of rondón – a Caribbean coconut fish stew. Finally, with great effort, we manoeuvred Hitchhiker into a wheelbarrow and dumped him unceremoniously over the edge and onto the bottom of the wicker basket. He didn't stir a wink. We positioned him as much out of the way as possible against one wall of the basket, and

Yara propped a lawn chair pillow under his head.

Rufus gave a low grunt of laughter as he voiced what we were all thinking. "Won't he be surprised when he awakens several thousand feet in the air supported by nothing but a straw basket."

I laughed, but then had second thoughts. He fell asleep in a bar and would wake up somewhere that would instantly terrify him. This felt a very cruel thing to do to a man who appeared to have a horrible case of air-terror PTSD, but what else could we do? He was the only one who knew what we were looking for: *WDO*, whatever that was.

Once the basket was loaded, Yara gave us a short lecture and guided tour of *The Lofty Copper*. It was just over forty years old, her father's purchase, and he had looked after it as if it was his second born. The top of the balloon, where the parachute valve was, including the suspension cables and gondola, or wicker basket, was some eighty feet off the ground. The balloon part was known as the envelope and was fifty feet across, made of rip-stop nylon. It had a volume of almost eighty thousand cubic feet.

The wicker basket was rectangular at six by eight feet and framed by steel rods and constructed with interweaved wicker. The basket was secured to the fireproof skirt of the balloon by suspension lines. Attached above our heads to the basket frame was an aluminum burner unit that fired flames up into the opening of the skirt. There were two burner units, typically attached to one propane tank secured in the basket. We would be bringing an additional two tanks for back up.

Also in the basket was a dropline – the long rope that was thrown to the ground – and some basic navigational instruments including a compass, altimeter, a variometer that measures the rate of ascent and descent, an envelope temperature indicator, and, finally, fuel gauges for the tanks.

Yara also pointed out that while it was true that the direction the balloon went was highly dependent on the direction of the winds, using the parachute valve to release or keep in hot air, we could change our altitude and tap into wind currents going in other directions if we needed to. I found this quite reassuring that at least we had some control over where we would end up.

Before we departed, Yara returned to her farmhouse to close up. She had family in Bilwi and would typically visit for four or five days before a relative would skipper her collapsed hot air balloon back to Providencia in a large fishing trawler. I had to admit, I admired her spirit of adventure and the island life she was living. Already, I imagined bringing Sarah and June here someday for vacation.

June.

Rufus had lent me his phone, and I was

able to have a brief conversation with Sarah on the drive here, giving her an update. Fortunately, I hadn't known about the hot air balloon yet and, despite what Rufus had said, guessed we would be taking some kind of boat. Even at that, she was quick to remind me of my sailing adventures of last year and to, "please be more careful."

"Careful? That's my middle name," I reassured her.

She quickly corrected me. "*Trouble* is your middle name, buster."

There was still no change in June's condition, hanging by a thread to her young life. At least, I reassured myself, she was no worse, which meant there was still time.

While Yara was closing up, Rufus was back on his phone sorting out his Gulfstream. When he returned later, it was with good news. The Gulfstream was fixed, in the air, and on its way to Nicaragua. He didn't elaborate how he was able to get permission to enter Nicaragua with the borders being closed, but I assumed money or old favors had changed hands.

Sitting alone – Hitchhiker remained out cold – I sat on the grass and alternated my gaze between the full moon and the coppery envelope of the balloon, wondering what prompted Yara, or perhaps her father, to paint it this color. Something related to local customs, maybe? Looking at all the ropes and rigging, or suspension lines as she called them,

I was reminded of Rufus' sunken sailboat, the *Rumrunner,* and all the rigging that worked the sails. Ropes and rigging that could get tangled about things and cause all manner of disasters.

I suddenly pulled off my backpack, opened it, and retrieved my Rambo survival knife. Normally, for my hiking adventures, I kept a similar knife and its sheath attached inverted to the front of my left shoulder strap for quick and easy access with my right hand. You never knew when you were going to run into a bear in the forests around Lake Superior in Northern Ontario. I knew I was fooling myself that a knife would make any difference, however, it was still a comforting thing to have. I attached the knife and sheath to the shoulder strap and then donned my backpack once more. Let the tangles come what may. I would be ready.

***

The trade winds were ferrying us along gently towards our destination when a deep, gravelly voice asked, "Please tell me this is a sedative related, bourbon-induced hallucination, and we're not really in the gondola of a hot air balloon?"

We were three hours into our air journey when the sedative and alcohol leached enough from Hitchhiker's blood that he finally awoke. He was sitting up with his back against the wicker basket wall, holding his head in his hands.

Yara handed him a water bottle and said, "You should really drink this."

Hitchhiker accepted the bottle and then immediately eyed both Rufus and I, as if thinking, *you're not trying to knock me out again, are you?*

I gave him a reassuring smile and asked, "How are you feeling?"

"Surprisingly good. I have just enough tranquilizer left on board that it's less air terror and more air fright at the moment."

"My name is Yara, by the way. And I'm your captain." She gave him a confident smile and extended a hand, which Hitchhiker shook gently.

"Pleasure to meet you, Yara. I'm very happy to know that neither of my two accident prone colleagues is in charge."

He drank thirstily from the bottle and then inhaled a deep breath. He did look calm.

Yara cracked a red glowstick and offered up a feast of local foods along with cerveza. Hitchhiker declined, saying that he didn't want to push it.

"You should stand and take in the view, my friend," Rufus said, reaching with a hand. There really was no view to be seen at this point since we were so high – almost ten thousand feet – and there was nothing but the moon and darkness. I wondered if this is what it felt like to float in space.

"No. No, thank you. I'm very comfortable where I am. May I ask what, exactly, we are doing in a hot air balloon? And where we are … and why?"

Rufus and I took turns explaining, ping ponging his questions back and forth until he seemed somewhat satisfied. I decided I would give him a little more time to feel better, maybe even until we landed with both feet on terra firma, before asking him some vital questions we needed answers to. Namely, what the hell was WDO? Did it have anything to do with the special ingredient we were looking for? And where, exactly, are we going in Bilwi?

I shouldn't have waited.

ACT III

A Life for a Life

Present Day

December 8th, 2021

The linearity of time fragmented, like an icicle thrown to a concrete a floor. Memories of the last few minutes floated randomly in front of my eyes as I lay washed up on the sandy shores of the Nicaraguan coast, dripping sea water from every pore of my body. My shoulder throbbed, but the sharp, stinging pain was gone. My eyes burned and the taste of salt filled my nose and mouth. I was on my back, staring blankly into the cloudless predawn sky trying to rearrange those memory fragments into a coherent timeline.

I remembered hanging from Yara's hot air balloon by my one lousy arm. Lousy, because it was the shoulder I had dislocated in a mountain biking mishap seven years earlier, and it had never quite returned to normal. Rick, my orthopaedic colleague, had needed three attempts to reduce the shoulder. He had later assured me that this was a good sign, and that it meant the shoulder was tightly in the socket and unlikely to dislocate again.

He couldn't have predicted I'd one day be hanging by that one arm thirty or more feet above the Caribbean Sea by a rope coiled around my wrist.

But what happened next?

How did I get loose?

My head flopped to the side, peering over the towering trees that dotted the coastline. Far-off in the distance, I could see remnant black clouds tapering off and rapidly moving west. As fast as it had come on, it had passed, typical of tropical places, now you see me, now you don't. I was gazing at the puffy white clouds that trailed behind the blackness, swirling and whirling – eddies and vortices – when the pieces of my memory puzzle suddenly fell into place:

Hitchhiker and Rufus were in the balloon pulling frantically on the rope. Hitchhiker was yelling something; however, the storm was ferocious, and the winds whirled at hurricane levels. I felt a sudden upward jerk on the rope – an updraft? – and the dull throb in my shoulder instantly became an excruciating, sizzling pain as it clunked, like I'd cracked a really large knuckle. I nearly blacked out. The hand of my good arm reflexively went to my dislocated shoulder for sympathy and support. This was fortunate, because I came upon my forgotten survival knife that was fastened to the shoulder strap of my backpack. I unlatched the Velcro with my one hand, drew the knife, and reached for the sky with it, attempting to slice the thick rope.

I couldn't reach it, though. With my shoulder dislocated, my left arm was longer than my right, and, no matter how I forced, I couldn't get the blade of the knife above my coiled wrist. The rain was pummeling, making it difficult to see, and high winds continued to buffet me all over, like a kite in a squall. I glanced into the distance for a second and could just make out the coastal treeline. We were almost on top of it.

I pinched the lower part of the rope that was hanging down to the water between my feet, as if I were trying to climb the rope for one of those high school fitness tests, and, with one final burst of adrenaline, pushed my body upwards and swung the knife in a wide arc at the rope above my coiled wrist, praying I didn't cut my hand off.

Then ... gravity took hold, with that disorienting sensation you get when falling in a dream. I watched the balloon jettison upwards and thought I could just make out Rufus' voice bellowing a cry of despair through the winds. My legs and arms flailed Roadrunner style. I could feel remnants of the rope still clinging to my wrist. I still had the knife in my hand and wondered what was smarter: to hold on to it so I knew exactly where it was? Or throw it away so I didn't accidently stab myself when I hit the water. I relaxed my hand, and the knife seemed to float next to me, falling at the same

9.8 meters per second squared that I was.

And, although it happened in seconds, it felt like forever: falling and falling. I was reminded of the exhibitionist high divers of days gone by who would land in a kid's wading pool with no more than a few feet of water in it from a ridiculous height and somehow survive. I prayed I would be so lucky.

I hit the water in a back flop position and lost consciousness for a brief moment on impact, which was a very good thing, because the force of the landing somehow relocated my shoulder. I sank, snorted, sputtered, and then reflexively attempted to swim before I realized the water was only four or five feet deep. I stood and gasped for air, sucking in raindrops and saltwater spray. As I wiped the salt water from my eyes, I realized my shoulder wasn't hurting anymore. My blurry eyes sought out the hot air balloon but could only see dark, ominous clouds. Maybe ... maybe it worked? Maybe, with my cutting free, they gained enough altitude to clear the treeline? I could only hope. If they did, where would they end up?

I waded through the shallow waters of the Caribbean Sea, pushed along by three and four-foot waves, until I arrived at the shore and collapsed in a heap of primordial protoplasm on the beach.

Time drifted by. Minutes? Hours? It was hard to tell. I lifted my head and noted an oval, orange globe cresting the watery eastern horizon. Already, the temperature had risen several degrees. I sat up gingerly and tested the integrity of my body parts. Nothing seemed broken, but I knew I would be finding all manner of bruises in every imaginable place over the next few days. My wrist, around which the rope had been coiled, was raw and bleeding. I rotated my dislocated shoulder with only mild discomfort but, in the process, noticed a nasty gash on the backside of my forearm. Closer inspection revealed a deep cut through fat with a few tendons showing. This would need fixing. I turned my wrist to look at the palm side. Had my wrist been turned in this manner, I would have cut where arteries lived – inadvertent suicide. A weird, lucky break, I supposed.

Something in the water caught my eye – perhaps a floating log? – and I was reminded of the red kayak I had flipped on St. Mary's River two years earlier – the last time I had washed up on a shore. And this reminded me of abandoning the *Rumrunner* in the middle of the Atlantic Ocean last year. I inhaled deeply and then released a lengthy sigh. What was it about these Covid adventures that always had me near death in water? The water gods, apparently, were not my friends.

I was marooned on a beach, separated from my friends, somewhere on the east coast of Nicaragua. At least, I hoped it was Nicaragua. Realistically, we could have been blown anywhere. Honduras? Costa Rica? I scooped a handful of wet sand and tossed it aimlessly. A tightness filled my throat, and a chill passed through me.

My friends? For all I knew, the balloon had crashed, and they were all –

My daughter? I imagined if June could speak, she would say something like, "Help me, Daddy. You are my only hope."

I am her only hope.

What could I do, though? I had no idea what I was looking for, other than I suspected it was some kind of flower. And no idea where it was, other than somewhere along this 360 km coast. Why the hell hadn't I demanded more information from Hitchhiker? I trusted him. Him and all his Big Pharma spy bullshit. He was supposed to be here. My eyes ached to release their sorrow, but I clamped them shut until the feeling passed. There would be time enough to let it out another day. Now, it was time to step up to the plate and be my daughter's Obi Wan Kenobi.

I released the shoulder straps of my backpack and removed it, noting the empty sheath for my survival knife. I unzipped and reached deep to the bottom for my first aid kit. When I pulled it out through a mess of t-shirts, underwear, socks and a small bathroom kit, a folded brown envelope fell onto the sand; it was an envelope I didn't recognize. I placed the first aid kit on a flat rock nearby and looked more closely at the envelope. My name was written in black ink in precise block letters. Writing that I was sure belonged to Hitchhiker.

Inside, I found a piece of paper. As I unfolded it, I realised it was a map, which triggered the question once again, *Where the hell am I?*

From within the folds of the map, two small wallet sized photos fell onto the sand. I picked one up and studied it. It was an image of one of the most beautiful flowers I had ever seen. Three long white petals and three sepals folded around a central tubular structure that reminded me of the bell of a French horn. Deep in the bell, the pure white color metamorphosed to the yellow of a dawning sun. All this beauty supported by a majestic and thick green stem. On the back of the photo, three words were printed: *Aurora Phalaenopsis Orchis*. Underneath those three words, in brackets: White Dawn Orchid.

That's what Hitchhiker was referring to: *WDO*.

The second photo was a close-up picture of a bee that looked like any other bee I'd ever seen. On the reverse was written, *Euglossa cyanura* Cockerell.

I scratched my chin and wondered about the two photos. The first was obviously the flower I was looking for, but the second, I wasn't sure. Did I need both?

I pushed the first aid kit aside, opened the map, and placed it on the flat stone. The map appeared to be hand drawn and focused on the east coast of Nicaragua and a town called Bilwi: The town Hitchhiker had referred to before passing out on the seaplane. Within Bilwi, to the south and somewhat inland, was an area marked with a large red "X," like buried treasure on a pirate's map. Above the "X" was written another town name: "Lamlaya." Under the "X," three letters were scrawled: "WDO."

Two years ago, without my knowledge, Hitchhiker had taken a potentially dangerous drug from my backpack that I was planning to administer to my wife in a last ditch effort to save her life. This time, he had somehow snuck this envelope into my backpack, although I had no idea how he managed to do it since it virtually never left my back. Once again, he was saving my ass from afar. I looked to the sky and hoped desperately that he and my friends were okay.

For the first time on this journey, I knew what we were looking for, and I knew where to find it. Now, all I had to do was figure out where I was on the map and how to get there.

Child's play.

***

I stood knee-deep in the Caribbean Sea about one hundred feet from the beach. The water was now calm and still, with a few ripples here and there and a murkiness that belayed the recent flash storm. I don't know how my distraught brain could have registered them when I waded into shore a few hours earlier in the middle of the storm, but it did. Two massive cell towers a couple of miles inland, maybe five or six miles apart. Add to that the long peninsula that formed the northern land mass of the inlet I was in, and an opportunity for navigational triangulation presented itself, like a gift from mother nature ... and the cell phone companies.

I sloshed back to the beach, knelt in the sand and used the edge of the White Dawn Orchid photo to triangulate my position on the map. I was no more than thirty miles from my buried treasure. Despite the storm, Yara had been nearly bang on with her directions. I pumped my fist. Had she been here, I would have given her a big thank-you hug.

Still, it was thirty miles. On foot, averaging two to three miles per hour, it would take me the whole day. There was one other possibility, though. Based on the map, just past the treeline, there appeared to be a dirt road. Hitchhiker's map was a little sketchy in this regard, sparse on details as the distance from the "X" increased. He would have assumed that Yara would land the hot air balloon significantly closer to our destination than I had landed. I was deep in thought when a drop of blood plopped onto my precious map. In the rush to "find myself," I'd forgotten about the laceration on the back of my forearm. In this environment, there was huge potential for infection from any number of unusual organisms. I needed to clean and close the wound.

I set my map aside and opened my first aid backpacking kit on the flat rock. I had modified this kit somewhat to make it a little more robust. I removed a small apothecary type brown three ounce vial that contained pure alcohol – better than iodine since you could also use it to start a fire, if you had to – opened the lid, held my breath, and poured it over my wound. Fire-like pain instantly coursed up my arm. It intensified even further when some of the alcohol dribbled down to my wrist, where the rope had flailed my flesh raw. Despite the pain, I smiled. There was no way any organism could survive that onslaught.

The laceration was five centimeters long and gapped approximately a centimeter. I dabbed it with a sterile gauze and inspected. The sheath of one tendon was torn but the tendon itself was intact. Nothing to be concerned about – just a flesh wound. I thought about using Steri Strips to pull the wound edges together but quickly realized that because of the location on the back of the wrist there would be too much stress when I used my hand, and the wound would quickly dehisce. It needed stiches. No easy task with one hand.

I dug through my kit and found a vial of

Xylocaine, a local anesthetic. With a prepared syringe, I drew up 5mL and then injected the edges of my wound. The stinging wasn't nearly as bad as the alcohol and quickly faded as the Xylocaine took effect. A little more digging produced sterile gloves, a small needle driver, scissors, and a 2-0 Nylon suture. This is where it got technically difficult, and I quickly realized that it was impossible to tie a good knot with only one hand. I adapted and used my teeth. Not the most sterile of techniques, but it worked. When I was done, the wound was completely closed with a half dozen horizontal mattress sutures. I rubbed Polysporin along the incision to ward off mouth organisms and then dressed it with an airstrip. I also rubbed the Polysporin over the macerated skin around my wrist and then wrapped it with sterile Kling. To be complete, I found two cephalosporin antibiotic tablets and downed them with the last of my water along with two Ibuprofen capsules.

I rotated my previously dislocated shoulder a couple of times with minimal pain, looked at my forearm bandage and the Kling around my wrist, and then mentally patted myself on the back for a job well done. I was ready for my road trip.

But first, my heroic self-care completed, I needed to pass out for few minutes.

***

When I came to, I was lying on my side, almost in a fetal position, with my backpack positioned under my head substituting for a pillow. A word about my backpack. I've had this extraordinary pack for over a decade and, prior to Covid-19, used it mostly for hiking and snowshoe treks deep in the woods surrounding the rugged terrain of Lake Superior. When Covid began, it accompanied me on my journey to Florida at the beginning of the pandemic to save my wife. It was with me on my treacherous trans-Atlantic crossing with Rufus a year ago to England to make peace with my dad and bring home the potential cure for Covid. In the process, it survived the sinking of the *Rumrunner* and a night treading water in the freezing November Atlantic Ocean. On this current journey, it has been with me in my SUV, on the bus, on the floatplane, on the hot air balloon, and on this beach.

Over the years, I've stuffed every nook and cranny of it with the best of survival tools. It's like a magic Harry Potter bag where, when I'm in need, whatever I wish for can be found somewhere in the pack.

So, it was no surprise to me that when I shifted my head, I was awoken by something hard digging into the base of my skull. Something that I'd forgotten. Something that was tucked away in a nook. Something I needed.

My eyes sprung open, and I bolted to a sitting position. My head spun for a minute before my vision cleared, and then I ran my hands over my pack trying to determine where the nook was. Before long, I had delivered a compact emergency GPS satellite communicator, a gift from Sarah years ago to make sure I always came back alive from my solo treks.

It was small, maybe the size of a large, old-fashioned pager. I powered it on and waited for the LED screen to come to life. This little device could generate an SOS signal via an iridium satellite system anywhere in the world, including Nicaragua. In this case, though, I didn't want the SOS feature since I wasn't in any immediate danger, and this was supposed to be a stealth mission. In fact, the last thing I wanted was to alert anyone I was here. The feature I was most interested in was the limited two-way texting. Although I'd never needed to use this device, I had kept the subscription up, so, in theory, it should still allow me to send off a message and maybe receive one. As I recalled, the receivers of the message were pre-set to my emergency contacts only. That would be Sarah.

The question was, what message could I send that would help me find Rufus, Hitchhiker, and Yara. Or, at least, help them find me.

The screen brightened and my heart sank. My ongoing battle with modern technology continued: the battery was almost dead – my own fault since I hadn't charged it for months. By the time it locked into the satellite system, I had time for maybe one text message with a limited word count. A trill of beeps indicated that the tracker had locked on to a series of satellites. I took a quick breath and tapped in:

"Send to Rufus: I'm on beach and heading for destination. XOXO."

I heard a beep, which I think meant that the message had been successfully sent, and then the GPS went dark.

Hopefully, Rufus and friends would meet me where "X" marked the spot.

***

I found the dirt road not more than a few hundred feet inside the forest canopy at the edge of the coastal treeline. It was wide enough to accommodate one small car, and nothing more. Some of the rainwater-filled potholes were as big as a child's wading pool, which made me think of the diving exhibitionists again, stopping me in my tracks as I contemplated how good it felt to be alive. It seemed unlikely I'd see much in the way of vehicles along this road. I tightened the straps of my backpack, grit my teeth, and followed the road north.

The foliage was thick and dense, blocking out much of the daylight. The sounds of local nature reverberated, and the earthy odors of a fresh rainfall permeated the air. The road swooped and curved, following the hilly coastline. It took only a couple of hours for the layer of wetness on the road to evaporate and turn to dust. It was a strange contrast to see large rain-filled potholes surrounded by desiccated gravel. I'd never been to Central America, and the sights, sounds, and smells were foreign and captivating. At least, in the beginning. It didn't take long before the boredom of one step after another kicked in. I tried some walking meditation, but the gurgle of my hungry stomach interfered. Then I tried counting steps, a substitute for my iPhone Health App. I got as high as 859 steps and then lost interest. It occurred to me that smartphones had a very boring existence. I was belting out *On the Road Again*, when I heard my first non-nature, man-made sound: the rumble of approaching tires.

I turned my head 180 degrees and witnessed a cloud of dust coming my way that quickly materialized into a bouncing pickup truck. I hugged the trees on the edge of the narrow road and took a page out of Hitchhiker's book by sticking my thumb out. I needed to make up some time, and either I would get a ride, or I wouldn't. I didn't see how I had anything to lose.

I would be proven wrong.

***

The vehicle that stopped alongside me

was a strange sight: a small, blue Datsun pickup littered with brown rust holes mounted on four gigantic tires suitable for negotiating deep potholes. In the back of the pickup was a loose orange tarp that partially covered a variety of tools: a skill saw, a crowbar, a chain saw, various types of drills, etcetera. The windows were tinted, and there was a long pause before anything happened. Finally, the passenger window rolled down, and I could see the driver reaching over to work the manual window crank. A billowing cloud of thick smoke escaped through the open window, and I wondered how the coronavirus would perform in this kind of environment since I no longer had a functioning mask. My "peace mask" had finally died, drenched by salt water. I still had it tucked away in my pack, a memory token of my fifteen minutes of fame.

There was still the matter of my outstanding PCR test, the supreme court of rapid test tiebreakers. The morally perfect doctor would be thinking twice about putting this stranger at risk; however, I was the desperate father who would do anything to save his daughter.

And maybe sacrifice a few people along the way?

With a hand wave, he gestured for me to come closer. I approached cautiously with my map in hand. My Spanish was very limited and largely based on the French fluency I gained from my time in Montreal attending boarding school. I assumed I'd be using a lot of mime to get my messages across.

The driver appeared to be in his mid-forties and had a patchy, black, scruffy beard. His eyes were glazed over, and the cab reeked of cannabis. He unlatched the door, pushed it open, and invited me in. I gave this some serious thought: the idea of getting into a truck with a stranger who was clearly high and probably drunk. Also, I didn't do well with smoke of any sort. In confined spaces, it typically gave me an instant headache. I liked to think of it as a form of smoke claustrophobia.

What choice did I have, though? Time was precious, and it could be hours before I crossed paths with another vehicle. I plastered a good natured smile on my face (per Hitchhiker's teachings) and took a seat. I closed the door but struggled to engage the latch. Eventually, it clicked ... after we were well underway. I reached for a seatbelt and found none. The floor under my feet was littered with empty beer cans. This was concerning, but not as concerning as what lay on the floor behind our seats: a sawed-off shotgun. This pickup was a two-seater with a small space behind us where two jump seats were located. The shotgun lay on the floor with a box of shotgun shells rolling around beside it.

What the hell have I gotten myself into?

Hitchhiker's rule #2: engage the driver in conversation.

"Hi," I said, perhaps a little louder than I should have. "Do you speak English?

He shook his head slowly from side to side. I wasn't sure if that meant he understood English but didn't want to talk, or he simply didn't understand.

As expected, the road was rough, and we were getting pushed around hard. With some effort, I unfolded my map and then tried to catch his eye with it.

"I'm going here, Lamlaya." I had to yell to be heard over the roar of his engine. I pointed to the "X" on the map and repeated, "Lamlaya."

I couldn't tell if he actually looked at it, but he nodded and said, "Si. Si."

He then reached over and turned on his radio … loud, like jet-engine decibels loud. He must have had some kind of custom sound system upgrade. Then he opened the ashtray and lit a fat joint with the automatic lighter. I hadn't seen a lighter like that for decades. He exhaled a frothy cloud of smoke, smiled, and then offered it to me.

I politely declined and then proceeded to cough up one entire lung as I felt a vice secure itself around my head. He smiled, shrugged his shoulders, turned up the music even louder, and then floored the gas pedal. In one way, this was good, because it meant less time in this cab. In another, it probably meant certain death from a car accident. He careened around corners like a Daytona 500 race car driver. I wasn't sure how he could even see through the thick cloud of smoke that clung like cobwebs to the front windshield. I felt like a toy action figure in the hands of a child amped on Sugar Pops. My hands were locked to the dashboard, but still, I was thrown, bumped, jolted, shaken, and even stirred. The forest whizzed by my passenger window in a blur. All my senses were being assaulted in one tortuous ride that went on for at least an hour before it, unbelievably, got worse; a car was coming from the opposite direction.

My driver glanced at me, and a sly smile crept into his face. He worked the stick shift, once again doing the exact opposite of what I would have done, which was hit the brakes. We were almost on top on the oncoming vehicle – I could literally see the whites of the other driver's eyes – when he jammed the brakes and pulled over to an area at the side of the road, which must have been meant for exactly this purpose: to let other cars pass. He let out a boisterous laugh, rolled down his window and waved his hand outside of the truck. When I looked out the back window, the other driver was doing the same. It was a game to them. Something they probably did all the time. I slumped into my seat, and the driver smiled at me and punched me lightly in the shoulder, a kind of "I gotcha" punch.

Yeah, you got me alright. Asshole.

He slowed down at this point and settled into a more comfortable pace. The road seemed to improve also, with less pothole swerving. I was even able to let go of the dashboard to rub the sweat from my eyes and massage my temples, which were throbbing like two gouty big toes. There was a clock on the dash that I hadn't noticed until now. It was just past 10 AM. If Rufus, Yara, and Hitchhiker hadn't crash landed, they would certainly have purposefully landed the balloon by now.

What would they do next? I wondered if they weren't already arrested. Our original plan was to put down on a beach close to our destination, out of sight of the authorities. Now, who knows where they ended up? If only I could call Rufus.

I studied the cab once again, easier to do now that we weren't ricocheting all over the interior. There was no trace of a mobile phone. The driver hadn't once reached into his pocket, something I was sure he would have done by now. Still, it was worth a shot. I looked at his face, and his eyes were half shut and his jaw was hanging loosely. The one hand he had on the steering wheel was limply manoeuvring it, almost as if he was on autopilot.

Shit. He's dozing off.

"Hey," I said, trying to get his attention.

It was my turn to lightly punch him in the shoulder. He didn't seem to like that. His eyes sparked open, and he gave me a glare. "Do you have a phone? Teléfono?"

"No," he replied curtly, shaking his head.

Suddenly, the forest overhead opened up, and we were bathed in sunlight. We passed a sign on the side of the road that I couldn't make out through the dust-caked passenger window. The road widened to accommodate a second lane with a weatherworn white hash mark dividing the road in half. Sparse buildings – perhaps shacks would be a better word – popped up here and there.

He abruptly pulled onto a narrow shoulder and hit the brakes so hard I almost flew through the front window. He then reached over to the map I had kept open on my lap and tapped the "X" with the tip of his index finger.

"Here!" He said.

Then he stared at me hard and made the universal sign of money with his other hand, rubbing his forefinger and thumb together.

Crap. He wants payment for the ride.

I reached inside my jacket to retrieve my wallet. This was a mistake. While I was doing that, he grabbed his shotgun from behind the seats and put it on his lap. I quickly opened my wallet to show him it was completely empty. I shrugged my shoulders and said, "Sorry. No dinero."

He did not look happy. His left hand squeezed the butt of the shotgun, and his right tore my wallet from my hands.

"Hey! I yelled, "You can't take my wallet."

This was obviously a completely stupid thing to say since he did have a shotgun. I quickly changed my attitude to a much healthier one.

"Take it," I yelled, putting both of my palms in the air towards him. "It's yours. You take it."

He sifted through the wallet and pulled one credit card out after another, looking them over and rubbing his thumb over the chip area. He nodded his head. This seemed to satisfy him. I supposed, from his perspective, even though he didn't have the PIN numbers, he realized he could at least scan up to a few hundred dollars per transaction. Good money for a quick drive. He shoved the wallet into his jacket pocket and pointed with the barrel of his shotgun at my door: my cue to leave, and I was quick to take it. I opened the door and stepped out with weak and shaky legs. I slammed the door shut, anxious to be rid of him, but not before he shouted, "Gracias."

The pickup took off, spinning its rear tires and spitting rocks and dirt in my direction. I tried to step to the side, but my knee buckled. My head was throbbing like it was in a medieval torture helmet. I leaned forward with both of my hands on my knees, trying to catch a clean breath of fresh air that kept eluding me.

Holy Fuck! I was just robbed at gun point.

I vomited a variety of Columbian local delicacies from my in-flight meal onto the grass at the side of the road, retching over and over until my throat ached and tears joined the party.

So much for my first solo hitchhiking effort.

***

I convinced myself that the vomiting was the result of the claustrophobic haze combined with the roller coaster ride, and not so much the terror of having a shotgun pointed in my direction. I was feeling better and trying to get my bearings.

I really didn't care about the wallet. The cards were all useless anyway, courtesy of … Big Pharma? If Big Pharma was *they*, then *they* may have saved me a bundle. And won't shotgun guy be surprised when none of the cards work. He might even come back to track me down. I doubted it, though. The guy clearly had multiple addiction issues, and I would be forgotten as soon as he smoked his next joint.

No, I didn't care about the wallet. It was losing the picture of June that really upset me. It had become a bit of a crutch, and I had turned to that picture multiple times after Hitchhiker reminded me that I had it in my wallet. Now, all

I had were my memories, and that would have to be enough. It had only been three days since I last saw June, but it felt like eternity. She felt so far away, and I had no idea what was happening to her.

I walked back to the sign we had passed and confirmed I was in the small town of Lamlaya, which was right above the "X" on Hitchhiker's map. Beyond that, I really had nothing to go on, other than I was looking for a white flower ... and maybe some bees. I walked to a "T" in the road and followed it toward the coast for about a half kilometer before encountering a series of houses. On the front porch of the first house was an old woman sitting on a bench under the shade of her porch roof, preparing some sort of vegetables on a small table with a pruning knife.

I approached her with a smile and the picture of the flower in an outstretched hand. I said, "Hola," as I showed her the picture and then mimed a questioning look with my shoulder's shrugged, waving my other hand towards the horizon.

"Hola," she replied. She slowly stood, and I could almost hear her knees creak. She then pointed to a side road a few more houses down the main road and said, "Por ahi," which I assumed meant something like, "over there." More than ever, I wished I had my phone and it's Google translate feature.

I bowed my head, muttered, "Gracias," and followed her directions.

It was another half kilometer down this side road before I came across an old sign with peeling paint that had an image of a large bee on it, much like the photo Hitchhiker had left for me. It was a little tilted; the post holding it up having come loose with the erosion of the heavy rains. Beyond the sign, at the end of a long dirt road driveway was a farmhouse. It all made sense now, why Hitchhiker had left me the picture, so I would know to look for a bee farm.

In front of the farmhouse, in ankle high grass, stood an easel with a canvas on it. It was facing an inclined meadow across the road that gleamed white in the noonday sun. It was about an acre in size, fronted by a white picket fence with a gate, and nestled on the other three sides by forest. It looked like someone had gone to great efforts to grow the flowers and maintain the grounds. Even from the road, I could see large multicolored rectangular shaped boxes with movement around them and could hear the low thrum of buzzing.

My heart skipped a beat as I realized this must be the home of the White Dawn Orchid. After a treacherous three-day journey consisting of cars, trucks, buses, a floatplane, a hot air balloon, and a near-death hitchhiking experience, I had finally found what I was looking for. The missing ingredient I needed to make a cure that could save my daughter was right there in front of me.

The steady spike of adrenaline that was keeping me going faded a little as I approached the meadow, and I suddenly realized how exhausted I was. My mission was almost complete.

Or was it?

***

Something was wrong. I stepped over the short three-foot fence that separated the road from the meadow, and my adrenaline spiked again as my worst fears were realized. Sabotage! The ground was carnaged with the petals and stems of the flower I had come all this way to find. Someone had cut them all down, right to ground level. Bees were everywhere, flying irregular patterns, looking as confused as I felt.

I squatted and rested my ass on my heels as I picked up one of the delicate flowers and inspected it. Traces of clear liquid still oozed from the cut end of the stem. Whatever had happened here hadn't been that long ago, perhaps in the last few days. I stood abruptly and threw the flower to the ground. I knew a dead flower was of no use to me. I turned, jumped the fence, and ran across the road to the farmhouse.

I need some answers.

I was drawn to the easel that stood

solemnly in the front yard. There was a small painter's stool next to it. I looked past the canvas and admired a perfect replica of the scene in front of it, as it would have been visualized at night, with a glistening sea of White Dawn Orchids blazing majestically under the full moon. It was breathtaking and magical.

A voice behind interrupted my reverie. "Like?"

I turned to find a very stooped elderly man, holding a beekeeper's bonnet under his arm. His face was aged and well wrinkled, but his eyes remained sharp. There was an aura of sadness about him in the way he held his head and the sloop of his shoulders.

I replied, "Hola. Si. Like very much."

I then pointed to the field and said, "No like. No like."

I paused for a moment before showing him my picture of the flower and then waved my hand towards the meadow. "Qué?"

"Inglés?" He asked.

"Yes, English. Do you speak English?"

He wabbled his hand, as if to say, "Not very much."

He reached for a large sketchbook that was on the stool and flipped it open. I saw pages and pages of preparatory drawings related to the moonlit scene of the White Dawn Orchids. He turned to a blank page and quickly drew pictures of the meadow and the orchids. He then added men in military garb holding machetes and scythes. A tear dropped from his eye on to the page, and I quickly understood. A group of men had come and cut down his orchids. Big Pharma? It was clear to me now that someone really was trying to stop us from creating a cure. And stop us they had. This was the end of the road.

I borrowed his sketchbook and turned to a new blank page. I was no painter or illustrator, but once upon a time, in my teens, I had dreams of becoming a cartoonist. That dream was overtaken by dreams of becoming an astronaut, and then an architect, and on and on in the way young boys try to find their path in the world. I used his pencil to draw a series of images that told my story, beginning with a map that roughly described where I was from. Then a hospital, followed by a picture of the Covid virus with an arrow pointing to a baby-size stick figure. Here I said, "June, June, June," until he repeated it, and I was sure he understood this was my daughter's name. He nodded his head steadily as he followed along.

The next part was more difficult. I drew a syringe and needle with a Covid virus next to it. Then I placed my picture of the White Dawn Orchid on the page next to the syringe and drew an arrow to it. Finally, I made a big "X" over the Covid virus and then pointed to myself and said, "Doctoré, Médico," nodding my head.

His eyes grew wide with understanding

as he nodded his head also and said, "Mmm, Doctoré."

A long moment passed as he seemed to be processing everything I'd shown him, and then he slowly turned and walked, with the wobbly, shuffling gait of the aged, back to his farmhouse, waving for me to follow him. I realized for the first time since leaving the beach that there was no feeling of Covid here, in this part of the world. No one was wearing masks and there were none strewn on the ground. There was no sense of hesitancy at being within someone's six feet of personal space. This didn't mean Covid-19 didn't exist here. It just meant, perhaps, that they saw the whole evolution of the pandemic it in a different way.

I thought we would be going into his house, but we passed right by it, through his back yard, and onto a small dirt path that disappeared between two large trees in his backyard. We followed this path for ten minutes until we arrived at an old wood gate that was as tall as I was. We stood there while the old man fiddled with the latch, and I could hear that same low thrum of buzzing audible near the meadow of dead orchids in front of his farmhouse: the sound of bees. My heartbeat ratcheted up a notch. Could he have a second "secret" garden of orchids? Something Big Pharma didn't know about?

We passed through the gate, and it opened

into a small clearing a fraction of the size of the one in front of his house. A clearing resplendent of vibrant, glistening White Dawn Orchids. He turned to me, and his toothy smile glowed as bright as the orchids themselves.

He pointed a forefinger at my chest and said, "Doctoré .... Por June."

***

We sat on his front porch in two well-worn, slant-backed, grey wooden chairs, nursing a cup of tea – with a dab of honey in it, of course – that sparked a grumbling stomach. The old man had dug up and packaged six orchids in a large crate with appropriate aeration holes. He watered them, closed the crate, and handed it to me. He had a grim look, like he was giving away one of his children, although I think his sadness stemmed more from the loss of his bigger family of orchids. I wondered what would happen to all the beehives he was nurturing in the large meadow. Would the bees fly away to greener, more flowery, pastures? I hoped Rufus and all his money could help the beekeeper recover from this disaster. A disaster that I was probably in some way responsible for.

Now, I had to find out what happened to my "team" and somehow get these orchids to the lab in Montreal. The old beekeeper lived off the grid with a set of solar panels on his roof. He had no landline and no cell phone. He explained with more illustrations that his truck was in "the shop" getting repaired and wouldn't be back until tomorrow. I had found what I came for but had no way to leave.

I pulled the satellite tracker from my backpack and stared at this dead, and presently useless, piece of technology, wondering if there was any way I could hook it into the beekeeper's grid. Since I didn't have the specialized charging cable with me – why does every piece of electronics have its own specially designed charging cord? – it seemed unlikely. I could only hope the message I sent from the beach reached Sarah and was relayed to Rufus or Hitchhiker, assuming they were still alive, and assuming Rufus still had his phone, and it was still working. A lot of assumptions.

As well, whether they received my message or not, it might take them several days to find this place, depending how far away they ended up. Or would they even try? If they didn't get the message, wouldn't Rufus hire a helicopter, or something, to go back and look for me, thinking I might have drowned or been injured and unable to move. I had so many questions dancing around the gyri of my brain. So many possible scenarios.

The bottom line, though, was that I was now stuck here with the beekeeper. Hitchhiking with the orchid crate would be impossible – not that I ever wanted to hitchhike again. If my friends did not show, I would have to find a ride, and even if I did, where would I go? I had no money, and I was in the country illegally during a Covid lockdown with their borders shut to all traffic. If the police or militia got wind of me, they would surely lock me up, if only for reasons of quarantine. They wouldn't care about my personal issues.

It was late afternoon, and long shadows cast from trees surrounding the field darkened the desecrated orchid burial ground. A reminder of another day coming to an end. I had started this journey early Sunday morning, and it was now Wednesday, four days later. The thought that hung over me like a black cloud during this entire trip remained ever present, W*ould I be too late?*

I was sulking. Tired and with all hope drained, I was running on ice and making no mental progress. I had no plan and there's nothing worse than a doctor without a plan. Well, I supposed a bad plan was worse than no plan at all. There it was. That icky feeling that things were sometimes meant to happen for a reason, and that it would be best to just allow it to happen. To get out of my own way and let the universe unfold.

I released an exceptionally lengthy sigh that caught my newfound friend's attention.

He asked, "Estas bien?"

I got the sense of the question and mimed wiping tears from my eyes – there were maybe some real ones there – and then yawned to show I was also tired. I then took up a fresh sheet of paper and drew a stickman figure of myself with the crate of orchids standing next to a truck. I drew an arrow to the truck and then looked up at him.

He nodded his head and said, "Mañana. Mañana."

"Tomorrow. Tomorrow," I translated in my head. His truck would be back tomorrow, and he would be happy to give me a ride. Now, if I could only figure out where to go.

He then pointed at me, placed the palms of his hands together and then put them next to his ear in the universal sign of "dodo, or sleep."

He was inviting me to sleep over. He rocked himself forward off his seat and pushed himself into a standing position. He brought his fingers to his mouth a few times and then stepped inside the house. He was getting some food, or maybe dinner. I was a stranger, a foreigner he could barely communicate with, and yet he was treating me like an old friend or a relative. If the shoe were on the other foot, and he was sitting on my front porch back home, would I have done the same? I wasn't so sure. There were good people here. Not everyone was like the asshole who stole my wallet.

I tilted my head against the back of the

chair and inhaled deeply, sucking in the vibrant odors of this place, and allowing my eyelids to grow heavy. The sounds of wildlife seemed to amplify, and I felt nature envelop me in its gentle warmth. As my breathing deepened, scenes of the past few days drifted before my eyes, like clips from a movie trailer: June in her hyperbaric incubator with Sarah hovering over her; a sister I never met being coddled in my mother's arms; the faces of various counter-people who turned me away, all melded together; Hitchhiker's terrified face as the floatplane took off; Rufus with his arm over my shoulders, staring down through the clouds; Yara when she first showed us her prized possession, *the Lofty Copper*; the look of desperation on Hitchhiker and Rufus' face when they tried to haul me back up into the balloon; the drugged out face of the driver who stole my wallet; the gentle, understanding face of the old beekeeper.

The scenes then seem to swirl around one and other, like they were caught in the tornado from the Wizard of Oz. The voices and emotions were still distinct, though. At least the good ones. June's hiccuppy laugh that melted my heart; the determination and strength in Sarah's voice when she gave me permission to do whatever it took to save our daughter; Hitchhiker – the full-time intellect – and his Spockian logic, sarcasm, and wit; Yara's energetic whoops and hollers as *The Lofty Copper* took us skyward; and finally,

Rufus, with his joyful Jamaican accent …

"My friend, why are you asleep on the job?"

'What?' I asked myself, confused.

"This mission isn't over." Hitchhiker's voice.

'The mission?' I muttered to myself, lost on another quantum plane, deeply dreaming.

"Yes." Yara's voice. "You remember. Dragging us all into the sky. Into the hurricane."

It's all my fault. I brought this on. I pushed for this. Their blood is on my hands.

I was squirming in my chair … until I felt a big hand push down on my shoulder and heard Rufus' voice as clear as a baritone's final operatic note.

"It's time to go home, my friend. It's time to wake up."

My eyes fluttered and gradually opened. It felt like I was underwater, looking through a murkiness that was gradually being diluted into clarity by the purest drops of the rainforest.

As my world finally came into focus, the faces of all my friends materialized in front of me: Rufus, Hitchhiker, Yara. Even the beekeeper.

Am I still dreaming?

"You were truly dead to the world, mon."

"How …? Where did you come from? How did you know where I was?" I asked in a scratchy, dry voice, trying desperately to organize the questions pinballing around my skull as I sat up.

"How do you think we knew, Mark?"

Hitchhiker asked as he knelt in front of me next to Rufus and put a hand on my other shoulder. "You're the one who sent the message."

***

Even though we had only been separated for a day, our reunion was emotional on a haven't-seen-you-since-high-school-and-thought-you-were-dead kind of level. In fact, apparently, they *had* thought I was dead and, after they landed the balloon, were trying to figure out their next course of action – search for me, or come here to get what they needed to save my daughter – when they received Sarah's text message, email, and phone call. Tears flowed freely from Rufus and Yara, and even Hitchhiker had a twitch in his eye that he couldn't seem to control. So many questions instantly received the answers they needed to quiet my harried mind, that I suddenly felt whole again and was able to refocus and re-energize. I had gotten out of my own way, and the universe had provided.

Deep hugs were exchanged all around as I caught bits and pieces of their adventure. They assured me that I would be brought up to speed in due course, but the clock was ticking, Hitchhiker reminded us, and we had to make haste. In the driveway, was an ancient tourist type truck. The cargo bed was made of four rows of seats protected from the elements overhead by the remnants of a ragged yellow canopy supported by a steel rod structure. There was no enclosure to the cargo bed. This was the kind of truck that was low on safety and high on visibility. A man I couldn't see stood on the other side of the truck in front of the open driver's door, smoking a cigarette.

The beekeeper was deep in conversation with Hitchhiker, who, of course, spoke fluent Spanish. When they were done, I was escorted to the truck carrying my crate of orchids. I placed the crate in the front passenger seat and then turned back to the beekeeper to say goodbye. At first, it was going to be a good old-fashioned handshake, and then I remembered everything he had done for me, and everything he had lost because of me. I wrapped him in a heartfelt, thankful hug.

I asked Hitchhiker to translate that we would help him rebuild his business, but Hitchhiker told me that he had already sorted that out. As I was about to get on the back of the truck, my backpack slung over my shoulder, the old man reached out with another small crate that appeared to have bees in it.

He said, "Por June," and smiled.

I smiled back and asked Hitchhiker to explain to the beekeeper that he was very kind, but that we didn't need the bees, only the flowers.

"What!" Hitchhiker exclaimed, his voice rising. "Has your brain turned to mush in this tropical sun. Of course, we need the bees. Why do you think I left you the photograph in the envelope?"

"Well ... to know to look for a bee farm."

As I spoke, I knew deep down there was more to it.

"Mark, mon, "Rufus interjected, "we need both the White Dawn Orchids *and* the bees to make our special ingredient."

***

Our tourist truck driver drove at a steady pace, deftly avoiding the larger potholes on our four-hour drive to the Bilwi Airport. Dusk was already upon us, and the truck's headlights bobbed erratically in time with the potholes. Yara accompanied the driver in the cab, while Hitchhiker, Rufus, and I, held on for our lives sitting in beltless seats across from each other in the cargo bay. Of all the things I was missing from home, smooth asphalt was fast rising to the top of the list. Rufus assured me that we only had an hour on the dirt road before the ride became more "comfortable."

Despite the roar of the engine, the wind blowing at us, the constant squeaking of the shock absorbers, and the crushing sounds of rubber on gravel, Hitchhiker was quick and keen to launch into a detailed explanation about how the bees were required, in addition to the orchids, to make our secret ingredient: It had something to do with pseudo-copulation and the commensalism symbiotic relationship between the bees and the flower. Apparently, the chemical that we needed from the orchid was only produced during a short period of time (a few days) after the plant had been pollinated, and the bee was the transportation system for that pollination. To make the timing even more precious, the White Dawn Orchid only blooms for two to three weeks and only twice per year. We had been incredibly lucky in this regard.

He went on to explain – pausing intermittently to protect his mouth with his hand from the dust cloud that would envelop us when we stopped for any reason – that our orchid used a particular kind of mimicry to fool the unsuspecting drone bee into mating with it. Over many thousands of years, parts of the orchid near the flower had evolved to resemble the female version of the bee, promising sex to the drone. The drone, after an unsuccessful attempt to mate, flies off in frustration looking for a cold shower (my words, not Hitchhiker's), and, in the process, carries a pollen packet attached to its abdomen onto the next orchid. From that moment of the bee unknowingly fertilizing the orchid, we had approximately 48 hours to harvest the chemical we needed to fabricate our special ingredient.

Given the timing, it was essential to have

the bees as well as the orchids brought to the lab in Montreal for Rufus to harvest the chemicals required to make the special ingredient and complete the cure. Hitchhiker was disappointed that I hadn't picked up on the importance of the bees.

I wanted to say, "Sorry, Hitchhiker, I was busy sewing up my forearm and relocating my dislocated shoulder when your photos fell into my lap after I'd fallen out of a hot air balloon into the Caribbean Sea during a hurricane and then been robbed at gunpoint. Somehow, my frazzled mind didn't make the connection," but I held my tongue. Hitchhiker had moved intellectual mountains to figure this out, all to save my daughter. At the very least, I owed him humble gratitude. Rufus sat quietly and smiled. I wasn't entirely sure he was aware of the need for the bees either.

Hitchhiker wasn't finished though. In fact, I realized he was just getting started with his explanation, which I suspected would terminate at the atomic, or at the very least, molecular level. Apparently, there were 32 species within the Euglossine bee family of Nicaragua, and we needed a very specific one called *Euglossa cyanura* Cockerell that only buzzed about in the area of the old beekeeper's farm.

He droned on and on (pun intended) explaining everything right down to the chemical structure of what Rufus and his scientists would harvest from the orchids in Montreal. He pointed out that, although it was a different flower and a different insect in Wuhan, the process was very much the same, and, in fact, it wasn't the Covid supply chains that had disrupted delivery to the Mayo Clinic, but a drought related to climate change that had wiped out the crops in Wuhan. Hitchhiker gave me a knowing look as he tied this conversation back to the one we'd had on the bus a few days earlier: It was all related to climate change.

I took some solace in the fact that, even if some rival company had stolen the orchids, they would not have been able to produce anything without the bees.

Finally, Hitchhiker ran out of steam, or perhaps subject matter – although this seemed unlikely – and sat back in his old, tattered, springy seat with a look of triumph on his face. It was like he'd been waiting days or weeks to tell me this, which begged the question:

"Hitchhiker, why the hell didn't you tell me all this earlier, like before we stepped onto Yara's hot air balloon or perhaps on the floatplane ride? It's not like there could have been any eavesdroppers in either of those two places. It probably would have been a good thing to know."

His look of cocky intellect somehow went up a notch. "Prior to meeting Rufus, I was concerned for listening devices. Remember, every smartphone can potentially eavesdrop. After the sedation and Bourbon wore off, I had planned to tell you either during the balloon ride, or after we landed. It never occurred to me that you'd jump out."

"Jump out?" I gasped. "How about fell out?"

He raised an eyebrow. "I assumed you intended to lighten our load so that we could clear the trees? Stupid heroics and all that?"

There was a bit of a pause as I reviewed the whole scene in my memory once more. "Well … let's just say, it was a bit of both."

I did try to let go of the rope.

Rufus piped in, "Incredibly brave, my friend. You saved us all and, hopefully, your daughter in the process."

My daughter.

Suddenly, the accomplishments and heroics of the last few days meant nothing to me.

We had to get home.

***

"Goodbye?" I asked in disbelief. "What do you mean?"

We stood on the tarmac of Bilwi Airport at the foot of the steps leading inside Rufus' Gulfstream. Rufus had re-sourced the needed parts, and his Gulfstream had been repaired faster than you could say the words, "Cash is king." Rufus had always known how to make his money work for him. Not long before *The Lofty Copper* had taken flight in Providencia, Rufus had coordinated the arrival of his Gulfstream to one of the few airports big enough to accommodate his jet along the east coast of Nicaragua.

"I can't come with you. I'm not exactly allowed in Canada," Hitchhiker answered, standing rigid straight, still wearing the same black trench coat he had started our journey with and still carrying the same black briefcase.

"What do you mean ...?" For some reason, as I gave some thought to his involvement with Greenpeace and God knows what other organizations, I wasn't remotely surprised. So, I tried changing tactics.

"Maybe Rufus can push some cash in the right direction," I countered.

"Perhaps. A complication that's really not necessary in the scheme of things. You must keep your eye on the prize, Mark: your daughter. Anything that comes in the way of that is, once again, excess baggage."

"*You*, are hardly excess baggage."

"My purpose is done, and my role in this adventure is complete. I *am* excess baggage at this point. And ... I have other things to do."

"What other things?" I inquired, incredulous of the idea that Hitchhiker would not be joining us on the remainder of the trip.

Hitchhiker placed his briefcase on the

ground, stepped forward, and gave me an awkward heart-to-heart hug. He looked me square in the eyes. "You don't need me anymore. I will find my own way home."

"But I do need you," I said pleadingly. I felt like I was saying goodbye to some version of my father all over again.

"You don't. You need Rufus and his scientists to make the cure for your daughter, and I'm confident he can accomplish this."

"How will you get out of the country?" I asked, knowing that I was grasping at straws.

He tilted his head as if he was looking at a child.

"Where will you go?"

He smiled, picked up his briefcase, said his goodbyes to Rufus and Yara, and then began walking back to the terminal. Before he was out of ear shot, he turned and yelled, "Eye on the prize, Mark. I'll be there if you need me."

The darkness of the midnight hour swallowed him whole, and he was gone.

THE NEXT DAY

December 9th, 2021

We were somewhere over Florida when exhaustion would not accept any more of my excuses and dropped, what felt like, a big hammer on my head in an attempt to ferry me off to dreamland. For days, it had been tugging at my every fiber and sending little neuronal messages to all parts of my body that it was time to turn out the lights, but I'd been able to ignore it. Not anymore. The dam finally burst, and melatonin flooded my body.

Still, my mind fought against the onslaught. I was tilted all the way back in my plush, leather Gulfstream seat, but couldn't get comfortable. The minute I closed my eyes and outside distractions lessoned, my inside world came to the forefront. My dislocated shoulder started to throb, and the wound on my forearm ached. Rufus had been kind enough to provide a sling from his first aid kit, and he had helped me apply fresh bandages to my forearm, commenting, "Nice work, Rambo." He also gave me a couple of tablets of Ibuprofen and Tylenol, which was finally starting to kick in.

I'd spent the first half hour of the trip on a FaceTime call with Sarah, courtesy of Rufus' onboard internet and a borrowed phone. The Cole's Notes summary of it all was that she was as much a mental wreck as June was a physical one. She cried for most of the call, and it was impossible for me to look at her and not physically share her distress. I welled up like a colicky baby, which was the exact opposite of what I'd intended in my efforts to support her. My battered walls had crumbled before her grief.

June was spiralling badly. A recent x-ray showed her lungs were already opaque with scarring from the virus. She was now requiring full pressure support from the ventilator. Incredibly, Dr. Bouliane had managed to get approval for off-label use of the monoclonal antibody treatment two days earlier. It had given her a 24-hour reprieve before the downward trend continued. She had maxed out her allowable time in the hyperbaric incubator at the beginning of the week, and they had even doubled the time with minimal improvement.

Hearing all of this, I immediately felt the absence of Hitchhiker and wanted to consult with him for new ideas. I knew, however, exactly what he would say, "You don't need new ideas, you need to get home and give her the cure. Believe in your father's work."

Believe in my father's work. I did believe, I

just didn't want my daughter to be the guinea pig.

Sarah reminded me of my pending PCR result from Walgreens. I checked my email: nothing. They had said two to three days, depending on volume. I was anxious to put the issue to rest, but there was really nothing I could do except wait.

I tried to give Sarah some of the highlights of our trip, but I could tell it was passing right over her head. She just needed me home. The Gulfstream was much faster than a commercial flight – I assumed rich people just had to get places much faster than ordinary folks – and Rufus guaranteed a tarmac to tarmac time of under five hours, which was amazing, given it took almost four full days to *get* to Nicaragua. If we'd had the jet from the beginning, we could have had a working version of the cure for June within 24 hours. Bloody Big Pharma. Rufus couldn't prove that they had blocked the delivery of the parts for his plane, but he had some of his people investigating and would get to the bottom of it.

Although Rufus wanted desperately to tell the story of how they managed to land the balloon and get to the beekeeper's farm, he felt it was too great an adventure tale to be hurried, particularly since everyone was so tired. Ideally, he wanted to tell it over a nice dinner and bottle of wine in Montreal after we'd slept a little, however, given the timing of things, it would likely be over lunch while his scientists at the lab finalized preparation of the cure.

With the two-hour time difference, we anticipated arriving in Montreal at 7 AM with delivery to the lab by 8 AM. Rufus expected it would take four hours to extract the special ingredient and prepare the cure. Strangely, much like our "special ingredient," we still had no official name for our cure other than "the cure." No doubt his scientists had a more technical name for research purposes, that we would later turn into something more palatable for the average person.

The final step was to administer the cure to a series of chimps in the lab before I left for home with a vial in my backpack destined for June. The chimp testing was more for phase 1 safety than anything else. The last thing I wanted to do was give June a drug that killed her on the spot from an anaphylactic reaction or something else unexpected. Rufus would have his Gulfstream refueled and standing by at the airport for the final leg of my journey. During the time of my flight home, Rufus would stay back at the lab and monitor the chimps for any unexpected side effects or untoward reactions. I was to call him for the go ahead when it came time to administer the drug to June. It obviously wasn't ideal. Normally phase 1 trials take months or longer, however, this was the best we could do under the circumstances.

There was, of course, the matter of my bypassing June's physicians and nurses tending to her in order to somehow administer this unproven and potentially lethal drug, but that was a problem I would deal with on the fly with Sarah's help.

Yara would stay with Rufus and when everything had settled, one way or another, he would make arrangements to fly her back to Nicaragua to retrieve *The Lofty Copper* as well as pick up the *Rumhawk* from the island of Providencia. My Highlander, the *Rumhawk, The Lofty copper;* we'd left quite a messy trail in our wake.

The incredibly complex weave of this multilayered plan burned through every axon in my brain until, finally, my mind had had enough, and I drifted off.

***

The mood was somber, heavy, and strained. Rufus had done his best to lift my spirits by ordering from Garde Manger in Old Montreal, one of my favorite restaurants from our time together in medical school at McGill. The restaurant wasn't open for lunch. Still, with his connections and financial resources, he was able to have the chef whip something together for a special order and have it delivered.

A limo had been waiting for us when we

landed and brought us directly to our lab to drop off the orchids and bees. A team of expectant scientists received the package eagerly and went straight to work. Rufus had consulted a biologist from McGill University, and she had assured us that, given the timing, the orchids had very likely already been pollinated and were primed to release the chemicals we needed. The bees were essential, but more for the long-term picture.

An hour later, we were in Rufus' Westmount mansion getting cleaned up and catnapping again. Yara was suitably impressed with Rufus' little shack.

Rufus was in the kitchen, prepping the food and drink, while both Yara and I sat comfortably at the dining room table. Rufus refused all help, saying it was his luncheon party, and his guests would sit, eat, drink, and try to be merry.

"Your friend," she said, "is very generous with his money, isn't he?"

"Never has there been a more generous friend," I responded. "And not just with his money. I don't think there is anything he wouldn't do for me or die trying."

I was reminded of the last time I was here, almost exactly a year ago. Right before we boarded his sailboat, the *Rumrunner,* and insanely and unsuccessfully tried to cross the Atlantic to get to England in the middle of November. I wasn't sure Yara knew that story yet. She would soon enough if she hung out with Rufus. And it seemed they would be together for at least the next couple of weeks.

"Well, he almost died on our balloon ride, that's for sure," she said.

"That's a story I can't wait to –"

"No, no, no. Did I hear balloon ride? Yara, milady, have you highjacked my tale of woe and excitement?"

She smiled playfully at Rufus, "Of course not, Rufus. You were a guest on my balloon. The guest always has the privilege of telling the story."

I watched them. The way they seemed to fall into step so easily. The entrancing smiles exchanged that always meant something more and were aimed at each other, like little cupid arrows. This was the most comfortable and happy I'd ever seen Rufus with any woman.

He delivered a variety of foods to the table, requiring three trips from the kitchen. It was a smorgasbord of crustacean delights with each lobster tail, razor clam, snow crab leg, oyster, and wild shrimp accompanied by its own unique French cuisine sauce. Not to mention the mound of New Brunswick sturgeon caviar and side dishes of homemade pastas. There was a bottle of Champagne, but it remained unopened. We sipped on sparkling water in tall glasses.

He then took up a position at one end, like he was about to deliver a speech, with arms outstretched and the palms of both hands flat on the table.

"Now, my old friend and my new friend …" He nodded to both of us, but at Yara in particular. "I realize we are not at the end of the mission. But we are so much closer than we were five days ago. This is in part due to the beautiful Yara. She, of the spectacular Caribbean isl –"

I stood abruptly and mimicked Rufus' posture. I knew how longwinded he could be, and I couldn't take the suspense anymore. "I'm hanging by a rope that's coiled around my wrist swinging above the ocean …. What happens next?"

Rufus' eyes narrowed, his brow furrowed, and his jaw clenched tight, like he's suddenly back in that moment. He inhales the deepest storytelling breath I've ever seen and begins.

"We were in a stalemate. Yara had fired up the burners all the way to get the lift we needed to clear the treeline, and you were hanging on for dear life, a counterweight."

"But you tried to pull me up?" I interjected. "Why not just cut the rope?"

"We couldn't see anything. It happened so quickly we had no idea how high we were above the water; how far you would fall. I was not going to allow my dearest friend to die, and neither was Hitchhiker. We pulled hard … and then the rope suddenly slackened, and we arrived at the frayed ends you'd cut, yourself, to save us."

Even now, I had visions of being pulled by *The Lofty Copper*, hanging by the end of the rope, and dragged into the trees – certain death.

"I cut the rope so that we'd *all* have a chance, Rufus."

"Well," Rufus said, "it worked. With Yara's burners producing maximum heat and the loss of your weight, we were launched upwards, as if by a catapult."

Here, Rufus took hold of a saltshaker and held it in front of his face. He then shot it upwards, climbing onto his chair to exaggerate the height.

"We went up and up, like a needle through the storm's eye, until we exploded through the clouds into space."

At this, Yara smirked. "We were above the clouds and above the storm. Not quite in outer space."

"Yes, milady," Rufus continued. "But it felt like space, so incredibly quiet all of a sudden. The roaring sounds of the storm had been left behind: The rain pelting the balloon and drowning us in rivers of water; the howling turbulence whirlwinding around us; the creak of the cables trying desperately to hold us together. All gone. The only sound was that of the propane burners firing flames into the belly of the balloon to keep us moving skyward."

"So, you rose above the storm?" I asked.

"That's brilliant."

"It wasn't entirely intentional," Yara admitted. "When we hit the center of the storm, I already had the burners on full. With the loss of your weight, it was like we were slingshot into the heavens. I had to fully open the parachute flap to let some of the heat out and slow our ascent."

"And then?" I asked, literally sitting on the edge of my chair.

Rufus cut in, "My friend, you won't believe it. We ran out of propane."

"The burners went out? Just like that?"

"Completely. The tank was empty."

"What about the two spares we were carrying?"

"Lost to the sea at some point."

"This was ... a good thing. No?" I asked, completely unsure if running out of gas could ever be a good thing.

"Umm. Well, it did slow down our upward thrust," Yara said, "but it meant we had no ability to control our descent."

That sounded incredibly bad, like losing the brakes on your car. I stuffed a crab leg in my mouth and tried to imagine the scene.

"What was Hitchhiker doing in all this?"

"He's very smart, our friend. Terrified of flying, but very smart," Rufus said. "One of the outrigger straps snapped during the storm leaving the basket wobbly. He moved himself around the basket trying to find the point of equilibrium and balance us out. Once he found it, he sat down crossed legged, and I believe he started to meditate."

"Seriously?" I asked. "He closed his eyes and meditated?"

"He did," Yara confirmed. "And it helped. He balanced out the basket beautifully, making it a much smoother ride."

"Then," – Rufus held the saltshaker with his arm outstretched, hovering high above the table – "we slowly lost altitude and began drifting down." He stepped off the chair and gradually lowered the saltshaker to the table.

"Wait. How high did you get?" I asked.

"Higher than I've ever been," Yara admitted, the whites of her eyes glowing. "High enough that we could see our breath."

"Damn .... Wouldn't that have brought you miles and miles away?"

"That's the strange part. The storm passed under us and off to the west. Behind the storm there was virtually no wind."

"So where did you land?" I asked.

At this, Rufus released a deep, hearty laugh, and repeated, "Mon, mon, mon. The adventure is not over, yet."

"Yes, the descent was a problem," Yara continued. "We were coming down slowly at first but began to pick up speed as the heat escaped through the parachute flap. I tried to close the flap, but I think it was frozen."

"So ..."

"We dropped like a rock," Rufus yelled.

"Okay," Yara corrected, "not quite that fast, but too fast to land safely without pancaking."

"Shit. What did you do?"

"Nothing. There was nothing we *could* do."

"But then?" I asked.

"Yara and I looked at Hitchhiker, still sitting crossed legged with his eyes closed and this absurdly serene look on his face. It was like he knew we were eyeing him because he spoke for the first time since we had escaped the storm, and said, "No worries. The sun will thaw the flap."

"And he was right," Yara said. "Moments later, I was able to yank the flap closed, and this slowed our descent."

"Still, without the burners, you must have come down hard?" I asked.

"Oooh, my friend. We came down hard many times."

I looked at Rufus quizzically. "Many times?"

"Three times, to be exact. The first time was in an open field. With the impact, Hitchhiker was jettisoned out of the basket, like a cannonball. Amazingly, he did exactly that. He curled himself into a tight ball and rolled, as if he were a bowling ball through tall grass. My friend, there is more to Hitchhiker than we think."

This, I already knew. The question was: how much more?

Truthfully, there was nothing about Hitchhiker that would surprise me at this point. The more I learned about him, the less I seemed to know. However, one thing was for sure, given how terrified he was of flying, he would certainly have been in a hurry to get off the balloon.

Yara continued, "Rufus and I were holding on tight, and when we lost Hitchhiker's weight, much as when we lost yours, *The Lofty Copper* sprang skyward again. Without the burner thrust, though, it was only a temporary reprieve. We hit the ground two more times before things got worse."

"Worse?" I echoed. "How much worse could it get?"

Rufus positioned two unlit candles opposite each other and strung two strands of spaghetti between them. "Imagine, my friend, that these are two high-tension power lines."

"Noooo," I said, in disbelief. "You ended up in power lines?"

I didn't know much about hot air ballooning, but I knew running into a power line was about the worst thing that could happen.

"Yessss," Rufus said. "After the third bounce, the balloon rose and lodged itself exactly between two power lines, trapped forty or more feet off the ground." He positioned the saltshaker between the two strands of spaghetti.

"How were you not electrocuted?" I asked.

Rufus bowed his head. "Perhaps, because we were on a mission of mercy?" He raised his head and looked at me with big eyes. God was with us, my friend, and so was our friend, Hitchhiker."

"What? I asked. "Didn't he fall out of the basket?"

"He did," Yara explained. "How he survived, I have no idea."

"Yara and I were in the basket with electrical wires running everywhere," Rufus said. "I tell you, Mark, I could feel the hair rising on my arms, and hear the electrical buzzing of death all around us. And then we heard Hitchhiker's voice from below. 'Don't move. Don't touch anything. Yara, make sure the parachute flap is fully open.'"

"I did what he asked," Yara said. "And the balloon slowly deflated."

Rufus continued, "Eventually, Hitchhiker got hold of the rope that you cut and was lightly pulling on us in this direction and then that one, trying to manoeuvre us away from the electrical wires as the basket fell.

Yara was standing now. Her hands outstretched and reaching upwards, as if she were holding *The Lofty Copper* in her hands. "The deflating balloon wiggled and wormed its way between the power lines and slowly collapsed to the ground."

"Hitchhiker reeled us in," Rufus said, "away from dangerous electrical lines, until our basket touched ground. I tell you, Mark, it was a miracle that none of us were electrocuted. And do you know what Hitchhiker said?"

"I can't fathom."

"He said, 'It was just a matter of physics and avoiding contact points.'"

Unbelievable, I thought. He fell – jumped out, knowing him – out of the basket. Survived. Came to the rescue, and then deadpanned some kind of Vulcan logic. Who was this guy, really?

"So, *The Lofty Copper* ends up in a heap on the ground under the power lines unscathed, and then what?" I asked, reaching for an oyster.

"We all walked away from it, like the final scene from a movie where everything is exploding in slow motion," Rufus said, now sitting back in his chair. "Except, without the explosions."

Yara was nodding her head.

"Rufus," I said, "you have more lives than the luckiest of cats. Have you ever thought of how many times you've almost died?"

At this, Rufus belched a deep laugh, stood, raised his glass, bowed his head, and declared, "My friend, I am happy to die, as long as I'm living my best life when it happens."

Yara smiled and looked at me. I grinned back at her and tilted my head towards Rufus, as if to say, "See what you're getting yourself into?"

"From there," Rufus continued, oblivious to our little exchange, "we got a ride from a big truck that had watched the whole fiasco and was coming to check on us. He gave us a lift to a nearby town, where we were able to rent that tourista truck and driver that we picked you up with."

I sat back in my chair, shaking my head in disbelief. Some crazy part of me wished I had been with them. I had a million questions going through my mind when the doorbell rang, startling everyone.

Rufus checked his phone. "They're done. They're here!"

He ran to the door and let in a delivery man who passed the tiniest of briefcases to Rufus. It was the size of a thick book with two latches on one side. Rufus dismissed the man with a thank you – he was apparently an employee at the lab – and then set the little briefcase on the table.

No words were said as he flipped the latches and opened the lid.

Inside, was a small vial of clear fluid protected by foam. It was entirely unimpressive.

"So, this is it?" I asked. "This is the cure?"

"Yes. We were able to make two vials. The other is still at the lab and has already been administered to a young chimpanzee of similar weight to your daughter."

I stared at the vial with competing emotions and a stomach churning with butterflies. This was everything I'd worked for. *We* had worked for. My father, Rufus, Hitchhiker, and now Yara. It was a team effort to discover it and make it. But it was going to be just me giving the drug to June. Sarah would be there, but only I would bear the brunt of that moment when I would take the liquid from this vial, draw it into a syringe, and inject it into my daughter's vein.

Rufus closed the lid and secured the latches. He took a deep breath and then passed it to me. He didn't need to say it, but he did anyway, "This is it, Mark. Your father's cure. For June. Protect it and go."

I placed it into my backpack – I could think of no safer and luckier place to put it. Rufus smiled knowingly and then led me to the door.

Before I reached the threshold, I gave Yara a big hug and thanked her for everything she'd done. For reasons unknown, a question popped into my head. "Yara. I can't believe I never asked you this, but what do you do for a living on the island of Providencia?"

She flashed a pearly white grin and said, "I'm a cop, just like my father."

Suddenly, it all made sense, and I smiled. "*The Lofty Copper* ..."

She grinned at me once more and slapped me on the back. "It was a pleasure having you onboard, Dr. Peace Mask. Next time you should stay for the whole ride. Otherwise, I might cite you for leaving an aircraft in midflight."

It occurred to me. "You're a cop and you brought us illegally into Nicaragua. You broke the law for us. You could lose your job."

She looked at me with a searing intensity that I hadn't seen before. "To save your daughter? And maybe the world? What other decision was there?"

A that moment, I wondered if Covid had killed her father.

I hugged her once more, and she whispered into my ear, "May God help you save your daughter, Mark."

I whispered back, "I've done my best, I just hope whatever God there is does the same."

I wiped a tear from my eye and turned to Rufus. He wrapped me in a massive bear hug and then pushed back to look me in the eyes. There was a glistening teardrop on his cheek, and I wasn't sure if it was his or mine.

"There's a limo waiting for you outside that will take you to the airport. My Gulfstream has refueled and will take you directly to your airport. I've arranged for a limo to be waiting for you there. You will be standing next to Sarah and June within a couple of hours."

"Rufus … I can't thank you enough for everything you've done. And I'm so sorry for everything I've put you through."

"It wasn't so bad, my friend. We survived another great adventure, didn't we?" He winked. "And I've met someone extraordinary because of you." He tilted his head in Yara's direction, let loose a hearty laugh, and then slapped me hard on the back, much as Yara had.

It's like they're cut from the same mold.

I swung my backpack over my shoulder and ran out the door.

***

"You have it?" Sarah asked.

"It's in a protective container," I answered, patting my backpack secured in the seat next to me. My phone was on speaker, lying on the armrest. Except for the pilots, I was completely alone on the Gulfstream. It was a level of luxury I simply could not appreciate at the moment.

"Where are you, Sarah?"

"I'm in the parent's lounge, taking a break. The sounds of the ventilator get to me after a while. All I can think about is the air being pushed in and out of her scarred lungs, over and over again." There was a lengthy pause, and I wondered if I'd lost the signal, until she said, "I'm so tired, Mark. Tired of the ventilator, tired of the incubator, tired of the nurses and doctors, tired of this hospital. Tired of all of it ..."

"I'll be there soon, Honey, in just over an hour. Rufus is in the lab as we speak monitoring the chimp that received the test dose. Just before we administer the drug, we'll call him to be sure there's no unexpected reactions. You understand this isn't to see if the new drug can kill Covid, right? There's no time for that. This is just to make sure there's no problems with the drug."

Silence.

"Sarah? We *are* still on the same page, right?"

I could understand if she'd changed her mind over the past five days, sitting there staring at June, wondering if this new drug would kill her, or make her worse. This was the thought that was eating my innards. The heart-wrenching polarity of what we had to do. Would the drug save her or kill her? There was, perhaps, an even worse outcome in some ways, though. What if it did absolutely nothing? What if we secretly gave her the drug, and nothing happened? Like taking an antibiotic for a common viral cold.

I shuddered to think about it. Watching my June slowly circle the drain over weeks or months before finally succumbing. That would tear us apart.

"Yes." Sarah responded firmly. "We are on the same page. She's lost so much weight. The virus is eating away at her, Mark. I can practically see the little bastards ripple under her skin as she lies there helpless. Isaac told me he has no more tricks up his sleeve. If there's anything we can do ... anything at all, we have to take the chance."

And then she added, "I trust your father, Mark. I trust him with our daughter's life."

The images from my dreams of the sister I'd never met suddenly came to me. My father would surely have given anything for a cure to save her. It would be poetic if his life's work saved the granddaughter *he'd* never met. However, one thing my work in the ER had taught me was that poetic justice was a thing of fiction and fairy tales with very little footing in the real world.

We have to take the chance.

Sarah was all in. Fully committed. Was I?

Could I be the weak link on this team?

No. Of course not. I was already doing practice visualizations, running mock scenarios in my head of how it would happen when I got there. How I would leave my fatherhood at the door and be completely in clinical mode, as if I was working in the emergency, with my walls high, thick, and impenetrable. How Sarah would watch the door for nurses. How I would set the small briefcase down on the changing table, open the latches, and withdraw the vial. Take a syringe from the nearby equipment cart along with a needle. Check in with Rufus for the go-signal. Draw up our Covid cure that still didn't have a name, and then inject it into June's IV. I would watch the cure flow into her veins and then flush the IV to make sure all the precious little medication we had went into her body ... and she would recover.

That's exactly how it will go.

***

Six days earlier, I walked this hall with a sinking feeling of despair. My daughter was that rare child who was infected by Covid and became sick from it. Really, really sick. With a more terminal outlook than most cancers.

Today, I held in my backpack a cure that was nothing more than an idea my father had nurtured in the depths of his mind for decades, a seed that he'd watered with literature and nourished with a lifetime of experience dealing with infectious diseases. Once again, I felt my father's presence with each step, the same ghost I felt in his thought lab a year ago, when I pulled the manuscript from his safe. It had all come down to this moment, where two generations of Spencers would come together and fight to save a third generation from an infectious disease that was killing her. Whoever didn't believe in the concept of alternate universes was clearly leading a dull life.

I paused to inhale deeply and then passed my ID over the scanner that opened the door to the neonatal intensive care unit. I walked through an anteroom past the nursing station, noticing one nurse at her computer terminal, and then stood at the door leading to June's room. I looked through the window and saw Sarah sitting exactly where she needed to be, at

June's side, with one hand through a porthole, rubbing her back.

I looked once more towards the nursing station and was pleased that Dr. Bouliane was nowhere to be seen. I entered.

Sarah flinched when she heard the door open and withdrew her hand from the incubator. She looked up at me from her seated position, and then launched herself into my arms. We melted into each other and then stood forehead to forehead, mask against mask, with no words yet exchanged, each of us digging deep to keep our shit together. We pulled our masks down and kissed, like we'd been apart for a lifetime, drawing strength from each other. Sarah then went to the door and leaned against it. No one was coming in except through her.

I pulled my borrowed phone from my pocket and tapped Rufus' name. All he said was, "All good, my friend. All good."

I took the small briefcase from my backpack and placed it on the changing table, exactly as I'd visualized in my mock mental simulation. I flicked the latches and opened the case. For a second, my vision blurred, and I thought the vial was gone. The blurriness dissolved, and I realized the vial was exactly where it was supposed to be. I grabbed a syringe and needle from the equipment cart and levered the vial from its protective foam cocoon. I inserted the needle and drew the contents of the vial into the syringe. Everything was going as planned.

I inserted the needle into an access point on the baby's IV tubing. My eyes went blurry again, and I shook my head to clear my vision. When I could see clearly, I was staring directly at the baby's face. My baby. My June. My walls collapsed at once, and I fell to one knee, paralysed with fear. The smallest endotracheal tube was sticking out of her mouth, her body was emaciated with all her ribs showing like a holocaust survivor, and she was limp and lifeless. Her chest inflated and deflated mechanically in time with the ventilator. Her eyes were open and unblinking, and I was hypnotized by their emptiness. A tear squeaked out and ran down her hollowed cheek, and my thoughts immediately turned to the last moments I had with my father in the ICU in England, moments before Covid killed him.

I closed my eyes to refocus and get back on task. My thumb was on the plunger of the syringe. What the hell was I waiting for? This savage virus was steeling my daughter's lifeforce, her soul.

We had to take a chance.

But the bittersweet dichotomy of my life and death decision was being suffocated by generations of emotions, my father's death, my sister's death, the millions of people who'd died from Covid.

The millions who'd died from Covid.

June Fitzpatrick's face flashed before my eyes, the older woman from the island who became my friend on the plane ride to Toronto last year on my trek to retrieve my father's manuscript. The woman who'd succumbed to Covid. The woman I'd named our daughter after.

This wasn't just about June Fitzpatrick or my June. This was about every other June out there who couldn't defend themselves from this deadly disease.

A little voice whispered, "But you could kill her with this. You would be her *kill-her*."

My fingers holding the plunger went limp, and suddenly Sarah was at my side. She set a hand on either side of my head, looked deep into my eyes, and with pure love and a determination only a mother can know, pulled me out of my quagmire of indecision. She wiped a tear from her eye, placed her hand over mine, and together we pushed the plunger.

***

Everything seemed fine. I wasn't sure what I was expecting. Some sudden change in her condition? A parade of dancing nurses and doctors to come through singing, "She's all better. She's all better." The respiratory technician to waltz in at the and, in time with the music, pull the endotracheal tube out?

Sarah and I both stood at the bedside staring at June. Watching. Hoping. Waiting for something to happen.

And then it did.

The lights on the incubator lit up like fireworks on the first of July. Actually, more like R2D2 in an angry moment with C3PO. June's spine arced and her limbs went rigid. Something out of an *Exorcist* movie. The beeps from the incubator became a steady hum. Bad. Bad. All bad.

The nurse crashed through the door yelling, "She's coding. Her heart's stopped."

My heart had stopped at this point also, drowned in guilt.

The nurse noticed the syringe still hanging from the IV access point and then looked accusingly at us. "What have you done?"

An overhead announcement was made. "Code Pink, NICU. Code Pink, NICU."

Moments later, Dr. Bouliane burst through the door. The nurse who'd found the syringe immediately showed it to him. His eyes darted towards us, and he frowned. A nurse handed him an EKG print out of June's heart rhythm just before she crashed.

Both Sarah and I were clutching each other, trying to will the nightmare away. He approached us and barked something completely unexpected.

"Mark. Were eggs used in the preparation

of whatever it is you gave June?"

"What?"

"Eggs, Mark, eggs. They're commonly used as a medium to hold antivirals in suspension."

He continued, pressing now. "I know from June's family history that Sarah's mother has a severe egg allergy. It can be genetically passed on."

"I'm not sure, I can find –"

I was reaching for my phone when Dr. Bouliane yelled to the nurse, "It doesn't matter. Give her 2cc of epinephrine."

Then I got it. My medical brain came to life, and I was following Dr. Bouliane's train of thought. June could be having a basic anaphylactic reaction. We'd never given her eggs before, so it was possible …

The nurse administered the epinephrine.

"Defibrillators," Dr. Bouliane yelled.

The nurse attached two tiny pediatric sticky pads to June's chest.

"Clear." The nurse yelled.

June's chest heaved and contracted. Everyone looked to the monitor at the head of the incubator. The line was still flat.

"No. No. NO!" I yelled. "Again."

The nurse looked to Dr. Bouliane who nodded his head and then hit the defibrillator button again. June's chest heaved once more, and, as it relaxed, the flat line on the monitor squiggled, and then we heard the sound of a living heart. "Beep. Beep. Beep ..."

***

Rufus confirmed, our cure did indeed contain egg products holding the active ingredients in suspension. June's heart came back online and grew steadily stronger in response to the standard treatments of epinephrine, oxygen (which she had already maxed out), antihistamines, a beta-agonist, and cortisone (which she was already on as well).

Dr. Bouliane had no choice but to kick us out of the hospital. What we'd done could be construed by some courts as assault. We fought to stay, but the nurses threatened to call the police and Children's Aid Society. NICU nurses did not take lightly to their charges being "assaulted."

I came clean and explained everything to Dr. Bouliane. I even showed him the preliminary make-up of the drug we'd given June. He sympathized, gave us both hugs, and, off the record, said he probably would have done the same.

While he was understanding, I was quite sure the hospital would not be. Insurance companies dictated administrative policies when it came to patient care, and we'd clearly crossed a legal boundary from which there was no return.

We left the hospital solemnly escorted by security.

Dr. Bouliane promised he'd keep us informed. As with the hyperbaric incubator, he was clearly intrigued by the drug we'd given June and the notoriety that would come with any kind of success.

His parting words: "What if it works?"

FOUR DAYS LATER

December 12th, 2021

It was as if one life had been exchanged for another. This was the only way I could think about what happened without every vengeful cell in my body picking up a weapon and going on the hunt.

Three days after Sarah and I gave June my father's experimental cure, we received two phone calls.

The first was from Dr. Bouliane mid-morning, presumably after he had finished rounding on his patients. Both Sarah and I were home, still barred from the hospital, pending review. This was something I was used to, but brand new for Sarah. According to Jenna, Sarah's sister, rumors were flying through the hospital at warp speed. We were the Bonnie and Clyde of the healthcare world. A full spectrum of opinions was rendered, ranging from courageous and brilliant to careless and stupid. Mostly though, Jenna said, anyone with kids claimed they would have done the same thing if they could have.

Sarah had no regrets whatsoever and repeated over and over that she would have made the same choices. As was commonly the case, the angels on my shoulders were more wanton to battle it out, and I continuously replayed every moment of that week backwards and forwards, sifting it through my analyser looking for faults, something I would have done differently. It would have been another story if June had spontaneously recovered after the injection. Then, the end would have justified the means, and likely all would have been forgiven. And, maybe, I would have forgiven myself.

We wandered about our house in a daze. A scrapbook of June's photos was left open on the kitchen counter. Archie received more walks in a day than he would normally get in a week. We tried to catch up on various T.V. shows but couldn't concentrate long enough to see an episode through. Once, we even drove by the hospital and parked where we could see the NICU windows.

I kept in touch with Rufus, who was still monitoring the chimp for any side effects: there had been none. With a little more time, he was able to synthesize enough of the special ingredient to create three more batches of the experimental drug and had administered it to three chimps that had been infected with SARS-Cov 2, more of a phase 2 trial. It was too early to see results yet. We stopped calling it "the cure," because, thus far, it hadn't cured a damn thing.

And then the phone call from Dr. Bouliane came.

"Mark, it's Isaac. Can you put me on speaker? Sarah needs to hear this."

We were standing around the kitchen counter, and I activated the speaker. His voice was clear, and there seemed to be a certain energy to it.

"I just finished rounding on June. I examined her closely and looked over her latest blood work, including a chest x-ray. We've sent off viral titers, but the results are still pending. I also discussed her case with a pediatric colleague at Toronto Sick Kids to be sure."

Here, he paused, as if he was organizing the words in his head before articulating them. Once you said something to a patient's parents in our line of work, it was difficult, if not impossible, to take it back.

"She's better and improving. We think your experimental drug worked, Mark. It worked." He choked up and took a moment to compose himself. The implications of a working cure to someone who dealt with the sickest of patients was profound on every level. Then, of course, there were the implications to the world.

She's better and improving, echoed through my skull.

Sweeter words had never been spoken. Sarah and I deflated into each other's arms as weeks of rigid tension evaporated, and tears of joy flowed. The knot in my stomach, that I had no idea was there, loosened.

We both spoke nonsensically, trying to find words that could express our gratitude.

Isaac tempered his previous statement with the usual disclaimer in critical care type cases, “Now, you know, she’s not out of the woods yet. She’ll have a long recovery. We may not know the long-term consequences for years. And there’s the potential for Covid long haul symptoms ...”

Some of it registered. Most of it didn’t. Our daughter was improving. For the first time since she became sick, there was a true glimmer of hope.

***

The second phone call came late into the night and was from Yara. If the first phone call was delivered from heaven, the second most assuredly came from hell, and poor Yara was the bearer.

“Hello? Mark? It’s Yara.”

I was awoken out of a deep sleep earned by a week or more of mostly nothing but cat naps interspersed with raging, non-mindful musings: The kind of distracting, racing thoughts that are the enemy of sleep. But now, with the news of June, the musings had settled, the racing thoughts had slowed to a crawl, and I was able to drift off.

I hadn't silenced my phone, ever ready for a call from the hospital. The ring tone that slipped into my dreams was the whistling part of Bobby McFerrin's, *Don't Worry Be Happy*, a tune that summarized my feelings of the day.

"Yara?" I said groggily, a sleep deprivation headache building at the base of my skull. "What's going on?"

There was a pause, much like Dr. Bouliane's, except laced with ominous undertones. The kind that sent little spiders dancing up and down your spinal cord and ignited a small fire in the pit of your stomach.

Something bad has happened.

"It's ... it's Rufus," Yara croaked, struggling to get it out. "There was a fire."

"Rufus? A fire? What? Where? Is he okay?"

Suddenly, I found myself sitting in bed, alert, like someone had stuck a syringe of adrenaline directly into my heart. Sarah began to stir next to me. There was quiet sobbing on the other end of the phone, and it seemed like forever before Yara answered.

"Mark ... there was a fire at the lab." She sniffled and I could hear the ruffling of tissue paper before she resumed. "Rufus was there by himself, working late. Someone kept calling Rufus' landline. I was sleeping and, when I realized he hadn't returned home yet, I picked up the phone thinking it was him, but it was one of the firemen at the scene. A man who knew Rufus and recognized the building. When I told him Rufus was at the lab working late, he immediately hung up."

Sarah was now sitting next to me, and I put the phone on speaker.

Yara continued, "When he called back an hour later, he said they'd found Rufus ..."

There was that dreadful silent moment that I recognized as a lead-up to words that would change my life. Evil words that I wished I could put back into the genie bottle. Yara was sobbing openly now, her restraint spent.

"He didn't make it Mark. I'm so very, very sorry."

My walls were once again up instantly, like the Enterprise's shields, protecting a psyche that had been relentlessly pounded by heavy artillery over the past weeks. My voice turned cold and robotic.

"How did the fire start? Does anyone know?"

She whispered in a pitiful, strained voice. "They think it started in the electrical panel in the basement. Old faulty wiring."

The lab was in Old Montreal, set up in a heritage building. That was Rufus' style. The wiring would no doubt have been renovated, but some sections would still be very old.

"Fuck!" Was all I could muster. Where was

the poetic justice again? A man goes to every length to create a cure that could potentially save millions and then pays for it with his life? That wasn't right.

"Are *you* okay, Yara?" I asked

"No," she replied. "No, I'm definitely not. We were just getting to know each other. He was a good one, Mark. Someone I could have had a future with."

"What will you do?" I asked.

"I have no idea."

NINE DAYS LATER

December 17th, 2021

My lungs burned acid as I gasped for air, reaching with my right leg for step 127 in the Clock Tower of Old Montreal, a replica of Big Ben in London and also known as the Sailor's Memorial. Cool December temperatures turned my breath to a cloud of vapor as it left my flared nostrils, like a horse on a wintery morning run. My quads quivered with an effort that I welcomed as a physical distraction from my grief, however, aching muscles did little to relieve the pain in my heart.

I had to leave. Get some air. Get away from that place.

The wake was unexpected, bizarre, gut wrenching, and everything I wanted and didn't want all rolled into four hours of agony.

Unexpected, because of the sheer number of people that shuffled through – literally, thousands. I had no idea how connected Rufus was, how much philanthropic work he had done for the community of Montreal, and how many friends he had. Leaders and followers of every organization from: McGill University to Université de Montréal; United Way to UNICEF; Black Lives Matter to LGBTQ; politicians, Québécois entertainers, and scientists. The diversity of people in attendance spoke magnificently to Rufus' character.

Bizarre, because of the Covid rules that governed everything. No more than fifty people were permitted in McGill's Thomson House during the wake at any one time, which resulted in a lineup extending out the door and down McTavish Street. A procession of masked and sanitized people walked through the stately limestone building, respecting social distancing while trying to convey the depths of their sorrow.

On the receiving end of the condolences, Winston (Rufus' father), Yara, and I stood as figureheads, physical connections to an adored man who had stepped through the veil. The situation with Yara was awkward, to say the least. She was a complete newcomer who found herself on the inside of a man's life she barely knew and would never get to know. I did my best to buffer her and, in some ways, the Covid restrictions were fortunate in keeping everyone at a masked distance. She was simply introduced as Rufus' friend. At times, she was on the receiving line and, at others, disappeared safely into the background. She had already decided she was leaving for home the following day, and I wondered if I would ever see her again.

I pushed my way up the circular, red, metallic stairwell, drowning in a sea of masked faces from the last four hours and reliving memories of my many years at Rufus' side. I paused for only a moment to stare out of a graffitied window at La Grande Roue de Montreal – the tallest observation wheel in Canada – before inhaling deeply and moving on. Each step was made up of concrete poured into a red metal stair frame and labeled in reverse order of the step number. The very first step being 192 and then counting down until the final step – number one – at the top. I'd raced Rufus up and down these steps all through medical school, typically after a full bellied smorgasbord of celebratory Garde Manger foods, marking a dozen milestones during our four years of medical school.

After I arrived in Montreal, I'd made my way to Rufus' house and found Yara in a state of aimless bewilderment, wandering the many hallways in Rufus' Westmount mansion, staring at photos on the walls. She was in shock. A huge life-rug had been pulled out from under her and she was struggling to find her place in this new world that the man she'd met only nine days earlier was no longer a part of. Her hug seemed to transmit all her sorrow directly into my body and, for the first time since I'd received the phone call, Rufus' death suddenly became real, and I broke down in tears.

The next day, I picked up Winston from the airport. He was Rufus' only surviving family, and I'd loved everything about him from the first time we'd met at graduation. He'd retired years earlier from the fishing industry and kept busy with his true love, entertaining bar crowds in Jamaica with his Bob Marley covers. Gifted with a natural born stage presence, it wasn't hard to see where Rufus had learned his storytelling skills. He was a perfect focal point for the wake, dressed in an ancient wide-lapeled black suit, offset with a colorful red tie decorated with guitars. He carried himself with the quiet dignity of a man who knew the worth of the child he'd lost and radiated a proudness for all to see.

A sign on the wall indicated that I was 37.1 meters above the ground when I heard the steady clicking, and the mechanisms that ran the four faces of the clock became visible. The stairwell narrowed, and the step numbers became a blur as I ran my hand over my jacket pocket to make sure the small container hadn't escaped. *It would be just like Rufus to escape at the last minute,* I thought to myself.

Neither Rufus nor I were particularly religious, however, we *were* spiritual. Over many a pitcher of beer at Gerts Pub, we had explored every angle of every religion and concluded that there was some greater power that connected all of us, a power that was intimately intertwined with nature. Beyond that, we decided that everything else was smoke and mirrors. It gave me comfort to think that the essence of Rufus, call it his soul, was somewhere beyond eyesight and understanding. Somewhere happy.

Rufus had named me executor of his will, but the only parts that I had been privy to thus far regarded the details of the funeral. Anything to do with the finances was being closely guarded by his lawyers and notaries until some later date. Part of his instructions included cremation, with all his ashes going home to Jamaica for a formal funeral except for a small portion that I was to do with as I pleased.

I broached the last step sucking wind like someone who had burst from deep waters after being trapped long passed their limits. My body and mind were numb from head to toe. And this was a good thing. In fact, it was exactly what I needed to break through the final barricades holding back my grief. It was time to let it out, and maybe move on a little bit.

I crouched into a ball with my elbows on my knees and let the tears flow freely, unchecked, my back propped against a concrete wall surrounded by barred windows overlooking the four cardinal directions of the port. I withdrew from my jacket pocket a small urn engraved with a sailboat that contained my portion of Rufus' ashes and stared at it. I wiped my eyes, pictured Rufus at dinner, arms flailing as he told the story of his latest adventure, and smiled as I remembered his words, *"I am happy to die, as long as I'm living my best life ...."*

Rufus had always lived his best life.

Facing east towards the Jacques Cartier Bridge and La Ronde, I stood, unlatched the lid of the tiny urn, reached through the black metallic window bars, and slowly tilted the container until a wisp of wind, like a hand, reached inside and caught Rufus' ashes, pulling them skyward before floating down on a network of air currents. I watched as the stream of ashes, grey ribbons on the wind, gently spiralled into the rushing blue waters of the Saint Lawrence Seaway.

"Goodbye, my old friend," I whispered to the wind. "Until we meet again."

CHRISTMAS EVE, 2021

I was sitting on the couch watching *The Grinch Who Stole Christmas* with June on my lap. Our Christmas tree glowed brightly in the corner of the living room dressed from top to bottom with ornaments, many of them heirlooms given to us by my mother. Our ancient fireplace crackled a holiday warmth from real logs and a real fire, permeating the air with the faint smell of oak.

"This should be called *The Virus Who Almost Stole Christmas*, right June?" I raspberried her pudgy belly and she giggled hysterically. "And if it hadn't been for your Uncle Rufus, you may have been stolen from us." More giggling.

June had bounced back incredibly well and was released from the NICU a week earlier. She hadn't yet regained her lost weight, but she was eating like a starved horse, and we had no doubt she'd be back to normal before long.

Cognitively, she didn't seem any the worse for wear either, although it could be years before any Covid caused learning disabilities showed up. At any rate, her sense of humour was back, and for me that was the best of signs since a good sense of humour was associated with a strong intellect.

Sarah waltzed into the room wearing a onesie pajama outfit adorned with reindeers, almost as tacky as an eighties Christmas sweater. She was carrying a gift-wrapped box in one hand and a hot chocolate – with a little something in it – in the other. She placed my drink on the table, kissed me on the cheek, and then handed me the box.

"Merry Christmas Eve, dear."

I looked at the box for a moment and then realized ... "This is the box that Darrell the retired dentist dropped off. It's for me? I thought it was for June."

"Hmm. Maybe it's for both of you. Open it."

I lifted one corner of the candy cane wrapping paper, gently squeezed June's hand over it, and pulled. Her eyes went wide as she felt the paper rip. She then grabbed another corner with her other hand and became the Tasmanian angel, tearing the wrapping paper to shreds as she laughed uncontrollably.

Underneath was a box with a picture on it that I recognized immediately, a World War II Spitfire plane, just like the model I'd build for my dad when I was a child. This one, however, was already built.

"I didn't think you'd have time to build model airplanes, and June is still far too young, no matter what you think."

"Where did you get it?"

"Where does one get anything these days? The global internet shopping center."

"It's amazing." I took it out of the box and held it in my hand, flying it around, making airplane noises as I once did as a child. Dive bombing June's face, eliciting more whoops and hoots.

"And guess what?" Sarah asked.

"No idea. Did you get me a model of the Apollo spacecraft, also?"

"Hmm, maybe next year. No. Remember who delivered the package?"

"Sure. Like I said, Darrell from down the road."

"Well, I just heard something through the grapevine. Guess who was diagnosed with Covid a couple of days after delivering this parcel?

"Nooo. Seriously? He was going door-to-door delivering Covid as well as packages? He must have been mortified when he found out."

Sarah looked at me queerly, as if I wasn't catching something she was throwing. And then it clicked.

"Holy shit! It wasn't you or me. It was Darrell. He gave June Covid."

It wasn't me.

It took a while for this to sink in. All that guilt I'd been harboring somewhere deep inside was washed away, just like that. The PCR result from Walgreens had never materialized, and, with everything that had happened afterwards, I'd completely forgotten about it. Until this moment.

I stood up, holding June in my right arm and gave Sarah a long kiss. "Best Christmas gift ever, Honey. Thank you."

She trotted off to the kitchen to make herself a Christmas beverage, and I plopped back down onto the couch with June. I picked up the plane again and stared at it, thinking about my father. How proud he would be that his theories proved correct. An old man in his basement, all by himself, who, beyond all odds, had discovered a cure that could be used not just for Covid but any viral disease. Fifty years earlier, and he might have saved *his* daughter, the sister I'd never met.

Rufus and the lab were gone. But I still had the original manuscript along with all our study data backed up safely. Already, as word spread of June's miraculous recovery, newspaper articles were popping up all over, *The Christmas Covid Miracle Baby*. Television news reporters were constantly leaving messages on our voice mail, looking for interviews. Several pharmaceutical companies had already tried to contact me. The same ones who'd refused us in the beginning. I was having none of that, though. I'd promised myself that I wouldn't even be thinking about this until the new year. This was a hard promise to keep. People were still dying from Covid – particularly children – with this latest Omicron wave.

Sarah bellowed from the kitchen, "Don't forget to call your mother."

It was time. I hadn't talked to her since I returned home. Sarah had talked to her regularly to keep her abreast of June's progress, but I wasn't ready, until now. I had to get something off my chest. I moved June, who was now sound asleep, stood, reached for my new phone, and dialed England. There was a five-hour time difference, so it was late, but not too late. My mother was a night owl anyway.

Her landline rang three times before she answered with an onslaught of questions. "Hello? Who's calling this late? Is that you, Mark? What's taken so long for you to call your mother. I was worried sick about you."

I paused, calculating my words. No takebacks. "Hi, Mum. It's good to hear your voice. Merry Christmas."

"Well, you timed that perfectly, Son. It's exactly the stroke of midnight here. Merry Christmas to you, also."

I was still struggling to find my words.

"What's wrong, Mark? My mother instincts are humming."

"How could you not tell me I had a sister?"

"This is still bothering you, is it?" She asked.

"Very much so," I answered. "I feel like I was denied an important part of my childhood and my family history."

"I'm sorry you feel that way, Mark. I wish I'd told you sooner, but I couldn't. Your father wouldn't hear of it. And remember, it wasn't your childhood. You weren't even born yet."

"But I had a right to know."

"You did have a right. Partly, I think your dad didn't want you to think of him as a failure. His own daughter died of an infectious disease that he couldn't cure. That destroyed him for a long time. The wound was too deep. But it also motivated him. Surely you can relate to that after what you've gone through. And surely you can forgive your father after what he did for June and ... maybe the world."

Suddenly it clicked. For some reason, I felt guilty that my daughter survived, and his daughter had died. It was a weird sort of intergenerational guilt. My father and I seemed to be on parallel journeys through different times, and I didn't want to become the man he'd become. The man who'd orphaned me for his work. I lifted the plane and flew it softly through the air. June was sound asleep on the couch. I would be a good father, I vowed. A better father. And what more could one generation hope to pass on to the next besides "better."

"Mark. Are you still there?"

"I am, Mum. It's all good. I wish dad was here to see June, to see what his toils had wrought."

"I miss him more than you can imagine, Mark."

Sarah walked in from the kitchen, holding a mug and a plate of cookies, smiling to herself, humming a Christmas tune. She was my everything, and more than I could ever imagine wanting.

"And I miss you, Mum. Thanks for being so understanding."

"Well, that's always been the thing about you, Mark. You've always been so deep inside your head. It's like you have a committee in there discussing your every move. You always did require a lot of understanding."

Sarah heard this and was nodding her head up and down in agreement, giving me an I-told-you-so smile.

"I suppose you're right." I agreed. "That's just the way I'm built, I guess."

"No matter, Son. We all love you exactly the way you are."

I rolled my eyes, "Alright, thanks, Mum. I'll call you tomorrow when June's awake and you can talk to her."

"I'd like that. Love you, Mark." And then she shouted, "Merry Christmas, Sarah," and hung up.

I pondered our conversation and wondered, *how do mothers always know exactly the right things to say?*

"Good conversation?" Sarah asked.

"Yes. I think it put a lot of things to rest. Much less expensive than therapy." I smiled.

Sarah placed a blanket over June and then offered me a gingerbread cookie, which I happily accepted.

"Do you think she's down for the night?" I asked.

"I doubt it. She's done nothing but sleep for the past month."

I lowered myself to the couch, and Sarah squeezed in beside, snuggling into my shoulder. She said, "Numbers are on the rise again."

"Yup. Omicron is taking over the playing field."

"What happened with the whole Spanish flu thing? I thought we were supposed to have a couple of big waves, then it would all taper off. Now it looks like nothing but variants for the foreseeable future."

"Thanks to globalization, I guess. We're just going to keep bouncing new variations of Covid-19 all over the globe. Our fast-paced world means fast-paced viral delivery everywhere. They didn't have that back in 1918."

"I suppose you're right," Sarah yawned. "It's kind of depressing."

We watched some actual, non-streamed, live T.V., with commercials and everything. There was a marathon of old Christmas favorites on. Frosty was next. Strangely, each commercial brought up a memory of the past week.

The van spot reminded me of Harold and Maude, and how lucky I was that I had developed a network of close friends. Two of them had driven to Pellston and brought my Highlander back for me – after paying Clint his $100 Denver Boot fee.

The Visa commercial reminded me of my trip to the bank to sort out my stolen cards from my hitchhiking debacle. I explained the situation, that none of them were working before being stolen anyway, so I wasn't too worried about fraudulent transactions. She spent considerable time perusing her computer before confidently stating that, to her eye, all my cards had been active and working fine prior to being stolen. She ascribed my issues to a temporary "glitch in the system," which was code for, "I have no idea what happened." Fortunately, there were no unexpected expenditures. I assumed the temporary glitch had lasted long enough for a frustrated stoner thief to toss the wallet. The teller reissued a set of new cards, and I was back in the world of digital purchasing.

A commercial for Air Canada reminded me of my phone call to Homeland Security to find out why I was on the No Fly List, and how I could get off it. This took infinite transfers and a half day on hold until, finally, someone in charge said, "Sir, I have no record of any Mark Spencer being flagged." I recounted my story from the

Pellston Airport, and the gentleman said, "Sir, there must have been a glitch in the system because you're good to fly anywhere you would like." I was suspicious once again that the man at the Pellston airport had taken me for a ride. Or, more literally, his brother had.

A commercial for the latest Apple iPhone drew my attention to the same phone now sitting on the armrest of my couch. I had cancelled everything to do with my missing smartphone, and it was a simple matter to download all my pertinent info from the cloud. I looked back on my time without my phone as a learning lesson. Hitchhiker was right, my observational skills and general presence of mind were definitely enhanced when my phone was absent. I made a promise to myself to cut down on screen time, but I was doubtful it would last. It was too much of a link to society, and, more particularly, family.

Photos of my "peace mask" taken from the van video had indeed gone viral. I'd already had offers from mask companies to model masks they had created copying the Rorschach peace sign chocolate milk blot on my N95. I still had the original mask in a drawer somewhere, which I'd kept as a souvenir of my social media fame.

An ad for a local funeral home brought back all the sorrow of Rufus' wake, along with something else. A little kernel that had been lying dormant in the back of my mind, wanting to pop but being smothered by all the grief. It occurred to me that all the scientists from the lab came by to pay their respects, counting their blessings that they hadn't been there that night. All of them except the one fellow that Rufus had wondered about .... I pushed this thought aside, saving it for another day.

Frosty had blended into Rudolph and somewhere in there Sarah had drifted off, purring a light snore. I let my head tilt back and was about to follow suit when my phone erupted with a FaceTime video call. I grabbed it off the armrest and tapped the accept button.

Hitchhiker's voice filled the room. He looked stressed, and he never looked stressed.

"Merry Christmas." He said, a tinge of urgency to his voice.

I checked on June, who was still slumbering, rose from the couch and gently tilted Sarah sideways, lowering her sleepy head to a pillow. I walked to the kitchen and whispered, "Merry Christmas to you to, Hitchhiker."

I hadn't seen nor heard from him since that last day on the tarmac in Nicaragua before we boarded the Gulfstream. I released a long sigh. It was good to see his face and know that he was alive and well, but his phone calls always seem to come at the price of my stress level.

"I sent you a Christmas gift," he said. "It should have been delivered to your front porch.

Holiday blessings to Sarah and June."

And the screen went blank. I sighed again. More Hitchhiker antics.

I stepped softly to the front door, into the vestibule, and peered through the window. Sure enough, sitting on our front porch was a rectangular Amazon package about the size of a shoebox. I quietly opened the door and stood on the porch, dressed in my onesie adorned with snowmen, and scanned the darkened, deserted street in front of our house. A light snow was falling and, when I looked to our circular driveway, I could see a set of tracks that did not lead to either of our cars, and a set of footprints that stopped just short of our steps. I picked up the package and stepped back inside, locking the door behind.

I brought it into the kitchen and used a serrated knife to quietly open it. Inside was a folder and an old flip phone. I hadn't held one of these in decades. I was not the least bit surprised when it rang. I instantly clamshelled both hands around it to dampen the noise and then flipped it open between rings.

"How much do you know?"

I rolled my eyes. "Hello, Hitchhiker. How are you this fine Christmas Eve? You do know it's a holiday, right?"

"Yes. Yes. Reality doesn't wait for holidays. I'm fine, and I'm sure you're fine also now that your daughter is recovering. This isn't a social call."

"I gathered that when I picked up this flip phone. Incidentally, *why* am I talking into a flip phone?"

"The phone you are holding is a burner. It's analog, untraceable, and uses different cell towers than your digital smartphones. In other words, it's secure. At least for a while."

Great. We're into the spy stuff again.

"Excellent. I have a burner phone. I've always wanted one of those."

"Save the sarcasm. We have work to do."

"Okay. I'll bite. How much do I know about what, Hitchhiker? What exactly are you talking about?"

"Rufus' death, of course."

"I know he died in a fire. Faulty wiring in the electrical panel at the lab. Bad luck. You were missed at the funeral, by the way."

"Funerals are for the family, not the dearly departed. And I wouldn't have known anyone there except you and Yara. I'd just spent two days on a bus sitting next to you and more time than I care in a hot air balloon with Yara. Not to mention, I'm not welcome in Canada, remember."

I shook my head. He always had an answer.

"Where are you, anyway? Back home in Kentucky?" I asked.

"Open the folder."

I did as I was told. It was a typical

legal envelope, not unlike the one my dad sent his cryptic letter in a year ago that began my adventures on the high seas to England. I cut the seal and tilted it until a half dozen 8 ½ by 11 glossy photos slid onto the counter.

"What do you see?"

"It looks like satellite imagery of some sort of warehouse. They all have a kind of greenish tinge to them."

"That was your lab in Montreal before the fire. Look more closely at the southwest corner. What do you see?"

"The detail is remarkable," I commented. "There's no way this is Google Earth."

"What do you see?"

"Well. Looks like a vehicle of some sort is parked in the alleyway in the back of the lab."

"Good. Now follow the time signature on the photos."

It took me a second to locate a time signature code in the lower right hand corner. "This is the day the lab burnt down."

"It is," Hitchhiker agreed.

"I see someone with a baseball cap standing in front of the back entrance. Hey, how come I can see anything at all? The time signature reads 20:37 hours. It should be pitch black."

"Infrared."

Not Google.

"Okay. Then the person partially

disappears on the third photo, and I can see the door open. There's no one in the fourth photo, and it looks like the same person coming out and getting into the vehicle in the fifth and sixth photos."

"If you look closely, do you see any difference in the person going in and the person coming out."

I studied two of the photos side by side for a moment. "Yes. He, or she, is carrying something on the way in, which they don't have on the way out."

"Correct. Do you recognize the time of the photos?

I sighed once again. "Yes. It's right before the fire broke out."

"Wouldn't that door normally be locked?" Hitchhiker asked. "Particularly, if Rufus was alone in the building."

"As far as I know that door was always locked. It was more of a fire exit." Which apparently didn't work for Rufus. "What are you saying? That Rufus was murdered?"

"Yes. He was murdered." Hitchhiker never beat around the bush.

"Wait. Rufus had cameras all over the building inside and outside. Wouldn't that have shown something?"

"The footage from that side of the building was blank," he answered.

"And you're saying this is the work of Big

Pharma?"

"Who else has the greatest motivation? You were on the verge of one of the greatest breakthroughs in medical virology history. They stood to lose billions if you were successful in bringing it to market. The warehouse and Rufus' life would be nothing to them. Interestingly, your daughter's successful recovery probably lit the fuse."

No way can anyone blame my daughter's survival for this. No bloody way.

"Big. Bloody. Pharma. I thought this was all put to rest. The error with the No Fly List, all my cards not working, the waylaid part for Rufus' Gulfstream ..."

"What reason did they give you?"

"Every time, they said, 'It was a glitch in the system.'"

"Who do you think the glitch in the system was?"

I put the phone down on the kitchen counter and brought both hands to my temples in frustration. I felt a tightness in my chest that worked its way into my jaw and realized I was clenching my teeth. I took a deep breath and picked up the phone.

"Also," Hitchhiker continued, "you know who destroyed all of the beekeeper's White Dawn Orchids."

"I know. I know. It had to be Big Pharma. But how did they know it was there? We were so secretive?"

"My contact tells me there was a security breech at the Mayo Clinic and documents establishing possible locations of this particular White Dawn Orchid were digitally stolen."

"Shit. Wait! There was more than one location?"

"Of course."

"And ..."

"All destroyed."

"Dammit, Hitchhiker," I whispered harshly. "I don't know why, probably wishful thinking, but I thought I'd put all of that Big Pharma spy stuff behind me."

"That's exactly what they wanted."

There was that *they* again. The all-powerful *they* that hid in the basements of the world wreaking havoc at their leisure. It was one thing to assume an enemy existed, it was another altogether to know. I worked with Big Pharma every day: Every time I prescribed an antibiotic, a pain killer, or an antihypertensive. Most every drug and all the beneficial effects they provided for humanity came from Big Pharma. It was hard for me to think of them as nothing but evil, conniving profiteers' hell bent on world domination, as some people suggested. I had to believe there was just one rotten apple in this basket I toiled in daily.

"Do you think it was the company that made us that wildly lucrative offer?" I asked.

"They are at the top of my list of suspects."

"Do you have any proof? Any evidence?"

"I'm building a case, step by step, piece by piece."

"We have to know for sure, Hitchhiker, before we take any action. Critical thinking, right?"

"Of course. There is *only* critical thinking."

I sighed heavily. "Alright. What do we do?"

"You. Nothing. Just keep the flip phone nearby. When I have more intel, I'll call you. I'm sure you want the same thing I do."

"Which is?"

"Justice for our friend, Rufus. He was only trying to save innocent lives."

His ... was an innocent life, I reflected.

"Hitchhiker. You weren't just a member of Greenpeace, were you?"

"Let's just say, I did good work there, and that's where I was recruited."

He paused, as if allowing that little tidbit to sink in, before saying, "Time is up, Mark. I'll be in touch."

The line went dead.

I closed the flip phone and tucked it away in a seldom used drawer in the kitchen for now. Should I tell Sarah? What would be gained at this point? She needed to focus on normalcy for a while. No. I would wait to hear from Hitchhiker again before telling her anything. I placed the folder with the satellite photos into my backpack. I would transfer them to my filing cabinet later, where they would be lost to prying eyes in a sea of papers.

It crushed my soul to think that Rufus may have been another, albeit indirect, victim of Covid. Was there no end to the way Covid would kill people? I knew I could never let this rest. Hitchhiker had planted a weed that would always find a place to take root inside me until I dealt with it. But not now. Not today. Not this month or next. There were no time constraints on justice. The priority was to set up another lab or collaborate with one that was already operational and deliver this working cure to the world. And that too could wait a little while until the Spencer family was whole again.

I walked into the living room where June and Sarah remained sound asleep, and Charlie Brown moped on the big screen. I turned off the television and then lifted June from her comfy place and carried her to her bedroom. Apparently, she *was* out for the night. No doubt, I grinned to myself, she already intuitively understood that Santa wouldn't come to our house unless she was asleep. I deposited her into her crib and pulled a blanket up to her little chin. I kissed her on the forehead, inhaled that wonderfully innocent baby aroma, and marveled at the beautiful bouquet of her life to come.

The End

AUTHOR'S NOTE

Mark Twain may have said, "Never let the truth get in the way of a good story." And so, in keeping with the spirit of that statement, here are some "truths" that have been, shall we say, modified in the writing of this book, along with some clarifications.

The hyperbaric incubator for pediatric Covid patients does not exist. At least, it didn't when I wrote this book. It was based on a paper called: *How a portable negative pressure incubator for COVID-19 was created with minor modifications," by Abhyuday Kumar, et al, and was published in Acta Paediatr, 2020 Nov.* (https://pubmed.ncbi.nlm.gov/32881055/)*.*

The paper describes a modification to an incubator that creates a negative pressure environment with the intention of protecting healthcare providers and family from a neonate afflicted with the SARS CoV 2 virus. In light of the success treating adults with hyperbaric chambers and positive pressure, I adapted their idea to create a positive pressure environment in an incubator. It seemed like a good idea to me and works for storytelling purposes, but it really is just conjecture.

Denver Boots are typically applied in large cities to deal with repeat parking violation offenders. The concept is that the boot will only be removed once the tickets have been paid. The Denver Boot scam described in this book is a well-recognized one. Typically, the scammer applies the Denver Boot surreptitiously and sits in a tow truck awaiting the victims return, whereupon the scammer approaches the bedraggled and frustrated driver with his ability to remove the boot ... for a fee.

It is never easy killing off your darlings. I wanted to show in a big way that Covid-19 and the pandemic caused collateral damage that far exceeded the direct effects of the disease itself and killing off Rufus seemed the most dramatic way to do that. The Montreal Clock Tower, or Sailor's Memorial, had taken on some importance in the second book as a launch pad for their great seagoing adventure, and I thought it was an appropriate place to end things with Rufus. Of note, The Clock Tower is only open in summer. Since this scene takes place in the middle of December, I had to take some creative liberties with the timing.

The discussion between Mark and Hitchhiker on the Greyhound bus about artificial intelligence, climate change, and future pandemics was harvested from an article by David Von Drehle titled *In the Mind of Humankind* found in a Time Special Edition collection called

Artificial Intelligence – The Future of Humankind, as well as the article *Deadly Climate* by Jeff Goodall from the January 2021 edition of Rolling Stone Magazine (the one with the scantily clad photo of Miley Cyrus on the cover ;-).

Blunton's Bourbon is completely made up to sound a little like Blanton's Bourbon. So don't ask for it at your local watering hole.

The White Dawn Orchid (along with its Latin Aurora *Phalaenopsis* Orchis) does not exist. My expert botanist cousin, Kevin Kubeck, warned against using an orchid because, well, "it's always an orchid. There are a million other cool plants out there, but it's always an orchid." So, I went with an orchid ☺. The pseudo-copulation and the commensalism symbiotic association between orchids and bees is based on solid science.

A last word about Covid-19, variants, and vaccines. Current evidence and clinical experience evolving from the thousands of scientific studies done to date worldwide suggests that while vaccines may not prevent you from getting sick, they will *diminish how sick you get.* In particular, you may escape the lung scarring and pulmonary problems that arguably become the worst symptoms of Long Covid. In the acute phase, you may even escape death! In this book, June was saved by a fictional cure. You may not be so lucky.

ACKNOWLEDGEMENT

A special thanks to my wife, Andrea, for her ongoing and eternal encouragement. Always the first to read, she is my sounding board, my soulmate, and, well ..., "my everything."

My writing partner, learning partner, and longtime friend, Laura Cody – we continue to toil away and push each other to new heights despite life doing everything it can to interfere.

My cousins Kim (the beekeeper) and Kevin (the botanist) for their technical expertise in creating a plausible and interesting source for the "the special ingredient." A further shout-out to Captain Kim for all her feedback and suggestions: AD-28!

Dr. Gary Fausone for his frontline insight as an American ER Doc into some of the clinical and scientific aspects about the current state of Covid and vaccines.

Lawyer and pilot Jeff Broadbent for his flying expertise, constructive feedback, and wonderful suggestions.

Matt Goodall for making some damn-fine food at his new restaurant, *Peace*, and making me feel like I've travelled to a big city without ever leaving home.

Cynthia Clement once again for her incredibly detailed knowledge base of the publishing process.

Chris Belsito for his ongoing support and public relations know-how.

Dr. Brynlea Barbeau for her feedback on all things medical and for keeping my moral compass in check when writing about unfortunate souls afflicted with addiction.

Amy Wheeler Reich for her eagle-eye and incredible attention to detail. There's a reason she's in charge of book club!

Hannah Priddle, always eager to read and my link to younger generations. Congratulations on completing your Master of Education!

Kelly McDavid for her encouragement, support, thoughts, and suggestions. She's a hell of a lot more than just Connor's mother! Although, that's special too.

Dr. Lewis Palmer, for always being one of the first to test the waters. I fully appreciate the time commitment.

As always, none of this would be possible without Connie and Murray Elder. Love you both dearly.

ABOUT THE AUTHOR

Graham Elder

Dr. Graham Elder was born in Montreal and attended McGill University for thirteen years, completing degrees in Physiotherapy, Medicine, and Orthopaedic Surgery. He now lives with his wife and two children (when they are not at university) in the small town of Sault Ste. Marie in Northern Ontario, cresting the shorelines of beautiful Lake Superior, where he runs a busy surgical and academic practice with writing time divided between scientific publications and novels.
Learn more about the author at:
https://www.twodocswriting.com/about-graham-elder/

A COVID ODYSSEY

Snapshots in time of the Covid-19 pandemic as told through the escapism adventures of ER physician, Dr. Mark Spencer.

A Covid Odyssey

A race against time to bring the cure for a deadly virus to a dying spouse.

Although the COVID-19 pandemic is ravaging the world, Dr. Mark Spencer's small town in Northern Ontario is largely unaffected other than being in lockdown and preparing for the potential onslaught. When his wife, Sarah – already attending a conference in Florida when the borders close – becomes deathly ill, she is admitted to a local hospital with minimal resources to treat Covid patients. As she spirals downward and with time running out, Mark concocts a plan to bring her an experimental anti-viral drug that might save her life. He must first, however, cross the Ontario/Michigan border and then travel 2000 km through a pandemic American landscape. Along his journey, he encounters a variety of unusual characters that bring into question the very foundation of his scientific beliefs.

Will Mark arrive at the hospital in time to save his wife?

No matter what, Mark's life will be forever changed by his Covid Odyssey.

A Covid Odyssey Second Wave

A physician's harrowing intercontinental journey to uncover a dying father's potential cure for Covid-19.

Dr. Mark Spencer's life has finally returned to some degree of pandemic normalcy when he receives a heart-breaking phone call from his mother, who lives in England. His estranged father, a well-known virologist, has Covid and is being admitted to hospital.

That same day, a letter arrives in the mailbox claiming that his father has discovered a cure for Covid-19, but that, for reasons unclear, Mark must go to England to retrieve it.

Deciding that the possibility of a cure outweighs all else, Mark embarks on a gut-wrenching transatlantic trek that will ultimately push his resilience to the very limit.

Will Mark's treacherous voyage deliver him in time to uncover his father's secrets?

Join Dr. Spencer as he once again tackles the pandemic landscape in A Covid Odyssey – Second Wave.

Book two in the Amazon five-star trilogy: A Covid Odyssey.

A Covid Odyssey Variant Reset

How far would a father go to save his dying daughter?

Alpha, Beta, Gamma, Delta . . . Omicron . . . Greek letters that have plummeted our world into chaos and tragedy.

Dr. Mark and Sarah Spencer are the proud parents of baby June, now four months old, born during the pandemic. The deadly Delta wave is waning, but there is a new variant on the horizon, the ferociously contagious Omicron that has a mortal predilection for infants. Somehow, despite every conceivable precaution, June has it and is quickly spiralling downhill.

Thanks to his father's research, Mark has spent the last year developing a drug that could cure not only Covid but all viral diseases, potentially changing a world on the verge of lockdown implosion. His team is close, so close, however, the well of their special ingredient has run dry, thanks to supply chain disruption. But an alternate source has been found in Central America at a location known only by one man.

Mark embarks on a transcontinental journey to beat the clock and save his daughter. There's a catch: A billion-dollar industry, Big Pharma, that wants to stop him.

Using every conceivable manner of transportation, Mark and his two friends will risk everything to save his daughter.

Wouldn't you?

Join Dr. Spencer as he struggles through the pandemic landscape for a third time in A Covid Odyssey – Variant Reset.

Manufactured by Amazon.ca
Bolton, ON

29636445R00229